Stone Devil Duke

A Hold Your Breath Novel, Volume 1

A thousand reasons to hold your breath, and one to let it go.

K.J. Jackson

DEDICATION

– FOR MY FAVORITE KS

CHAPTER 1

The hack looked innocent enough.

But recognizing innocence had never been his forte.

Innocence had only sparked for a brief moment in the life of Devin Williams Stephenson, twelfth Duke of Dunway.

Devin looked at the shattered wheel on his carriage, the lantern's light he held cutting through the thick fog, a remnant from the earlier drizzle. The rogue barrel had splintered the spokes on the left rear wheel, and it was clear he would travel no more in the comfort of his carriage this night.

He looked up through the heavy mist, searching for his coachman. The evening had already piddled on too long, and he had only been on the town for two hours. He needed to get to the club, talk to Lord Roberts and Lord Vanes before they were so deep in their cups that business could not be conducted, and then he could use Killian's coach to get home. Killian had best not balk at that—Devin was, after all, only out in society for his good friend's benefit.

Devin liked things simple. No superfluous chitchat. No posturing. The minimum in everything, from his attire, to the very few people he allowed in his life. Simple in, simple out.

He rubbed his shoulder that had banged into the wall of the coach when the crash happened.

The evening was quickly turning into less-than simple.

The uneven clomping of a nag on cobblestones preceded the appearance of his driver through the fog. His coachman avoided Devin's eyes as the hired hack came into view.

"Is your shoulder well, your grace? I am terribly sorry at the inconvenience."

The duke paid his driver well, and knew the man took great pride in his job. Pride that was sorely beaten as he presented one very sad-looking coach as alternative transportation.

"It is quite all right, Monroe," Devin said. "There was no real harm done. The wheel will be an easy fix."

Uneasy, his driver glanced over his shoulder at the hack. "'Tis the best I could do right quick, your grace. There were no hack stands close, so I flagged it down. I checked out the inside, it seems right clean enough. The driver might be a bit sick, all balled up and grunting away like that, but I already paid him and he seems right willing to get you to the Red Horn quickly. Says he knows where it is."

Devin scanned the hack, which, at one time, had obviously been an aristocrat's fine carriage. Matching footman stands and ornate carvings gave evidence of once-possessed grandeur, but now the coach sat grungy from London's filthy streets.

Atop the carriage, the hack driver hunched over, coughs racking his body, but he kept his head down.

Resigned, Devin nodded. He had been in worse coaches in his day. "It will do, Monroe. You will handle the carriage?"

"Yes, your grace. It will be repaired by tomorrow." He pulled the step on the hack.

Dismissing his coachman, Devin got into the carriage, sat on the bench without the torn upholstery, and leaned tenderly back on his shoulder. He must have hit it harder that he realized.

He scanned the coach interior in the dim glow from the outside carriage lantern. Musty, and the whole of it had seen better days. He wondered how the hack driver had come about it. Most likely gambled away by one of the ton's ever-indulging drunks. Devin had no patience for men who gambled and drank away fortunes that were hundreds of years old. The dead deserved more respect than that.

Leaning forward, he glanced out the coach's window and noticed the fog had thinned. Small favor, for he suddenly found himself lost in an effort to stop thinking about the dead. It happened too frequently in the rain and fog, and the crushing guilt still caught him off-guard. He had yet to master how to live with his past.

Blasted rain. He lived in the wrong damn country.

He could now see through the lifting fog to the passing buildings, and Devin noticed they were not on the correct route to the club.

They had, in fact, taken quite a few unnecessary turns. The stench captured by the fog grew. Devin searched the buildings, looking for a touchstone—damn, Blackwaters gaming house passed by—they were deep into London's east side. And now they were on a deserted street.

So much for the look of innocence.

Popping open the trap door, Devin demanded the hack driver stop.

The driver slowed the horse and turned his hunched form to Devin. He coughed the entire time, and Devin had to wait for a pause in his heaves.

"Red Horn. The Red Horn Club on Pall Mall. My coachman said you knew the place?"

"Sorry, sir, I be taking a left on the next block, and we be right back on track."

The driver's voice perked Devin's ears. Something odd about how low and drawn-out the words were. Drunk? He sat back in the coach, trying to figure out what exactly was amiss about the driver. Devin couldn't see his face—the oversized black cloak he wore hovered over his head. The driver was small for his station, but then, he'd seen men much smaller handle six horses with ease. It was just the voice that threw him. Must be the wretched lungs he continued to try to cough up.

Devin attempted to relax. Killian would be annoyed he was late, but Devin only partially regretted the delay. The less time at the club, the better. He would go for Killian's sake, but that didn't mean he wouldn't try to minimize his time there.

"Damn." A woman's swear cut through the fog, followed by a pistol shot booming along the street.

A man screamed in agony outside of the carriage.

Devin's own pistol drawn without thinking, he flew to the floor of the coach, eyes out the window in the general direction of the continued bellows.

He saw no one outside the hack. But he heard the raged swearing of several men from the alleyways across the lane. Muggers. Which was exactly why he carried a pistol.

Blast it. That hack driver led him right into this. He should have listened to fate's warning and gone home when that barrel hit his coach.

Devin heaved a seething breath, readying his pistol. The driver was about to be the first one punished. Muscles tensed in anticipation, he moved, crouching along the carriage floor toward the door closest to the nearest building—he would need that structure to protect his back.

He reached for the door handle, poised to dash to the closest alley, when the door ripped open and the hack driver's head popped up in front of him.

"Please, sir, you must get out. You must leave." Words flew in a high-pitched whisper. "There is an alley behind me leading to a busier cross street. It is lit, and—oh, you have a pistol."

A woman's voice came from the hack driver. Him—her. Devin wasn't entirely sure. The dark hood still hung around the driver's face, and in the flickering light of the coach's lantern, the eyes that looked out from the hood were sunken and surrounded by dark circles.

She jerked back, scattering a look around herself, then looked back to him. "You can shoot, can you not, sir?"

"Yes," Devin said, outrage lacing his whisper, "I can shoot, and you will be the first to go."

"No, no, sir—"

A lone bullet tore through the carriage behind Devin. Wood splintered around the hole.

The horse took a few skittish steps, then amazingly, stood its ground.

"Damn." The driver looked from the torn wood to Devin.

It was a woman. There was no mistaking it.

"No, sir, you misunderstand." Her eyes veered over Devin's shoulder through the carriage window. Biting her lip, she took a deep breath, seemingly for tolerance. "I am not with them, but if I can count on your kind assistance, I am sure we can rid of them quite easily and justice will be served. There are four, and they are spread out in the two alleyways of this block on the opposite side of the street. I have already hit one of them."

She waved a pistol in her hand. "The carriage will be our best defense, and if we can draw them out of the alleys, I am sure I can dispose of all of them quite quickly."

Devin's eyes were still trying to catch up to his ears. A woman. A woman who thought she could shoot down all four of these muggers by herself. Or with just a tiny touch of help from him.

To prove to himself he wasn't crazy, Devin reached out and ripped the hood off the driver's head. Tied back, blond tendrils cascaded from under a black cap, down her neck, and disappeared into the cloak.

Hell.

The words that were stuck in shock finally loosened. Woman or not, he didn't trust that this was not part of a trap. "Why should I trust you?"

She shot him a withering look, then, apparently realizing that may not be her best angle, she gazed up at him with pleading eyes. Pleading eyes that refused to look pathetic, even surrounded by dark circles and smudges of London dirt on her face.

If anything, her eyes gave off a controlled smidge of merriment. "Truly, sir, is it not obvious?" She did little to hide the sarcasm in her voice. "I am damsel in distress, and I need you to save me."

Her words choked off as her tone went down a notch. "Oh, bother that. I was never very good at batting my eyelashes." She held up her pistol. "Clearly sir, I would have already shot you and stolen everything on your person if I was with them. I would also prefer not to be wasting precious moments standing here, chitchatting with you."

Point taken, Devin bit off a blaspheme and jumped out of the carriage, shoving his pistol back into his jacket. He took a small amount of satisfaction in towering over her slight frame. "What, pray tell, woman, is your plan for finishing off these four and getting us out of here?"

Devin grabbed and stilled the hand she held her pistol in, still precariously waving about. He already had a plan set in mind to finish off these four, but wanted to know what this woman was about.

She twisted her arm, trying to free her wrist. Devin wouldn't have it.

With a glare up at him, she grunted as she used her free hand to pull her hood back up over her head. "Quite simply, we need to first draw attention to the back of the carriage. Upon doing so, I can cross the street and sneak up on them at close range."

Devin's grip on her loosened, and she pulled her hand free.

"You, sir, will be my distraction at the back of the carriage, if you are so willing. The shot from your pistol should do." She bent over and reached into the tall black boots she wore, producing another pistol. Devin thought he saw the silver flash from one more pistol strapped above her boot.

Now she waved two pistols about as she talked. "With luck, I shall be done with them once and for all." She cocked the pistol she just withdrew. "Oh, and your name, sir?"

"D."

The side of her mouth pulled back, not quite into a smile, and she nodded. "D. Okay, yes, well, thank you, D., for your help. I apologize that you are in this position, but if you could get on with it, that would be most helpful." She flicked her wrist, dismissing him to go do his job.

Devin swallowed a deep groan. He had to admit—aside from the fact that he would be the one to sneak upon the muggers, using the skittish horse as a diversion—that had been his exact plan. But using this bit of a girl as diversion was definitely not part of the plan.

The devil. Did she think this was a game of lawn darts? They could very well end up dead, and she was acting as though this situation arose every night. Hell, for all he knew, maybe this did happen to her every night. Maybe she did this for fun, day in, day out.

Devin studied her. Even through the soot covering her face, he could see she was looking up at him expectantly, a determined glint in her eye.

It was time for him to walk away. This was already too sketchy. He needed to walk the hell down this dark street and get himself to the club.

But that glint in her eye stopped him. He couldn't place the exact why, but the glint masked something—fear, vulnerability—something that struck him so deep inside, he couldn't move his feet and do what his brain knew he should.

She shifted on her feet, not hiding her impatience at his lack of movement.

Devin's jaw hardened. "The horse is the diversion. I will cut across and attack. You will wait on this side of the carriage."

His advisement didn't go over so well.

"Oh no, sir, that will not do at all. I will compromise with you on the sneaking up part, if you think you are up to the challenge—quite gallant of you," she rewarded Devin with a quick smile. "It is best that we each take an alley. They will pay whether it is by my hand or yours. But not if you are to get hurt. That will not do. Nor will putting my dear horse in the line of fire. No sir, I am afraid your plan will not do at all."

Two more shots flew at the coach, ripping wood and interrupting the argument. Both ducked.

Jumping on the opportunity of an unguarded moment, the woman scooted past Devin to the back of the coach and fired a shot. She dropped that gun to the ground and pulled a pistol from inside her coat.

A shot was immediately returned at her, digging into the coach inches from where she slid back to hide.

"Damn, woman." Devin growled, and followed her to the back of the carriage, cocking his own pistol. He leaned out past her to survey the empty road, then sprinted across the street, his dark overcoat swinging in the night.

Back flat against the building lining the closest alley, Devin looked across the street at the coach, watching the woman as she juggled her pistols. Her tiny form shrank as she crouched around the corner of the coach, took aim, and shot again at one of the figures that had stepped partially out of the alley closest to Devin.

A wail pierced through the night. She had hit her mark.

At the scream, Devin slid along the wall to the edge of the building. The wailing had receded into the dark of the alley, and Devin glanced around the corner to find one man flat on his back and holding his leg, with another kneeling over him.

Taking advantage, Devin charged into the lane, splashing filth, and pounced on the back of unhurt man.

The mugger reacted to the threat quicker than Devin anticipated, and turned just in time to send both of them into the wall of the alleyway. Hitting the building, Devin dropped his pistol. The thug landed a step away from Devin and whipped out a knife. He advanced on Devin, stringy hair swaying and hand wildly swinging the short blade.

The two jousted for a moment, the thug forcing Devin into the open expanse of the street. They were in plain sight of the girl, and worse, an open target for the remaining two robbers in the other alley.

Devin swore as he dodged a blade swing at his belly. His instincts were rusty, and it was not only costing him valuable time, it was also thrusting him deeper into a situation he was annoyed to be in. He would have been happy to just run them off. But then they shot at him.

It was time to put this man down and off the streets for good.

Devin saw the woman run to the front of the hack and scamper up onto the driver's seat. Blasted. Now she was leaving?

Devin jumped away from another swing of the blade and snatched the wrist of the thug just as he saw one of the other muggers step out from the alley. He had a pistol leveled at Devin's head.

Devin spun, pushing the greasy man with the blade in between him and the barrel of the pistol. He twisted the arm behind the man's back and cracked his wrist. The grip on the blade opened, and Devin grabbed it from his hand.

Just as he gained angle and slid the sharp of the blade across the mugger's neck, another shot cut through the night.

The mugger with pistol aimed at Devin thudded to the ground.

Devin looked at the carriage. The girl stood tall on the driver's perch, arm straight out, hand shaking. She hadn't left. She stayed. She stood.

And she just killed the thug who was seconds away from shooting Devin.

Devin kicked off the body that had fallen onto the toes of his Hessians.

The girl scrambled off the carriage and, new pistol high in her hand, cautiously approached the alley where she had hit the first robber in the leg. Devin mimicked her approach at the second alley. Quickly finding nothing, he turned and followed the girl into her alley.

Hers was empty as well. The last two muggers had disappeared into the darkness, the only evidence, barely perceivable dark stains of blood hidden in the deep shadows of the alley. And they took his favorite pistol.

She turned, head down, well-hidden in her cloak, and walked past Devin out to the middle of the street. Devin followed, still heaving breath from the fight, staring at the girl. She didn't give him the slightest glance.

The girl froze near the man she shot and stared at the body in the puddle-soaked street.

Her voice crept out into the thick air, cracking in the lowest whisper. "The end, Papa...it is near."

Chapter 2

Devin's eyes narrowed as he strained to hear her.

She exhaled deeply, and Devin saw a single tear fall from her hooded face onto the street.

Realization hit Devin. This had not been a ruined robbery attempt. "Vengeance? It was vengeance?"

The girl jumped, obviously forgetting in her reverie, the man standing next to her.

"You had me—a bystander, a complete stranger, a fare—involved in a shoot-out—a lowly street fight, where I killed a man." Devin looked in disgust at the blood-soaked metal still in his hand and threw the knife down to the street. "For what—petty vengeance?"

The absurdity of the situation hit him, and a warped chuckle took Devin over as he stepped around the bodies to face her. "And not only are you, a woman, posing as a man—but you brought me into this."

Devin's jaw tightened. "Who were they? Ex-lovers? Customers? Your keeper's men? Oh, but that's right—" he threw his arms up— "this is about your father—did he send you here? Does he owe them money? Did he steal from them? Was he a drunkard? For that would certainly give evidence to his daughter's lack of decency."

Her gaze shot out from under her dark hood, eyes turned to fire. "My father was an honorable man. He died saving me. I will not allow you to speak of him in such a manner."

Her eyes challenged him, and when he made no reply, as quickly as the fire had manifested, it disappeared. She ducked her head again, hiding her face from Devin. Fire dismissed, anger hidden.

She stayed silent. No motion.

Devin waited.

Nothing.

The echo of a coach passing on the next street over reached them. Devin stared at the top of the black hood. Still, no words, no answer. Not that he particularly wanted to know what was going on.

Disgusted, he spun away and began toward the carriage. Time to grab his umbrella and be done with this mess. He didn't plan to be caught with, and have to explain, these dead bodies.

"It was not vengeance."

Her low whisper stopped him. Devin turned back, impatient, both not wanting and wanting to hear her speak. To hear some sort of explanation.

"No, sir, I assure you, it was not vengeance that drove me to this point." Her voice shook, still only slightly above a whisper.

Devin could see her eyes again, and he coldly assessed her. "What then, please tell, was your grand reasoning," his arm swept in a wide gesture over the bodies, "for the cause of this scene and the death of two men?"

Surprised that his own annoyance had blown past his usual even keel, he was fast coming to the realization he had allowed himself to be used by a stranger, this girl. He could have very well been killed, and it was just dumb luck that he was in the cab and possessed the combat skills he did.

What was her game? What if she had been alone? What if her fare had been some matronly spinster? The girl was a menace to society. To any innocent that happened into her cab.

Plus, who the hell was she?

Devin stifled a sigh in his chest. He didn't really want to know the answers to those questions. The plans of the night—along with his clothing—were now ruined. Nothing left to salvage. And he doubted that any answers coming from this insane woman would be able to soothe his utter aggravation.

Her face had fallen to the ground once more at his outburst. She stood, arms limp at her sides, a pistol loosely gripped in each hand. Blond tendrils escaped forward from beneath the black cap she wore under the hood. Deep worry lines on her brow were exacerbated by the dark soot that covered her face. Again, no answers came.

Patience never being top on his list of virtues to hone, Devin contemplated his limited options of getting home—either have this daft woman drop him off, or walk home—for he certainly wasn't going to tempt the fates and hire another coach.

He rolled his eyes. Trekking back to his townhouse would be it. He turned to the coach once more, only a step away when her next words stopped him dead.

"They have been trying to kill me for more than a year now."

Resisting at first, Devin turned back toward her. She shook.

"I am sorry, sir, you are right. You do deserve an explanation for the evening's," she hedged, stepping in front of him and searching for the right word, "misadventure."

The shake eased into composure, and she offered him a hopeful smile.

"Misadventure?" Devin's eyebrow cocked in disbelief.

"Please, sir, this is by no means an easy thing for me to recite to you. I have told no one of this. Nor do I want anyone to know. You deserve the truth, only because of your unfortunate involvement, but I plead that this remains between us. No one has, or must learn of this."

She paused, staring into his eyes as though she were weighing his soul, determining his trustworthiness. Uneasiness flickered in Devin at her assessment. Uneasiness that was immediately replaced with ire. What did he care what this girl thought of him?

She nodded to herself, decision made, and rushed on with her explanation.

"You see, these men, these four men, have been after me for a year now, because I was witness to a…terrible incident." Her voice stuck, wilting to nothing, and hinting that whatever had happened was far more traumatic than she meant him to believe. One deep breath, and she continued on.

"They did not get a chance at the initial incident to kill me, thanks to a fortunate interruption from several passers-by. But from that moment on, I was marked to be disposed of."

Remembering the pistols in her hands, she deposited one deep into a pocket in her cloak, and bent to re-secure the other around her calf over the dark breeches she wore.

It gave Devin a second to appraise her. Her eyes, though surrounded by dark soot to give the appearance of illness, were very candid. She was telling the truth—his instincts had never failed him when it came to liars. And her story, although remarkable, was not outside the realm of possibility—especially for a woman who drove a coach and shot a pistol.

"Obviously, they were not very adept at my disposal," she said, voice flat. "At our country home, I encountered three attempts on my life—"

"Country home—so you are of money, then?" Devin interrupted, surprised by the nugget of information.

Her jaw shifted askew as she looked up at him, startled, and clearly disgruntled at admitting that piece of information. "Yes. Can I continue sir? This is not very easy."

"What is your name?"

"Really, sir, that is not relevant." She shoved several locks of hair back under her cap. "All I owe you is the reason why you became involved in my problem on this eve. Nothing more."

Integrity. She had integrity, Devin decided, if she was intent on sharing what she felt she owed him, even if it meant a risk. But she offered very little of who she really was. And who she was had his curiosity piqued.

She cleared her throat, impatient, as she shifted her weight from one boot-clad foot to the other. "May I continue?"

He nodded her on.

"The first attempt I easily deflected—two of them tried to dispose of me as I was riding in the countryside near our estate. Shots were fired back and forth. They have terrible aim. I did get a bullet into one of them—I believe it went in an arm. The second attempt I barely escaped from. And the last attempt was a bit too close to home and my family, so I decided it was time to draw the monsters out on safer territory…"

"London—safer? Safe for whom?"

She blinked, surprised, as she shifted her weight again. "Why, my family of course—really, sir, you must quit interrupting me if I am to get this all out. We have been here too long as it is."

"I agree. Continue."

The horse hooked to the carriage began to fidget just then, and the girl immediately walked past Devin to affectionately stroke the nose of the white speckled horse. Calm once more, it stood still.

She turned back to Devin. "So I came to London to pursue them, hired a runner to do a bit of research on the men, and discovered, among other things, hijacking and robbing hacks with wealthy fares inside was a favorite pastime of theirs."

"So you decided to get robbed?" Devin rubbed his forehead at the idiocy. "And not by riding around in a hack but by driving one?"

"Yes, well…" She turned to stroke the horse's nose again, "Quite simply, sir, I needed to get to them before they got to me, and this was the most efficient way of doing it."

"Never mind the safety of your fares."

She sent him a withering look over her shoulder. "Do not be a goose, sir—I am not in the habit of picking up fares."

"Interesting, for that is usually what hackney drivers do."

She turned fully and took a step toward him. "Really sir, I am not given to putting others in danger. You were an anomaly."

"Yet, you took me as a fare and promptly dropped me in the middle of danger."

"You can thank your over-zealous coachman for that. He almost jumped on my horse, trying to get me to stop."

Monroe. Devin winced as he pictured his driver. Always over-exuberant in effort to please. That was what he got for hiring excellent help.

"Still, you placed me straight into danger."

"You were a fluke—and a lucky one, I must admit." She tilted her head, acknowledging the fact. "I truly only pick up fares when someone is overly insistent on getting me to stop. Which your man was. And, by the by, he should be acknowledged for wanting to please you so."

"I will be sure to reward him."

"Do not be sarcastic, sir. The poor man had no notion of what was to happen. Neither did I. I was actually quite fortunate they decided to attack my hack so quickly. I have only been doing this for several weeks now." She played with the edge of her cloak, hands restless and obviously anxious to get going. "And then tonight happened, which you participated in, so I do not need to recall that part of the story to you."

She pulled the edge of her cap down more fully onto her brow. "So then, can I offer to take you home, sir?" A smile broke through the layer of dirt on her face that somehow managed to be charming.

Devin almost broke out laughing for the sheer bizarreness of the situation. He rubbed his eyes. What the blazes was he doing standing in the middle of this dark street listening to this woman? He should have bowed out of this long ago.

But this slip of a girl with blond tendrils escaping everywhere and wide eyes had him—he hated to admit it—intrigued. And he couldn't quite walk away, even if it was the smart thing to do.

His anger had dissipated, only nuggets of annoyance still holding root, and he was left with a deep interest about the woman standing before him. He couldn't explain it, but he actually wanted to know much, much more about this girl.

She looked up at him, smile still in place, waiting for an answer to her last, subject-changing, question.

"Please, sir, do not stand there looking daft. Do you need to be dropped off anywhere in particular? Oh, but first," she said, looking over at the bodies, "we should rid the street of the, uh, vermin. I would be saddened if they frightened any children or ladies come the morning."

She stepped past him to the nearest body. "No. It would not do to have these evil men lying dead in the street for all to see."

Biting her lip, she gave a slight wringing of her hands, then looked up at Devin, hopeful. "Please, sir, although I do not wish to touch their bodies, I would at least like to drag them to the alley. If you would be so kind to help?"

Devin watched as she fidgeted above the body. She had started to shake again. He could only assume that seeing a dead body up close must be new to her. A pleasant surprise.

She bent over one of the men, gripping his arm, and tried to drag him toward the nearest alley. She managed to move his chest only a tick.

"Sir, please. I really could use a bit of help—I had not actually figured on this part of it and…and…" Her words trailed, and she dropped the arm. Hand clamped over her mouth, she stumbled backward as she stared at the dark blood that had seeped onto her left hand.

Devin strode to her, grabbed her slight shoulders, and steered her backward, propping her onto the wood siding of a building.

Her eyes didn't leave her bloodied hand while Devin deposited the bodies deep into one of the alleys. A constable would come by them in the morning and no doubt chalk the bodies up to a drunkard's fight.

He stepped back in front of the girl, noting the shaking had ceased. "Are you okay?"

She nodded, eyes closed, before words appeared. "I will be. Thank you for your assistance, once again."

She looked up at him, for an instant, unguarded. Her eyes. The sheer intensity in her eyes made Devin falter a step backward. Through unshed tears, utter hopelessness. They cut straight through to Devin's soul. It was only a second, and she looked back down, seemingly aware of what she had just accidently shown and ashamed by it. Devin's gut lurched.

Instinct sent his hand under her hood to the back of her neck, deep under a thick braid, and he stroked the center indentation with his thumb. She didn't pull away from the touch.

Seconds passed, and then, like lightning, she yanked away from him, realizing his hand on her was too intimate.

Clearing her throat, she briskly stepped by him, ducking to avoid his outstretched hand. She wiped her bloody hand the best she could on her cloak as she went to the carriage and then scampered up to her driving post.

"Please, sir, you are holding me up." She bit her lip as she anxiously looked down at him, pulling on thick black gloves. "I have to get my horse back to the stables and get to my home before the house awakens." She pulled her black hood around her face to cover escaping blond tendrils. "Where is your townhouse? I can drop you off on my way—it is the least I can do, after all your assistance this evening."

Devin walked to the front of the carriage and looked up at her. "Why not just let me drive you home? It will be quicker if I drop you off."

"No, sir, please, I really cannot allow that. I will not impose another dollop on your good will. Not after all the help you have given me tonight."

"It was really no trouble at all."

"We both know that is not true. But still, I must decline your generous offer."

"What is your name?"

Eyes narrowing, she gave him an exasperated look.

Devin moved to grab the bridle of the horse, effectively stopping the girl from leaving without him. He looked up at her hard. "We will not move from this place until I have your name."

"Please, sir. This is uncalled for."

"Your name."

"Fine. My name is Aggie." Her hand wrapped tight on the leather reins. She looked like she ached to strangle him with the leather.

A heavy sigh from her didn't deter Devin. "Aggie what?"

"Really sir, I do not have time for these games. Please give me your address, and get in the carriage before I leave you here."

"Your full name." Devin produced his best intimidating look. The one that sent both business associates, and chits of the ton, to cower in corners.

Her hands fidgeted on the straps as she contemplated his demand. Then her chin raised a notch. "Sir, I believe I have told you what I owe you. Please just drop the matter."

Her eyes closed and she took a deep breath. It did little to calm the defiance in her words. "I am extremely grateful to you, but I cannot give you more than I already have. This is about my family…and I…I cannot place my trust in anyone. Please do not take offense. And please, please, do not ask me to trust you."

Her eyes glimmered. She was pleading with him. Begging. And she was being honest. He had to respect that.

Devin let go of the bridle and nodded his acceptance of the situation.

A smile, tight, but grateful, broke through as she loosened her hands on the reins. "Thank you."

He told her where she could drop him off and climbed into the carriage. They moved through the streets at an even pace, this time with no rogue detours. As awkward as it was letting the girl drive him about town, it gave Devin minutes to contemplate the situation.

Why was she handling a problem as big as this alone? She obviously didn't lack courage—or stupidity—but why was she doing this at all, much less alone? What did those men really want from her? And why hadn't she just let the local constable handle the problem?

Devin stopped himself on that question. He scarcely believed her story himself, and could only guess what a constable's reaction would be. Not too kindly or supportive, he imagined. She was probably right not to bring it to the local law. But did she not have any male relatives? Where were they to leave her alone to handle this? And how in the blazes had she made it this far by herself?

The first of the far-off morning glow filtered in through the lifting night fog as the hack slowed to a stop.

"Sir?"

Her voice floated down to him, and Devin recognized the urgency in it. He complied with her need to leave by quickly stepping out of the hack. He began toward the front of the coach to talk to her before she left, but before two steps were made, the coach was moving again.

"Thank you again, sir, for your assistance," she said over her shoulder as she raised her arm in part thanks, part dismissal.

Devin swallowed a wry smile. Exactly expected after the night. He waited a moment until the coach turned the street corner, and then started after her.

He discreetly trailed the hack for nine blocks. Pausing alongside a townhouse a half-block back from stables, he watched as she stopped the carriage in front of them. He heard her whistle, and a young boy, maybe twelve, appeared in the street, taking the bridle of the horse.

She jumped from her perch, talked to the boy for a few minutes, then scurried alongside the stables away from the street. Devin cut in past the house he stood by, pulling back into the shadows just as the girl walked in front of him down the alley.

She was in the alley lane of the next street when her feet stopped. She swayed for a moment, looking for balance, and then grabbed a wrought-iron railing next to her. Turning and gripping the railing with both hands, she leaned over and threw up.

Hands still locked onto the railing, she sank, sitting on her heels, and Devin could see sobs racking her body.

He fought the urge to go to her, as an uncharacteristic sense of protectiveness swept through him. He resisted, but he could feel himself becoming involved. Hell, he was involved. No woman should have to handle such a threat to her life and family alone. And she would no longer.

He was part of this, whether she knew it or not, and he would finish it for her. It would take minimal effort on his part to have the last two men found and taken care of.

With a heave, the girl pulled herself upright and continued down the alley. She crossed three more streets, then ducked into the back door of a townhouse.

Devin walked from the alley to the street side of the house she disappeared into. He stared at her door, attempting to figure out why he even cared. He didn't take kindly to kittens. It wasn't in his nature.

Her eyes flashed in his mind. That instant. That instant she defended her father, green eyes flashing hell and brimstone. She was so quick to defend his honor, and that most likely meant she had a code of honor herself.

But she was clearly in more trouble than she could even imagine, and was either too dumb or too stubborn to know it. Devin figured on the latter. He sighed. Dumb was easy to help. Stubborn was an entirely other matter.

A sly smile tugged at the corners of his mouth. He knew her name. Knew her address. That was enough for a man with his far-reaching capabilities.

The smile found way to actually form.

CHAPTER 3

Aggie ran up the back stairs of her family's townhouse. It was no small feat that she had kept her curdled stomach from upending before she could get away from the stables. She didn't want to add more worry onto young Tommy's never-ceasing concern for her. Now she just needed to get upstairs and into bed.

She clicked the door closed as quietly as she could with her clean hand.

Moving through the house, she turned up the stairs, her boots thudding on the carpeted treads. She tried, but didn't manage to step light enough to avoid the squeak on the fourth step.

It made her pause, and in the early morning rays coming from the window above the staircase, she caught a glimpse of the dried blood still marring her left hand. She crumbled.

Sinking to the stairs, she leaned on the cherry staircase railing, legs drawn close to her body, breath choking off. The sun had risen, but the house remained achingly silent. The staff wouldn't be moving for another half-hour or so.

She was a murderer.

She had tried not to think of it while she was still dealing with her fare—she couldn't have the poor man believing she didn't know what she was doing. Even if she sure as hell didn't. And she felt horrible about his involvement.

So she had tricked herself into avoiding the severity of the situation by just not thinking about it. And by repeating over and over why she was doing this—why she had to do this. She needed to protect her family.

But the trick only lasted so long. Her throat tightened.

She had killed another human being.

Her eyes slipped down to her left hand. She couldn't avoid it any longer. The dark red had crusted into the corners of her fingernails. Human blood.

Her soul was marked forever. He was breathing, then cold. Her fault. Her conscious decision. And unforgivably, she had forced her fare into the same fate.

She leaned over as her stomach flipped again.

Worse, she would have to do it again. There were still two left. And then, their leader. He wasn't with them tonight, and he was the most important one.

Her head began to swim. The resolve she depended on to continually push her forward had just, quite cruelly, disappeared, stranding her on the stairs.

Numbly, her brain tried to talk sense into her body. She needed to harden herself now. It was her duty. Her family's lives depended on it.

"My lady?"

Aggie jumped, then sank back to the step, pulling her cloak around her breeches. She slipped her blood-encrusted fingers into the folds of the black fabric.

"My lady, are you well?" Peters, one of the three men she hired to protect her family both day and night, stared up at her from the bottom of the staircase, concern etching his brow.

Aggie couldn't unclamp her throat.

"I didn't mean to scare you my lady. I saw you coming 'round the back and was just going to check on the lock."

Thankfully, he chose not to mention her attire or her soot-covered faced. Reasonable, for she was paying for discretion, as well as protection.

Aggie took a deep breath, forcing her throat to open. "I am fine, Peters, just tired." She stood up, body angled to hide her hand.

"Are you sure you are not sick? You look as death had snuck up and spit on you."

Aggie looked him in the eyes, stilling her rolling stomach. Peters was the quietest of the men she had hired to protect her family, and by far, the strongest. She had come to like him the most, and she must truly look atrocious for him to openly question her.

"No, I am fine. Thank you for your concern, Peters. My mother and my sister?"

"Both sleeping in their rooms. All is well."

"Very good. Thank you. That will be all." Aggie turned with a nod, dismissing Peters, and trudged up the final stairs.

Her step faltered in the hallway outside of her mother's room. While Aggie didn't want to wake her, she had to consciously stop her heel from clunking onto the wood floor. Even if her mother did wake up, Aggie knew the questions about her attire, about her whereabouts until sunrise, would not come. To her mother, a blank wall held far more interest than her daughter.

Aggie's chest tightened, the bitterness warring with heartbreak as she silently lifted her heel.

Continuing down the hall, she peeked in on her younger sister, Lizzie. Her sister's nine-year-old slip of a form made only a slight mound under the covers, her breathing even. As hard as Aggie tried, she knew she was a poor substitute for their physically present, but mentally absent mother.

Aggie couldn't remember the last time she had seen her little sister laugh. Lizzie had withdrawn into her studies and rarely visited their mother, and then, only in the company of Aggie.

When this was done, things would be different, Aggie repeated to herself for the thousandth time. She would have the time to draw Lizzie out of her shell, and their mother would get better, come back to the land of the living. When this was done.

When they were safe.

Out in the hall, she moved back past her mother's room to her own, which was situated closest to the staircase. It had been Jason's room, but Aggie had taken it out of the necessity of being the last defense between an intruder and her mother and sister.

A man's room, dark mahogany furniture and paneling, polished off with deep maroons and emeralds. Just being in it made Aggie feel much closer to her big brother. She had so little of him left. And every day, she feared she lost more and more memories of him. Two years was a long time to keep hope alive. But it helped being in his space.

Aggie slipped into the room, noting immediately the ball gown she had worn much earlier in the night had been pressed and hung from where she had carelessly thrown it on a side chair. Dismissing her maid for the evening had obviously not squelched the girl's need to keep order in her mistress' life.

The gown hung by her dressing mirror, waiting to be inspected by Aggie before being placed with the rest of her assorted wardrobe. Aggie would have preferred to be able to skip the social activities of the ton altogether, but she had needed an excuse to be in London in order to track down her father's killers—her killers, if she didn't do anything about it.

Aggie went to the washstand and pushed up the too-long sleeves of the cloak and the black shirt underneath. The pale yellow gown hung next to her, a startling contrast to her current attire.

Bent over the porcelain basin, Aggie began to scrub ferociously at the dark red residue sticking deep into the cracks on her hand and nails. A splatter of the red water landed on the gown, and Aggie bit her lip, hoping it wouldn't stain. She didn't have the energy to deal with the gown.

Why had she bowed to her aunt and uncle's pleadings for her to bring her mother, sister, and herself to London for the season? It had seemed like the perfect cover, but now Aggie wished she had devised some other reason for coming to London.

Her aunt and uncle were determined that she have a fine season because of her traumatic last several years, and, Aggie presumed, marry her off in the process. Generous, but a complete intrusion on where Aggie needed to be spending her time— tracking down the men trying to kill her.

The blood along her nails was not coming out easily. Aggie grabbed a small brush and scrubbed harder. Her true purpose for being in London took so much energy and concentration, and the parties were a nuisance. Aggie was not in the market for a husband—taking care of her mother and sister needed to come first—nor was she enamored with the manufactured smiles and tedious gossip that seemed to entertain the masses.

Her hand rubbed raw and clean, Aggie unhooked her cloak and pulled off the comfortable black breeches, black shirt, and muddy boots, wrapped them in the cloak, and hid them in the back bottom of her wardrobe. Although certain that her overzealous maid had discovered them on more than one occasion, for the items were often much cleaner and more neatly folded than Aggie would ever bother with, she still wanted to maintain the pretense of secrecy with the items.

A shift went over her head, and Aggie went back to the washstand. She forced herself to look in the mirror she had avoided while washing her hands. She looked hideous. The black soot she used around her eyes had smeared to every inch of her face, save the streaks where tears had run. Two skunk tails on her face.

With a heavy sigh, she pulled off the black cap that had mostly hidden her hair. The water in the wash-basin was now pink with blood, so Aggie poured fresh water from the pitcher onto a handkerchief and dabbed at the dirt on her face. It was tedious—the soot didn't like to budge—but Aggie didn't stop until her face was rubbed pink, no trace of blackness.

Dazed, she turned from the washstand and trudged to the bed, falling on the cool covers.

~ ~ ~

Gasping for breath, terror gripping every muscle, Aggie shot out of the suffocating nightmare.

Sitting up, grasping her chest, a moment passed before the smell of roses filtered into her nose and she opened her eyes, realizing she wasn't alone.

"The dream again, dear?" Aunt Beatrix patted her leg through the royal blue blanket Aggie had shoved halfway off the bed.

Aggie closed her eyes, nodding, tears stuck in her throat.

"I guessed. You scared poor Hilde into scurrying out of your room and downstairs. She was afraid to wake you with you screaming." Her aunt squeezed her leg.

"I was screaming again?"

"Dearest Aggie, when will you share with me what makes you scream so? It cannot be good for your mind. You are so serene—too serene, truth be told—when you are awake. I know you cannot talk to your mother. It distresses me that you refuse to share what burdens you. Your father would be tormented were he here to see you in such a state."

Torment. That was a good word for what her mind manifested nightly. Not that she could tell her aunt of the demons that haunted her sleep.

There was a reason she remembered the faces of her father's killers so clearly. She saw them every night in her sleep. Coming at her. Guns drawn. Attacking her. Every vivid detail. Her father's cold hand slipping from her grasp.

Aggie braced herself, eyes closed. She couldn't think about it when awake. She may have no control over her dreams, but lucid, she had control. When they were dead, maybe, just maybe, she would find peace in sleep again.

"Please dear, I can already see that you plan on avoiding the subject once more, but I beg you to consider sharing. This does you no good. Your health is worrisome—you have been so tired these past weeks. And you sleep so late."

"What time is it?"

"It is after one. My dear, you must tell me."

Aggie opened her eyes and looked at her aunt. Those blue eyes, the same as her father's, held nothing but concern for Aggie. How could she tell her beloved aunt that she was only here to kill the men that murdered her father—that threatened her family—that threatened her? That she was the only one that could do it.

No, she couldn't tell her aunt that. Her father had demanded she tell no one. Only trust Jason, he ordered. Dying words.

She would honor that.

Not trusting herself to open her mouth, Aggie just shook her head with a weak smile.

With a tongue cluck, Aunt Beatrix pulled back from the bed to settle into her seat, and clasped her hands in front of her robust frame. "Well, if you will not talk, then we will move onward. Although you made an appearance at the ball last night, it was dreadfully short. And the two previous ones you missed with headaches. This will not do at all for your season."

"I am sorry. You and Uncle Howard have been so generous with your time, coming back from your travels, and I have been nothing but a burden."

"Posh. We are here for one reason alone, and that is to give you the season you deserve after the atrocities you have endured. We both do it with joy, but missing these important events—it does you no favors in meeting possible suitors." Aunt Beatrix studied Aggie's face. She leaned forward, seeing something above Aggie's eyebrow, and wiped it away.

"That's odd." Aunt Beatrix rubbed the black from Aggie's face between her thumb and forefinger. "It looks like ash."

Aggie's hand flew up, rubbing the spot Aunt Beatrix wiped. "I dropped some pins by the fireplace last night. I must have had some on my fingers."

Her aunt nodded. "You are a beautiful girl, Aggie, even after a horrible night's sleep, and not quite fully aged-out of marriage material. But time is gaining on you, my dear. I know you would like to wait until Jason comes home, but we cannot afford to wait for your brother to reappear."

"Thank you for your concern, Aunt Beatrix. I am tremendously grateful for you and Uncle Howard, but—"

"No. Nothing more. No excuses. The Samuelson ball is tonight, and I understand the guest list is most impressive. You will take an additional nap and we will be by at eight to escort you."

Aggie gave her aunt a half-smile. Aunt Beatrix was so very like her father. Always moving forward and allowing very little to veer her off-course.

"Yes." Aggie nodded. "I will be ready. Thank you."

Aunt Beatrix stood. "Delightful, dear. Until tonight."

Aggie stared at the mahogany door as Aunt Beatrix closed it behind her. All Aggie wanted was the serenity the country estate could afford her and her family. Serenity without the threat on her life, of course.

Life was so much easier outside of London. Aggie certainly hadn't been able to enjoy any of the season's events over the past several weeks, not as she had during her debut several years ago. In that carefree time. Before Jason disappeared. Before her father's murder.

The simplicity of that long-ago life hit her, and Aggie slid back down on the bed, pulling the blanket tight under her chin. If only.

Her mind wandered over memories of that simplicity, and before she knew it, she was drawing comparisons of the men of the ton she met years ago, to her dark-haired fare last night. He was of the peerage, that she easily deduced by the coat-of-arms on his carriage, but he was not the slightest like the easygoing men she had once flirted with.

Her fare had a darkness about him. It wasn't merely his dark hair and eyes, it was in the way he moved so easily in the night, like the darkness was where he belonged. The hooded expression on his face.

He had secrets—that, she could tell. Secrets that haunted him. She knew, because she saw that same look reflected back on her every time she looked in a mirror.

But whatever darkness he sheltered, he kept it in check. At least long enough to graciously help a complete stranger who— she hated to admit—needed his help in the midst of a skirmish that had her outnumbered four to one. She had come dangerously close to failing her family—and dying in the process.

And then he was kind enough to put up with her inexcusable breakdown after feeling the dead man's blood, still warm, on her hand.

Gracious, kind, and clearly dangerous.

Aggie realized she hadn't even asked for his full name. Rude. But no matter. It was clear he wasn't going to share, and she would not see him again. They clearly ran in different circles.

Plus, after she found the remaining two men and their leader, she would go back to Clapinshire, back to the country. But she still said a silent prayer in thanks for the man's fortunate presence in her coach.

Aggie rolled over in bed, squishing her face deep into the soft pillow, as the image of the tall man with the dark grey eyes refused to leave her mind. She couldn't help but imagine the peace and security the man's family must feel, knowing that he was protecting them, and always would.

The imaginings made her heart ache for the peace she feared would never be hers again.

If only.

CHAPTER 4

Devin's ire instantly elevated when he entered the ballroom, for the crush was thick and sure to hinder his search for Aggie. He moved down the marble staircase with cat-like ease, graceful and aloof.

"There you are." Killian Hayward, Marquess of Southfork, moved through the throng and joined him within moments. "I almost thought you had given up on joining us tonight."

"Apparently, there was no chance of you missing my entrance." Devin tilted his head in wry amusement at the crowd before them. Killian flanked his side and followed his gaze.

"It does look pathetic, does it not?" Killian shook his head in sympathy at the wave of commotion that was spreading across the room like wildfire. "I do not know how you handle it so indifferently."

Devin shrugged his shoulders.

"Well, quick, before the vultures set in." Killian inclined his head to the men, approaching from several angles, who were eager to confer with the two friends. "I have found out quite a bit."

"Tell me." Address in hand, Devin had easily found out her real name and about the functions she was to attend over the next several days. Bits and pieces of her story were still trailing in when he left for the ball. But he still wanted as much information on Lady Augustine Christopherson as possible.

"Most important, she is here."

That caught Devin's attention. His eyes quickly scanned the room, but he found nothing. "Where?"

"The left far wall. Next to the middle terrace opening."

Devin's eyes swept over the spot several times before he finally spotted her.

Cloistered by a matronly cluster of women, his search had passed over the group several times before her face was upturned. He recognized her immediately, even with a dirt-free face.

There was no mistaking her large green eyes. Even at this distance. Surrounded by soot or not—in the glow of a carriage lamp or in a well-lit ballroom—they were wholly unique.

A classically lined face, she was not an immediately striking beauty, not one that reached out and grabbed the jugular. She possessed a quiet, sophisticated beauty. The kind that the longer one stared, the more obvious the beauty became. Elegant beauty that would not fade over time.

"Is that what you were expecting?"

Devin shook his head, eyes not leaving her. No. He hadn't quite expected her to be so desirable.

"Me either," Killian said. "From what you described, I was thinking of a tiny little waif with a bulldog face to match her actions."

Killian snatched two glasses of Madeira from a passing tray. "And it looks as though your time is officially up," Killian said in a low voice as he handed the glass to Devin.

He turned from Devin, a smile plastered on his face as he attended the task of maneuvering the men now surrounding the pair. "Lord Smiton, Lord Torrent, so good to see you."

Devin afforded polite greetings, then didn't hesitate to tune the men out and shift position so he could keep Aggie in his line of vision. His eyes swept over her, assessing her.

Her attractiveness caught him off-guard. The soot-stained face he had looked at the previous night had hinted at, but not promised the real beauty she was. A slight frown settled on her face, telling him she was completely ignoring the conversation about her and concentrating hard on some issue.

She absent-mindedly tucked an errant tendril of honey-colored hair behind her ear. Her hair, soft with waves, was upswept in an elegant chignon, tendrils hopelessly escaping to curl about her slender neck.

The duke's eyes moved downward. Her cream gown was modest by society's standards, the neckline only teasing the graceful slope of her breasts—ample, and set upon a lean body.

She was enticing, and intriguing enough for him to expend the energy. Those eyes. That one brief moment she had let all the despair and hopelessness she felt portal into the world through those green eyes. She had tried to cover it up, but Devin had seen it. And it was, above all, what he remembered of her, what intrigued him, what haunted him. That one unguarded moment.

He wanted to help her.

His eyes ran back up her body, stopping at her bosom again. And, it turned out, he wanted her.

That part would be easy. Women were bees to honey when it came to his title and money. Aggie would be no different. The fact that women got his bed, and no proposal, never bothered any of them. It was understood by the women of the ton that his bed was all that was available. And it was rarely empty.

Aggie looked about the ballroom, nodding to one of the elderly ladies surrounding her. Devin saw a very poised, interested look slip onto her face, but it was not enough to fool him—he knew she was bored out of her breeches. Applicable because he had seen those legs in breeches.

Devin almost chuckled to himself when, within minutes, she flicked open her fan, waved it prettily before her face, and after a few exchanges, exited the ballroom for the terrace.

She was looking to escape the boredom of the party.

Devin smiled. A more perfect opportunity he could not have planned himself.

~ ~ ~

Aggie leaned against the black iron railing, gulping down fresh air, fighting the suffocation that had set in. She needed to be concentrating on the evening's plans, not listening to the smothering gibberish of gossip.

Aggie had never heard the gossip reach as high a pitch as it did when the Duke of Dunway made entrance. The murmur had started at the far end of the ballroom, and like a giant wave, swept through the crowd toward the far end where Aggie stood, jarring her from her thoughts.

"Aggie, my dearest, this one is to be avoided at all costs," her aunt said.

The matrons surrounding her flew into tizzies.

"The mother…"

"…the dreadful end of her…"

"…his horrific rage…"

"…should not be allowed into polite society…"

"…for only his title…"

On and on it went for several minutes, the ladies gleefully tossing about their gossip. The flurry and agitation of the people whispering about the duke soon began to cause feathers from the many headdresses to escape and float into the air.

Aggie had to stifle her laughter at the sight of a sea of flying feathers floating above heads. As amused as she was with the suddenly comical ballroom, she couldn't help but hear the many comments, and within moments, had pieced together the ton's story of Devin Stephenson, twelfth Duke of Dunway.

Aggie had raised herself onto the balls of her feet, peeking around the heads of the taller men in the ballroom in effort to catch a glimpse of the duke she was supposed to avoid. Neither interested, nor tall enough to gain better positioning to actually see the duke, Aggie rolled back down on her white slipper-encased feet.

She didn't know the duke, had never heard his name before, but made a mental note to avoid him. Attention and scandal—true or not, Aggie didn't really care—surrounded him, and Aggie could not draw any undue attention to herself by a chance meeting with the man.

Her thoughts had already shifted back to going over the plan for the evening, but the ladies surrounding her, of course, were not done, all vying for her fresh ear to gossip in.

So Aggie had flicked open her fan, flickered it, waited an appropriate five minutes, then excused herself to the terrace for fresh air.

Now, thankfully, she was in the clear night air. She took another long breath, enjoying the woodsy scent of neatly trimmed boxwoods wafting up from below the empty section of the terrace.

Tonight had to be the night. Everything was out in the open—the killers knew what she was up to. Even though it would be impossible for them to discern her from the hundreds of other hack drivers in her dark garb, they still knew she was going about town disguised as a hack driver. They would be looking for her. And she was going to let them find her.

Aggie leaned back from the railing and smoothed down the skirt of her delicate cream gown. Possibilities. She always had to run through them, again and again, questioning her own decisions. The only other option she could think of that would allow her to run amuck through the city without notice was posing as a lady of the night.

Playing a prostitute was again—as it had been when she first formulated her plan—not an option. She couldn't even begin to imagine all the trouble that could cause her. Terrifying. A hack driver was still the safest option.

Her lip slipped under her teeth. She had to sharpen her wits. Those remaining brutes would be out for her. With luck, she would stumble upon them quickly. And with a little more luck, she wouldn't overreact as she had done the previous night. She would also make certain not to put an innocent man's life in danger again.

Aggie fidgeted with her white gloves as she leaned her forearms on the railing. Her eyes closed with resolve as she worked through her forthcoming foray into the slums of London. Tonight had to be the night.

A warm breeze picked up, lightly caressing the tendrils that had escaped Aggie's artfully piled hair. She opened her eyes to gaze at the small formal garden below, thankful to be the only one taking advantage of this section of the terrace. Roses rode the breeze, mingling with the boxwoods.

Aggie could see countless couples strolling about the grounds and into the maze at the back of the garden. Laughter flitted up frequently from that area, and Aggie guessed that some of the couples had been gaily lost within. The night air enveloped her, and she allowed herself a few short moments to succumb to it, balancing one elbow on the railing to allow her hand to cup her chin.

Love must be the most wonderful blessing. The thought snuck into Aggie's conscious mind before she knew it was there. And the second she recognized it, she snapped at herself.

Thoughts of love were not a possibility, and she hated herself when she submitted to senseless snippets of an unattainable dream. She had her family to protect. She had herself to protect. Aggie shook her head and straightened as she cleared her mind free from fanciful notions of love.

She needed to get back to the task at hand—how to draw out the serpents that had slid into her life and were trying to choke the life out of her. Dispose of them, and she would be free. Free to get back to a peaceful life in the country with her mother and sister. Nuggets of hope filled Aggie.

A tendril of light hair caressed the sleek indent in the back center of Aggie's neck and gave her goose bumps. She reached back to tuck the piece into her upsweep, but bumped into something very solid.

A hand.

A hand at the back of her neck.

Not a piece of hair blowing in the breeze. A hand.

Whirling around, a scream stuck in her throat and came out as a tiny croak.

Her pathetic croak smothered into an exasperated groan when she saw what she spun to.

Staring down at her were the most unusual steel grey eyes she had ever seen. Eyes that were completely unmistakable—it was her fare from last night.

Her shock mutated into anger at being needlessly frightened. "Blazes bite your ass, sir. Only a hell-bound rogue would sneak onto a lady like that."

"Hello there, nymph." He inclined his head. "Not exactly the enthusiastic greeting I was expecting, but it will suffice. And it is good to know you have such a tongue."

"What—" Aggie's eyes darted back and forth on the balcony as she sputtered, "what are you doing here?"

What the blazes? How in the world had this gentleman just shown up at a party she was attending? Aggie fought for breath. And not only had he shown up, but he appeared with the audacity to tickle the back of her neck.

"Not the wittiest reply I have heard this evening, Aggie. But I realize after our last encounter you had hoped—nay, prayed—that I would fall into the dark, forgotten abyss of which you must throw many men."

He moved to the railing next to her, casually leaning on it. Body frozen, arms at her sides, her head followed him. She knew her jaw was open, but she couldn't quite manage to close it.

"You really must be more selective of the men you pick up in your coach, my dear. It would not do at all to have your dance card filled with past fares now, would it?"

His eyebrow cocked in mock question as he looked down on her. "Much less with the men that you have invited to a shoot-out."

A couple rounded the terrace corner from a shadowed cove on his last words. The lady's flushed face wrinkled in puzzlement at the comment, but the man at her arm smirked, obviously taking a different inference to the words, "shoot-out."

"Evening, your grace." The man tilted his head in passing as the couple passed on their way back to the ballroom. "Nice to see you out and about this fine evening."

Her fare nodded politely toward the gentleman and lady. Aggie forced her head to incline in acknowledgement at the passing couple.

The couple moved out of ear-shot, and her fare bent to whisper in her ear. "No need to worry about loose lips from those two. His heiress is inside looking for him."

Separating, the couple disappeared into the ball, and Aggie's eyes veered back to her fare, only to be met by his penetrating gaze. Her breath caught.

He was waiting for something from her. Patiently.

Then it hit her. Without mercy, the full implication of the man's greeting to her fare snuck up and clubbed her.

"Your grace…" Her earlier croak resurfaced. "Really? Your grace?"

She grabbed the fan that had been delicately dangling from her wrist and spastically twisted it in her hands. There was only one duke in attendance here tonight. She spun on her heel away from him, taking a step. Then she whipped back to him.

"Please, sir…" Voice trailing, she turned away again, then back. She stared at his chest, attempting another start at words. "I…"

It wasn't successful. Her mouth went dry. She lost all words, not even attempting to hide her shock.

Speechless, she stared at his chest, until the silence became awkward. Finally, realizing the twit she was making of herself, her eyes lifted to his.

What she saw in his grey eyes was complete amusement. Amusement at her uncontrolled emotions—realization, disbelief, outrage, and just plain dumbstruck. She'd shot through them all—openly displayed them, like an idiot. Easy amusement for the duke.

It was rude of her to react as she did. But even ruder of him to find laughter in it.

Well, no more.

No more uncontrolled reactions to the situation. The initial shock of his presence, who he was, and what that could mean to her plans, sunk in. He could ruin everything. And would be amused in doing so. Why else would he have sought her out, if not to decimate her plans?

Frustration with the situation that had just escalated out of her control, combined with the duke's smirk, catapulted her into whirlwind of indignation.

His smile. So smug. So completely in control.

Lips pulled hard, Aggie did the only thing she could, the only thing she could think that would shock the duke enough to wipe that arrogant smile off his face.

She flicked his ear.

Bold forefinger launching out from her thumb with mighty force, she went up on her toes and flicked his ear.

Stunned, his jaw dropped. But no words escaped out of his open mouth.

Taking advantage of his incapacitated state, Aggie stepped alongside him, their arms touching. She didn't look up at him, her eyes trained on the corner of the building. "Your grace, if you would be so kind as to follow me to the side of the balcony, there are some things that need discussion."

Not waiting for him, she stalked off, turning the corner and moving along the extension of the main balcony. Finding a nook closed off by lattice-work, where they would be out of eye—and ear—shot of the ball attendees, Aggie stopped, crossing her arms over her chest, fan swinging.

She turned to make sure the duke was following her. He was.

Aggie's heart sped into fast thuds when she realized that every step he took, every movement of his body, was lethal. She glanced around at the spot she had stopped in. Maybe out of sight and sound of the party wasn't the smartest move. But she couldn't back away now. She straightened as tall as she could as he stopped in front of her.

The heavy scents of the rose garden wafted up into the cove, and the two stood, both in stance for battle, glaring at each other, daring the other to make the first move.

Aggie deemed it would be her.

"Your grace, I realize what a shock this must be for you, seeing me here," she started, now in firm control of her emotions, and full of determination that he not ruin her upcoming plans.

"Rest assured, you need not worry about the threat of me spreading word throughout society about your cowardice," Aggie said. "Doing so would serve neither of us any purpose, even though, for myself, it would bring me great satisfaction to have your particular faults examined and heckled—but I have never much cared for the way society treats its weaker people."

She blustered a look that reeked of pity, ignoring the fact that his eyes had turned into dangerous thunderclouds, their deepest blacks promising destruction.

She sadly shook her head. "They can be so harsh—wolves weeding out the weak—and it is, frankly, distasteful to me. I will not play a part in such abhorrent behavior. So I promise you, no one will know of your cowardice."

Aggie's gut flipped. He looked very near to choking her.

It took every bit of Aggie's steel to raise her gloved hand and place it gently on his forearm. A pitying motion. He knew it, and his muscles flexed under her touch.

She knew she had gone much, much too far in calling him a coward. Especially when it was so opposite the truth. But it was the only way she could think of to rid herself of him and she couldn't stop now. She had to finish this. She needed to remove the threat he posed. She couldn't let him ruin her plans. Her life, her family's lives, depended on it.

"So, your grace, if it would be amicable to you, I would like to keep our little…shall we say…adventure, between the two of us?" Her look turned to concern. "Your grace, are you listening to me? You seem a bit pale. Are you feeling well?"

He took a menacing step toward her, closing the space between the two of them. "Yes, Lady Augustine, I am listening to you. And I am well, thank you for asking. While my recollection of last night's activities is quite different from yours, you are correct in your assessment of what would happen to my reputation if word spread that I was called out as a coward by a woman. You have chosen an interesting gambit."

Her eyes widened at his use of her name. Damn. He knew too much. Of course he did. He was a blasted duke. He knew whatever the hell he wanted. She took a step backward, hand falling from his arm, only to feel the iron railing press into her backside.

"But you are also wagering that I bear resemblance to the majority of men in society." He closed the space she had just maneuvered. "Unfortunately, my lady, you must know little or nothing of my reputation if you decided so quickly on such a useless tactic."

"Useless?" Aggie forced the word out through a choke.

The throbbing that had, until now, been constant along his jaw, disappeared into a smile. "You see, I simply do not care. I would give absolutely nothing to have society deem me an acceptable gentleman. In fact, I rather enjoy my notorious reputation in society—it keeps the wrong people away."

Aggie's shoulders slumped. "Such as young girls looking for a husband?"

"Precisely, Lady Augustine."

"Your grace—"

"Call me Devin."

"Your grace, I do not know you well enough for such an intimacy."

"You will."

He was too close, too overbearing for Aggie to create even the simplest thought. She looked over her shoulder, searching for air. She needed space before she crumbled to anything he demanded of her.

Aggie lifted her hand, her gloved fingers landing lightly on his chest. Completely improper, but she was stuck. Not meeting his eyes, she pushed gently, knowing she couldn't move him, but had to try. "Please, your grace, just a step." Her eyes met his. "Please."

To Aggie's surprise, he gave her one reverse step. It was enough.

The duke's eyes pinned her. He gave her space, but not a moment to catch her breath.

"Your brother. He is presumed dead?"

"My brother?" The topic switch snapped Aggie's mind back into working order. "No. My brother is presumed missing. Unreachable. Not dead. Whatever you have heard, it is not true. We received a letter from him months ago."

"Does he not know about your father? That the title is now his?"

Aggie shook her head. "Messages have been sent. We are awaiting his return."

The duke's eyes swept her face. Aggie swallowed at his look. He didn't believe her. But why should he? She was lying.

Aggie pasted a smile on her face. He had taken her over in one breath, and if she was going to get out of this, she couldn't let him control the conversation. "Your grace, I do believe I must be contrary to your statements about the importance of your reputation in society. I understand you are a close friend, and an even closer business associate of the Marquess of Southfork."

His left eyebrow lifted in surprise. She looked up at him, letting the challenge reflect on her face as her mind whipped through all the tidbits of gossip she had heard earlier about the duke. Why hadn't she paid closer attention?

"What do you know of Lord Southfork?"

"I know you are helping him gain power and money in society. I know that the men you need to impress to gain investment with, will, unfortunately, not take very kindly to a coward." She inwardly cringed at her own words, but she had to say it once more. Options were limited.

His jaw began to throb again. And he took back the step of space he had just given her. "Yes, Lady Augustine, you are correct about my situation with Lord Southfork. But you underestimate me if you believe that ultimately, I would not sacrifice my good friend's advancement in society, if it meant utilizing an opportunity to glorify the notorious reputation that I have worked so hard to earn. Killian will do fine, with or without my prodding of select gentleman."

He glared at her, assessing. "You, my dear, have much more to lose if I let it slip about last night's activities. And we both know it."

The duke paused, letting his threat sink in.

Aggie couldn't control a slight squirm as she stared up at the man. Damn him. There was no escape, and she had just led him to where she didn't want to go. What she didn't want to acknowledge. Of course he could ruin her. Ruin her plans.

His grey eyes flickered at her, and she was suddenly struck by the fact that he was a very handsome man. She hadn't slowed enough in her dealings with him last night to actually notice the fact, but there it was. Lording over her.

But he was also completely overbearing. And the worst sort of threat to her plans. One word to her uncle, and she would be shipped out of London back to the countryside, a sitting duck to be gunned down.

It was now obvious that she could not back him into a corner of compromise to stay silent about her nightly activities. A new approach would have to be employed if she was going to keep her nightly activities discrete.

The easy half-smile came back to his face. He knew he had her cornered. "My lady, I must inquire, how did you come about my connection with Lord Southfork so quickly? I had believed that you knew not my identity, until just a few short moments ago."

"You are correct in all that you say, your grace. I have everything to lose, and you have nothing." Even though it was the last thing she wanted to do, she conjured a sweet smile, nodding in acquiescence. Honesty was the only tactic she had left. "The information about you, well, you must have noticed it was no small stir you caused when you entered the ballroom—did you see the feathers above the crowd?"

Aggie was rewarded with a full smile from the imposing duke. If he stretched it, it might have even turned into the smallest chuckle.

"I knew all I could ever—or will ever—want to know about the Duke of Dunway within moments of your entrance."

The smile instantly left his face, storm clouds gathering in his eyes once more.

The change startled her, and she knew she needed to clarify. "Although, I believe at least ninety-eight percent of the information could only be considered fabricated gossip. Lord Southfork happened to fall into the two percent of truth that was flying about."

"Interesting ratio."

"It is rarely off." Aggie shrugged. "But you must understand, I need to request that we not be seen cavorting with each other."

"Some of the gossip scared you?"

"What?" Her head tilted in slight shake. "Oh, the gossip. The Stone Devil, is that what they call you?"

He blinked, almost stung, then a mask of indifference settled across his brow. "It is."

"Let me assure you, your grace, I am not concerned of your activities or of what people call you. I have met the devil, so you do little to frighten me."

"Then you would like to avoid me why?"

"It is clear you know too much about me. That is a threat. And that will not do."

"You have no idea what I will do with my knowledge of you."

"Exactly. With only a few words to the wrong person, you could ruin my only chance at saving myself and my family." Aggie looked away from his face at the nearest windows to the ballroom. "Beyond that, you are a dangerous man, your grace."

"Dangerous?"

"You produced a pistol far too fast last night not to be dangerous. Your skill in how you fight. Your skill with a knife. How you look at me." Aggie took a deep breath, eyes solemn as she looked up at him. There was nothing in those grey eyes that was good for her. "You are a dangerous man, your grace, and I have enough danger in my life at the moment."

He didn't answer right away, instead, his fingers slipped around her left hand and he raised it, palm up. The knuckle of his forefinger went to her wrist at the edge of her short glove. He ran his knuckle up the long winding scar that curved around her arm, from wrist to elbow. The line of the pink, slightly raised skin had deterred many men from her dance card, but Aggie refused to cover it with long gloves, as her aunt often suggested. It was an easy test of character.

"This looks recent."

The gesture, so small, so innocent, became entirely too intimate after a moment. Aggie knew she needed to pull away from his fingertips, but could only do so slowly.

"A riding accident. It causes no pain."

Not letting her escape the touch so quickly, the duke leaned in, the right side of his mouth lifted. "Do you not find your own work with a pistol dangerous?"

"Of course it is. But I am a woman. And I do what I do because I have to. Because I have been forced into it. Not because I choose to."

"There is always a choice, Aggie."

Aggie bit her tongue. Not for her. She didn't bother to argue. Her current state, what she had been forced to do, was something the duke could never understand.

"Your grace, although your reputation does precede you, I have no indication that you are the sort of man who takes pleasure in ruining the reputations of innocent women."

He gave her an odd look at the word "innocent."

Aggie chose to ignore the look. "I must believe that you would gain nothing by allowing our little secret out—except to hurt me. As a gentleman…" She let her voice trail off, looking up at him. As much as it grinded her pride, she allowed him to see the hope in her face, her hands gripped tightly about her fan.

His jaw suddenly flexed hard, and Aggie could see everything start to slip away.

"I guess we will just have to wait to see if I am a gentleman or not. And how close your speculation hits to the truth."

His words were clipped. Meant to be final to her request.

Still holding her breath, Aggie nodded. It was all he was going to give her.

She turned to the railing to hide her disappointment, gripping it with both hands, letting her fan dangle from her wrist above the crawling rose bushes.

"Your grace," Aggie's eyes were trained on the rooftop of the house on the other side of the courtyard, "there is one other point I mean to ask you about, for it doesn't seem to accommodate the rest of the information I have heard about you."

"Yes?"

"Why, your grace, did you attend this particular ball tonight?"

She turned back toward him. "There is little economic or social advancement for your friend Lord Southfork to make in this crowd. You are rarely seen out except for that mission. I frankly, see no reason for you to be here—and I, of course, would rather our paths never cross again. So if I knew what drew you here tonight, I could make an extra effort to avoid it and any further passings between the two of us."

The duke's eyes bored into her coolly, pausing before answering. Then he reached up to caress one of the tendrils that hung along her neck.

Startled, Aggie tried to not react and move her head away. She had cowered enough tonight.

He leaned down, mere inches away from her face, eyes locked on hers.

"My dear Augustine, for all the knowledge you seem to possess of me, of the world, I am truly surprised you have yet to figure it out." A thoughtful look crossed his hard features. "I am here for one thing, and one thing only. The answer, Aggie, is right under your nose."

Instinct sent Aggie's eyes downward. Past the duke's smartly tailored evening coat, only to land on the sight of a very pulsating, manly bulge, set off beautifully by the tight trousers he wore. Her eyes didn't linger, instead, flashing up to his, then to her clasped hands, which had immediately moved up between them.

"Ex…excuse me, your grace," Aggie stuttered out. She tried to catch her breath as she wedged herself between his unmoving form and the lattice wall. "I really must be getting back to my aunt. Thank you for the pleasant…conversation."

Clear of him, she snatched back a bit of her control but could feel the scarlet in her cheeks. Her eyes went to the farthest reach of his jacket-clad shoulder. "I trust our secret of last night will stay a secret. It is the only gentlemanly thing to do, after all."

She shot him one last hopeful look, trying to minimize the embarrassed scrunch of her forehead. She couldn't hold his gaze but for a second.

Not allowing him time to utter a response, Aggie lifted up her light cream skirt and half ran, half groped her way around the side of the house back into the ball, making a straight line to the comfort of her aunt's side.

The duke's bellowing laughter trailed her into the ballroom.

CHAPTER 5

Halfway home in her aunt and uncle's carriage, and Aggie had spent the entire time berating herself for her encounter with the Duke of Dunway.

She had acted like a twit. He had acted like an ogre. Any man who would throw a silly thing like nightly excursions as a hack driver into a lady's face, just didn't deserve to be called a gentleman, she fumed. Completely uncalled for.

After feigning a headache moments after returning to her aunt's side, she escaped the ball. Hopefully, with any luck, that was the last time she would ever have to see the man. And if not…well, she'd already decided to forget the whole incident and pretend she had never met him.

Aggie tuned in and out of her aunt and uncle's chattering, looking out the carriage window at the dark sky. Clouds were thickening, wet fury building, and that meant another night of sopping wet clothes.

She would do or suffer through anything to give herself peace when it came to her family's safety. Even if it meant London streets full of wet, mushy filth. Too bad tracking down murderers didn't allow for nights off.

Her thoughts unwittingly landed back on the Duke of Dunway. Disgusted that he popped back into her thoughts so quickly, she gave herself a shake. He was a problem, she couldn't deny it.

The infuriating man could unveil her activities without the slightest glance back over his shoulder. One who could destroy her plans—much too easily and much too quickly.

Sure, she was an oddity; she knew that. But she should have been inconsequential to a man with his considerable status and power—a hiccup in his life. Maybe he had forgotten their whole little scene on the balcony by now. And with luck, the inconvenience she had caused him the previous night in the street fight would also soon leave his mind.

With even more luck, she would find her father's other murderers tonight, and be done with the whole affair before he exposed her escapades.

"Aggie dear, are you all right? You look a bit flushed and preoccupied," her aunt said, worry evident in her brow. "Does your headache bother you overly much?"

Aggie forced a smile. "No, Aunt Bea, I am okay, just a little tired. You saw me earlier, and I could not get back to sleep today."

"Well, no surprise after the last year you have had," Uncle Howard said.

"Hush, Howard, she does not need you bringing up old memories."

"Really, Aunt Bea, it is okay. Rarely an hour goes by that I do not think of all that has happened."

Sadness touched both of their eyes as they looked at her. Aggie knew they wanted her to move on from the past. They had wasted no time or expense in surrounding her with gaiety to lighten her mood, but they knew they were failing miserably.

Aggie felt guilty that they had come back to town, leaving their travels, specifically to get Aggie out into society and hopefully find a suitable mate for her. Although she went to the functions with politeness, she never immersed herself in the fun, nor encouraged any man's attentions. They wanted desperately to help her move on with life, and she could manage very little to help with that endeavor.

"Oh, sweetie," Aunt Beatrix said brightly, bursting into Aggie's thoughts, "I was told, on good authority, that the Marquess of Southfork was inquiring about you tonight."

"The Marquess of Southfork?" Aggie hid the catch in her throat. "Do I know him?"

"No, I do not believe so, but maybe you have seen him? Dark-blond hair, handsome—extremely dashing—on his way up in society."

Aggie shook her head. "I would pay no heed, Aunt Bea. Rumors. I am sure it was nothing."

Nothing except the duke finding a way to ruin her life, Aggie thought.

"Oh, do not be so sure, sweetie. He is quite the charming man. Wealthy and well-respected, too. Howard, you knew his father?"

"Yes, yes, I do recall. Fine man, I remember. Sad ending though, I believe."

"Dribble on that, Howard. Anyway, Aggie, he was inquiring after you—we shall have to make certain to show up at some of the same functions as he over the next weeks."

"Really, there is no need to, Aunt Bea," Aggie said "I am positive it was of no consequence."

"There is no use in disregarding this. It will hurt nothing to gain proximity to the gentleman—I will make plans immediately."

Aggie produced a smile for her aunt. Satisfied, Aunt Beatrix leaned back into the cushions, a plotting look on her face. Aggie had learned long ago it was much easier to just placate her aunt, rather than waste time in trying to dissuade her from a course she had already set on. And she had decided to get Aggie a husband. The coach fell silent again and Aggie returned to running through the checklist in her mind to get ready for the night.

The carriage arrived at Aggie's townhouse, and after promises that she would attend the Appleton party the next night, she escaped inside with no more talk of finding a husband.

From the front window, she watched their carriage amble down the street, then continued quickly up to her room to change.

At the door to her room, Aggie paused when she saw light spilling out from the crack under her mother's doorway. A stab of hope went through her.

Quietly, she went and opened the heavy door. She was greeted with her mother sitting in bed, her now grey hair hanging tangled around her face, staring at nothing, her hand monotonously patting her thigh over and over.

Aggie swallowed hard and walked over to the single candle that was lit next to the bed, softly chattering to her mother about the beauty of the ball. There was no acknowledgement of Aggie's presence.

Aggie hid a sigh as she grabbed her mother's shoulders and gently pushed her back onto the pillows. The arm stopped moving, but her mother's face remained blank, eyes seeing nothing. Some days were better than others. But tonight her mother had slipped into her lost world.

Aggie snuffed the candle and turned to the door, her heart heavy in her chest. Grabbing the knob, she glanced back at her mother, now illuminated in the hall light.

Maybe, just maybe, if her father's murderers were brought to justice, the mother she had known and loved might resurface, if only just partially. Aggie would give anything to make that happen.

Aggie stepped into the hallway and quietly closed the door. She moved on to her sister's room. All was dark, and her sister was in bed, her breathing deep and even. Aggie turned to leave the room.

"Aggie—wait. Are you leaving again tonight?"

Aggie froze, her hand on the doorknob. She didn't turn around. "What do you mean, 'leave'?"

"Go out again—where do you go? I have seen you leave in those clothes. Those boy clothes. I worry." Her sister's voice sounded scared and so very young.

Aggie turned as her eyes adjusted to the darkness, and she saw her sister sitting up in the four-post bed. She walked over and seated herself next to Lizzie. "It really is nothing to worry about, Lizzie." Aggie smoothed a strand of curly blond hair out of her sister's face.

"I just have to go out sometimes. Do not fret." Aggie tried to infuse some enthusiasm into her voice. "We will soon be leaving London to go back to Clapinshire."

"But why do you have to leave at night?"

Aggie sighed. She didn't want to lie to Lizzie, but there was no way she would ever tell her the full truth. A half-truth would have to do. "I am looking for a way to help mother."

Lizzie's eyes turned solemn. "Mother," she nodded. "I understand."

Aggie kissed her cheek and stood up. "Now get some sleep and do not worry. Everything will be just fine. Oh, and Aunt Beatrix and Uncle Howard probably do not need to hear about this, all right? I do not want to worry either of them, okay?"

"Okay." Lizzie snuggled back under the covers that Aggie tucked around her.

Aggie moved across the room to leave.

"Aggie?"

"Yes?"

"Will Mama get better?"

Aggie forced a bright smile on her face, even as her heart broke for her little sister. "I hope so, Lizzie. I really hope so."

She closed the door and then leaned back against it. Her sister was too old for a nine-year-old. She had lost too much in her short life, and Aggie was determined that her sister's life be as normal as possible. She would allow no more loss to enter into Lizzie's already fragmented world.

Aggie knew she was a terrible substitute for a mother, but if she could give Lizzie that—that one thing—a life where she lost no more people she loved, then Aggie would be happy.

Wiping the corners of her wet eyes, Aggie moved back to her room. Quickly stripping down to her chemise, she went to her wardrobe. Digging down to the bottom, an exasperated smile appeared as she pulled out her recently washed and pressed shirt and breeches, along with her now-clean, tall, black boots and cape. Her maid. Never asking, never telling. She didn't pay her nearly enough.

Sitting on the bed, one candle lit next to her, Aggie pulled on the black breeches, then stood and gave a few quick jumps on her toes, relishing the comfort of them, even if they did fit a bit too snugly at the hips.

She pulled on the shirt, laced up the tall boots, and attached the large dark cloak about her. Onto her knees, she pulled a wooden box from under her bed.

Opening it, she grabbed the tin that kept the soot, and she spread the blackness heavily under her eyes for a sunken-eye look, then across her chin, forehead, and cheeks for the filthiest of appearances.

Pulling pins from her hair, she tousled her hair down from her upsweep, and retwisted it tightly, pinning it up and tucking it under the black cap she had swiped from the stables several weeks ago.

Going back to the wooden box, she pulled six pistols, one by one from their neat holders in the box. She checked each for a bullet and gun-powder, then strapped one above her left boot and one higher up on her right thigh. The other four pistols went securely into special pockets she had sewn into her cloak.

Stepping over to the mirror to study her costume, she was, as always, quite pleased with the entire effect. She looked like a skinny, dirty, down-on-his-luck hack driver. And she knew with a splash of brandy onto her cloak on the way out of the house, her smell would complete the disguise.

Aggie made her way out through the gardens and slipped through the back gate. Scurrying through the blocks of courtyards and alleys, she stopped behind the nearby stables. Tommy, the young apprentice to the Bow Street runner she had hired to help her gather information on her father's murderers, waited outside for her. Sunshine was already hitched to the carriage.

She had hired Tommy when she realized she would need someone discreet to ready her coach and horse every night. Tommy was a young lad, a bit scruffy, but he had the most intelligent eyes. Aggie liked him very much.

"Evening, my lady." Tommy's cap came off as he greeted her with his usual grin, which quickly turned into a determined look. She knew what was coming.

"My lady, I know it is not me business. I know what your answer will be. But I worry on your safety, my lady. You know well that there be plenty of men who can do this business for you."

He tightened his cap back on his head. "Just hire one of 'em, please, my lady. It could save you from much harm. And me from much guilt."

He did this every night she went out as a hack driver. And every night, he failed at getting her to veer off-course.

"Tommy, you know full well why I do this myself. I do not want any man being hurt or killed because of a confusion," she said, keeping the reprimand in her voice to a minimum. "I am the only one who can recognize these men for certain, and I will not risk someone else's safety, or the possibility that the job will not get done, just because I am scared or could get hurt."

His gaze fell downward. Aggie softened her tone. "Tommy, I realize you are only looking out for my best interest. And I know you believe I am in constant peril, but you must not worry. I know what I am up to, and I know how to protect myself."

He looked back up at her, worry still evident, but wanting to believe what she said.

"Your help has been invaluable to me, and the best way you can help me is to continue to find out as much as you can about the last two men and keep the coach and horse a secret."

Aggie put on her brightest smile. "I really do not know how I could continue safely without your help, Tommy."

That always got him, as she knew it would. He sheepishly grinned and apologized for questioning her plans. Aggie went to rub Sunshine's nose.

"But, my lady?"

"Yes?"

"At least let me accompany you for protection's sake?"

Aggie smiled at his question. It was always ask her not to go, then ask if he could come with. She walked to the front of the carriage.

"Tommy, you know I am counting on you to put in place the plan to protect my mother and sister if something should happen to me. You are the only person I can trust to do that without fail."

Resigned, Tommy shook his head. "Yes, my lady. Don't you worry nothing about your family."

Aggie smiled over his loyalty, handed him a small reticule full of coins, and turned to crawl up to the driver's perch.

"One more thing Tommy." Aggie looked down at her young friend with hope on her face. "Have you or your boss discovered out anything at all about the fifth man—the gentleman?"

Tommy's answer was the same as it had been since she had first hired him and his boss, and every time she had asked since then.

"No, my lady. I am sorry."

Aggie nodded in resignation, bothered once more that the man hadn't been found. It would seem that their leader was impossible to track, and the longer Aggie knew nothing of him, except for his evil face, the harder it would be to find him. Especially if she disposed of the other two.

If she couldn't get one of the last two murderers to tell her about their boss, she knew peace would be forever elusive. She could not rest until their leader was brought to justice.

With a deep breath to calm her nerves, Aggie thanked Tommy, and clicked Sunshine forward. She rambled off down the cobblestones, Tommy looking after her, admiration shining plainly on his face.

～～～

She had been gone from the ball for only moments before Devin found himself clear to make it to Killian. Both men had been deluged for some time by gentlemen eager to gain an ear to talk investments.

After watching Aggie scurry back to her aunt, Devin hadn't been back in the ballroom a minute before five men surrounded him, intent on gaining his attention.

He gave it to them, partially, while the majority of his mind worked on the slip of a girl that stood across the room from him, her face never fully losing the blush from the balcony.

She had been impossibly easy to find. Too easy, for a woman attempting to go undercover as a hack driver. He originally thought he'd talk to the girl, tell her he would handle the two remaining men. And that would be it. Maybe a dalliance if she was amicable.

But all that changed the moment she called him a coward. Not because of the insult, but because he realized how desperate she was. Only desperation would make her toss out lies like that. She lied about him being a coward. She lied about her brother. He could already read that in her.

Desperate people lied. And desperate people did stupid things. Like flick the ear of a duke. Like stick to a stupid plan, because it was the only thing to hold onto.

Devin rubbed his ear—the flick had actually stung. And then she had tried to blackmail him into silence. The little wench.

His eyes narrowed at her. He wasn't going to let her succeed at stupidity. She needed to be protected from herself, whether she liked it or not.

Devin wondered how long it would take her to produce the necessary excuses to leave the party.

He didn't have to wait long. Soon enough, he saw her rub her temples in a distressed motion, and her aunt's immediate sympathetic face. The aunt rushed off to find her husband, and within minutes, the party of three made their way up the grand staircase and out of the ballroom.

"Excuse me, gentlemen." Devin nodded to the four men surrounding him and stepped away to find Killian.

"Killian." Devin motioned to his friend.

"We shall continue this at another time, gentlemen." Killian nodded to the group and stepped from the ring of men.

The two friends walked up the staircase and paused at a quiet balcony overlooking the ballroom. Both leaned on the gold-leafed railing, looking absently out at the hall of gaiety before them.

"Whatever you said to her on the terrace must have been interesting, for she could barely contain her need to leave, or hold in the arrows her pretty eyes were throwing your way," Killian said, and took a sip of the Madeira he was holding.

"She called me a coward."

Killian sputtered and laughed. "A coward? What I would have given to hear that. Really? A coward? And your reaction?"

"Threats."

"Typical." Killian turned sideways, leaning on his arm as he looked at Devin. "Is it time to leave, then?"

"Soon. Is your business done?"

"Yes, enough for the night." Killian curiously eyed his friend. "She appears to be fine marriage material."

"Who?"

"Lady Augustine."

Devin shot his own daggers at Killian. "Yes, if you discount her panache for dressing up as a hack driver and trying to take down four men, each twice her size."

"Lends a certain charm to her, would you not say?" Killian took another sip of his wine. "We all, eventually, have duty to our lineage, Devin. An heir might be something you want to think about."

Devin harrumphed, stood straight, and turned toward the upper entrance of the ballroom. "Let us take our leave—if only to cease your idiotic insinuations."

Killian followed Devin, speculative smile playing on his face. "We have a coach to catch, don't we?"

CHAPTER 6

The night plodded along slowly. Rain had sputtered on and off. Her cloak kept her mostly dry, but her search thus far had remained completely fruitless.

Some insistent young dandies, deep into their cups and rich with the need to lose their families' fortunes, managed to stop Aggie. They tumbled into the moving carriage before she could stop them.

With a sigh, she started off to the Horn's Rooster, knowing that, of the gaming halls, it was one of the best for drunken young men of the peerage to go. The owner was of the good sort; she had seen him send many on their way before fortunes were lost on the flick of a card.

It was odd, the knowledge she had gained from the streets of London. If nothing else, this had forced her into a much wider view of the world than she had ever known.

The Horn's Rooster teetered on the edge of the east side, which was convenient—she would still have time to go back and poke around near the area where she had found the murderers.

Scouring the east end from her hackney perch was an inescapable part of finding the murderers, and she hated the sort of fares she was inevitably forced to pick up in that part of town. The drunkest of the drunks. The stench from within, and the cleaning that had to be done once a drunk spilled his night's supper on the floor of the carriage was disgusting. And it seemed to happen to her at least every other night.

Aggie dropped her fares at the Horn's Rooster, lucky to be rid of them so quickly, and nicked Sunshine along. Her favorite horse since seventeen, Sunshine was a key component in her plan, for Sunshine, without fail, obeyed every command of Aggie's. She had not realized how indispensable that bit of foresight had been until the previous night. In the country, Sunshine usually accompanied Aggie when she went out to practice her shot, so the horse was used to the sudden cracks of gunfire.

Trotting the white speckled horse down one of the rank streets of the east side, Aggie felt the first drops of more rain. She rolled her eyes as she adjusted the hood of her cloak.

At that moment, two men stumbled out in front of Aggie from a well-known brothel. Their rich clothes hung haphazardly about them, and their bawdy laughter filled the already loud street.

One of them was obviously very intoxicated, bent over, head hanging low, and struggling to keep upright as he staggered across the street. The other man seemed a bit more sober, helping his friend. The semi-sober man hailed her. They blocked her path and gave her no choice but to stop.

Aggie tensed, as always, when she took on a new fare. Her left hand held the reins, while she slipped off her glove and hovered her right hand over one of the pistols hidden in the depths of her dark cloak. Caution was key; there had been several times when she had barely escaped being mugged—or worse— from an unscrupulous patron.

These two men seemed okay. Aside from their unkempt clothing, they were obviously men of society. She looked down, suspicion evident, at the two men.

"Evening, hack," the semi-sober man said, high spirits in his voice. "It would seem my friend here needs a bit of help gaining transportation home. I would take him myself, of course, but I have not exactly finished of my pleasures here tonight." He nodded back over his shoulder.

The drunk friend started bellowing a raunchy song, aimed at the cobblestones. Words incoherent, it sounded more reminiscent of a howling dog than an actual tune.

"Yuss, sir," Aggie said in a low, slurred tone. She produced a pathetic cough for effect. "Jus ees long as he don't spackle in me coach."

The man laughed as he shoved his still bellowing friend into the carriage. "No, I reckon he will be okay, at least until he makes his residence."

The man gave Aggie the address and a few coins, and quickly stepped back into the brothel. She could hear raucous music and high-pitched laughter blaring into the night when the door opened.

She hesitated at the sound, thinking of her own innocence when she had first started charading as a hack driver. She knew the streets in the better parts of London well enough, but had to memorize maps of the areas she had never dared go into before, imagining that she would have to search hardest in those areas to find her father's killers.

But nothing had prepared her for the poverty or the lack of morals she now saw on a near-nightly basis. It had taken her several trips to a certain red-bricked building to realize that she was dropping off her fares, all men, at a brothel.

It hadn't been until the third trip that Aggie had actually registered the fact that there were a peculiar number of scantily-clad women milling about the front steps and lounging on one of the two well-lit balconies. That was where she had gotten her first proposition as a man. She'd passed on the offer, head tucked down.

She recognized such buildings now, and knew what they were for, but that didn't stop her from wondering, ears reddened, what exactly went on in such houses. Hearing certain words tossed at her from the balconies only got her so far in her imagination, and she was beginning to wonder just how many holes were actually on the human body. What her mother had told her years ago bore no resemblance to the harlot speak she heard night after night.

The bellowing behind her slowly tapered off, and she guessed the man was working on passing out. Aggie shook her head. Men and their carnal pleasures—after what she had seen on the streets, she wasn't so sorry that she never got married.

She clicked Sunshine on, her clomping hooves on the cobblestones echoing down the empty street. At least the drizzle had died off. It was late and only a few hours from sunrise. She wasn't going to find the remaining two murderers that night.

Get this fare home, and, for a change, she would bow to the needs of her exhausted body and be home before sunrise to get some much needed sleep.

Tap, tap, tap.

Aggie's ears perked.

Tap, tap, tap.

The insistent tapping came from inside the coach. Could the night become any less productive?

Aggie grumbled to herself as she pulled the reins. Her intoxicated passenger obviously needed to lose his dinner. Best that he did it in the street.

Hopping off her perch, she quickly opened the carriage door and swung aside, knowing the man was about to fly out, hand poised over his mouth.

Instead, an arm swept out, grabbing her wrist and yanking her hard into the carriage. Her shins banged into the carriage doorway. Before she could reach for a pistol, she was flipped onto her back and her free arm clamped into an iron brace.

Stuck atop her fare, Aggie went to her last resort, kicking. Thrashing as hard as she could, her boots made several hard thunks on the attacker's ankles. But then her legs were immediately captured between steely thighs.

She stopped squirming, realizing it was wasting precious energy. Through the terror haze in her mind, she heard her name being repeated quietly and smoothly.

A voice she recognized. A voice too familiar from earlier in the evening.

No.

It couldn't be.

Not again.

The duke. And she was sprawled fully on top of him on the floor of the coach, her body clamped tight to his.

"Your grace, let me go." She craned her head upward. "What of you?"

He chuckled over her obvious indignation, not loosening his hold. "My dear lady, how could I resist another one of our exciting midnight jaunts?"

Aggie blustered, wiggling again. "First, your grace, I am not your dear. Second, and more important, you were not invited on this particular midnight jaunt."

She pulled her arms with her wiggle, trying to free them.

"There, you are wrong, my dear. I was invited."

She couldn't see it, but she could hear the smile in his voice.

Aggie groaned, stopping her wiggle. She kept her head craned as far as she could off of his chest. "By whom, your grace? For it certainly was not I, and unless you count inviting yourself along, I would say you have no argument. You are not a welcome companion, and I advise you to let me go, remove yourself from this coach, and go back to the brothel to find your nightly entertainment there."

The duke's chest rumbled under her back. Aggie's breath tightened. He took her plight with amusement. She was fighting for her life, and he was laughing at her. Again.

"On the contrary, my dear, my presence is both necessary and invited."

Aggie couldn't reply, the burn in her chest taking all words. She stared at the pockmarked ceiling of the carriage.

"Fate invited me. Fate put me in your path last night, and I am honor-bound as a gentleman to adhere to fate's wishes. Fate wants you protected. I am obliged to bow to fate's wishes." His grip tightened even harder. "Cooperation, or not."

"Protection?" Aggie struggled, growling, giving another attempt at getting out of his arms. "Your grace—"

"Devin."

"Your grace, I do not require any protection." She twisted her arm and managed to poke an elbow into his chest.

"I, on the other hand, believe you do, Aggie. And I am seeing to it that you receive it."

He unclamped his legs that had snaked around her and released Aggie's arms and torso. He remained still as Aggie tried to keep a sense of propriety, awkwardly struggling to remove herself from their tangle.

Clawing herself upright, she shoved off the tiny carriage floor, not caring what limb of his she crushed in the process. She heaved herself onto the seat with the torn cushion.

"Was that necessary?"

The duke sat up, arms resting on his bent knees, and regarded Aggie. "Would you have come in to chat with me on your own?"

Aggie glared.

"Exactly. So yes, it was necessary." He went to his feet, reaching out and closing the carriage door. "You may as well accept the fact that I will be by your side if you decide to go on any more of these excursions, Aggie. For if I was not convinced before, I certainly am now, after the night I have had of following you about. For hours, all without the slightest notice from you—"

"You were stalking me?"

"Following. And yes, I was." He moved to the cushion across from Aggie, his long legs stretching out on either side of hers. "And your complete lack of observation that I have been following you since you left your townhouse has only proven to me that you need my protection."

Aggie started to shove the many locks of hair that fallen into her face back under her cap.

"Why are they trying to kill you, Aggie?"

She put her hands in front of her face, working on her hair. He could have this conversation alone.

"I have all night, Aggie. So you can hide that face of yours until the bright light of morning, or you can answer the question."

Aggie dropped her hands to her lap with a sigh. "I saw their faces, I guess."

"And your sister and mother. Are they in any danger, or are they only after you?"

"I thought it was just me." Aggie picked at the black soot that rubbed onto her fingers after touching her face. She didn't want to share, but her options were limited. "But then I was out of the house one day, and one of them—I believe it was one of them from my sister's description—showed up at our house. I do not know what was said, but our butler did not let him in. I immediately hired guards to watch my sister and mother around the clock after that."

"No guards for yourself?"

"We came to London soon after."

"So you could go after them on your own?"

"I see your look, your grace. You do not hide it well. I know you think I am an idiot. But I am doing the only thing I can think of for survival. I am the only one that actually believes of the threat I am under."

"You told others?"

"Yes. I told our local constable. You did not see how he looked at me. He laughed, then patted me on the head. I do not exaggerate. He patted me on the head." She shuddered, remembering the utter humiliation. "He did not believe me."

"I did."

"You had to. You were forced into it by circumstance." She bit her lip. "With all respect, your grace, you do not understand how men look at a woman my age. I am fanciful and full of dreams and drama and silly imaginings to them. Not harsh realities."

"So you tried once and gave up? What about your uncle?"

Aggie's eyes widened. "Please, your grace, do not tell anyone. I considered my options. And now...I am doing what needs to be done. I will not allow my family, and that includes my aunt and uncle, to be jeopardized—they are all I have. I am all they have."

"So your chosen option was to try to kill four men?"

"I do not take the deaths lightly, your grace. I am sorry you were involved. It is my soul that takes the marks of those deaths, not yours. And I do not intend for you to have another death on your conscience. Please, just let us part ways, and let me do what needs to be done."

"I think you already know I cannot let you do that, Aggie."

Her eyes took in Devin's face, and she was suddenly frightened by the man across from her.

She had thought of him as a nuisance and a threat to the exposing of her hack driving, but in that moment, he became much more. He became someone to not just ignore and hope would go away. He became a true threat.

A threat to her entire plan to put right the wrongs and to keep her family safe.

He would no longer allow her to continue on her mission as she had been. For some reason, he had decided she was his to protect.

Why? What possible reason would a man of his status have for getting involved with a girl in a ridiculous amount of trouble? It wasn't worth it. Aggie's eyes narrowed at him as she wondered what he really wanted of her.

Even worse, she wondered at her own reaction. She liked the man. She liked that he didn't cower from danger. Liked that he actually listened to her, even if he disagreed with every step she took. Liked his steel eyes. The concern in them. No one had looked at her with such raw concern in a very long time. It was that concern that held the most danger.

Like him or not, she had to get rid of him.

Aggie shook her head, eyes at the ceiling. What else could she say to remove this man from her shoulder?

She levelled her eyes at him. "Maybe I went about this all wrong earlier at the ball. I apologize. I should have thanked you, your grace, and then we could have parted ways." Aggie gave him a quick smile, folding her hands in her lap. "So thank you. I appreciate your help. Is that what you are really after? Acknowledgment of good deeds done?"

He smiled at her then, slow, drawn out. Aggie swallowed hard against what was coming.

"You can keep trying, Aggie, but I am going nowhere. Charm, blackmail, appreciation—all of them hold no sway with me. Have you not already learned I do what I please?"

Aggie bit back a scream. Of course he did what he wanted. Obvious.

"Your grace, once more, I do not need your protection. As for your stalking of me, well, you are no gentleman—truly odious behavior."

"And you consider yourself a lady?"

Aggie let her irritation show in the dagger look she shot him as she stood, trying to step over his leg and leave the carriage. Unfazed, the duke grabbed her arm and yanked her down directly into his lap.

"Your manhandling is out of control, your grace." Aggie lost no time in trying to break free, which merely caused him to clamp his arms around her again.

Aggie took a deep breath, attempting calm. It didn't work.

"Your grace, you have just grievously insulted me." She looked down her nose at him, the best she could from her close and awkward angle.

"I meant no insult, my lady, just merely noting the clothing." His hands moved along her cloak, patting the lumps. "Good God, how many pistols do you have in there?"

"Enough." Aggie bristled, then froze as a new realization struck her. "Blasted that."

The duke's eyebrows rose at her in question.

She sighed, her eyes darting off, distracted. "I presume the man who helped your 'drunk' self into the cab tonight was your friend, Lord Southfork…which means my secret is no longer a secret."

"Not to fear. Yes, Killian knows of your fetish for dressing up in men's clothing and your hackney skills. But he would never repeat the story to anyone, not even under torture, unless you, specifically, gave him permission."

"You trust him that much?" Aggie asked, disbelief clear in her eyes.

"Without doubt. I trust him with my life, and I trust him with your secret."

He looked hard into her eyes, and her breath caught. She was much too close to him, on his lap for heaven's sake. She forced out wooden words. "Yes, but the question remains. Do I trust you?"

Aggie searched his face, his eyes. Could she trust this man? Could she trust her very life to anyone other than herself? Did she even have a choice?

Calm resolve, clear as the day in his steely eyes, was all she saw in answer to her question.

How could she trust someone she knew nothing of? Someone she instinctively knew was dangerous. But dangerous to her? That was the real question.

Her heart stopped beating in the next moment. But not because of the duke.

Because a knife flew in at them through the open carriage window.

The next second, she was smothered.

~ ~ ~

In an instant, Devin had her flattened on the carriage floor.

Not taking a breath, not caring that his weight crushed her, he reacted before the knife had fully embedded into the worn cushion.

Devin stilled, listening.

Aggie's breath became hot and quick, and she started wiggling to escape from the shell he had enclosed her in.

"Aggie, it would do nicely if you could stop squirming for a minute," Devin said in a dead calm whisper. "I am going to get up, and I demand complete silence and no movement out of you. Do you understand?"

Harshness edged his voice, he knew, but he couldn't afford the slightest question from her. It was a damn knife that missed her by inches, after all.

A whisper went into his chest. "Yes."

He slithered his right hand between them, ignoring Aggie's gasp as he brushed past her breast. He fished, extracting one of Aggie's pistols from deep in her cloak.

Lethal grace lining his movements, Devin shifted off of Aggie, his foot gaining a small spot by her head, and positioned himself low against the inside of the coach. He pulled out his own pistol, leaned up, head back as far as he could, but with sight line to the street.

All was silent.

He waited.

Devin noted that Aggie had actually listened to him and remained frozen, lying on the floor, eyes wide as he got up from her. But now she slowly started to move her arms.

He cleared his throat. She stopped.

He turned his attention back to the street. Still silent.

Devin looked down at Aggie and pointed to the opposite carriage door. They had to remove themselves from the interior of the carriage, for this was the worst place to be cornered.

Aggie nodded. Scrupulously searching the street, Devin knelt, poised to react. Aggie crawled to the corner opposite him, pistol drawn.

After a minute, Devin glanced back at her.

"They are gone?" she whispered.

He moved over to her, hand going over her shoulder onto the door latch. It would be quickest to escape the immediate area by foot. "We need to get out of here. Are you ready to run?"

Aggie shook her head. "I am not leaving my horse."

Of course not. Of course her damn horse was more important than bodily harm to her—or him. She sure worked on saving herself in the worst possible ways.

A swear started, but Devin swallowed it before it escaped.

Even through the black soot covering her face, he could see the set of her jaw. She wasn't going to budge on leaving her horse.

"Fine. But you are staying in here."

"No. You need other eyes up there. And you know I can shoot."

Devin bit back another blasphemy. He knew he couldn't stop her, and he also knew they needed to get the hell out of there. Not giving her permission, he opened the door slowly, eyes scanning the street and adjoining alleys. Stepping out, he slid along the edge of the black coach, and crawled up to the driver's perch.

Aggie followed, drawing another pistol on her way. She joined him on the small seat, wedging herself in next to him. Devin grabbed the reins and sent the carriage down the street, moving west past Charring Cross without further incident.

They reached a respectable area, and he pulled off the main thoroughfare to a quiet residential street.

"Why are we stopping?" Aggie slid her pistols back into the pockets in her cloak.

Devin pulled the brake on the carriage. "Our conversation is not done, Aggie. Down you go. Back into the coach."

"What? Why? What is wrong with staying up here and conversing? We can chat on the way back to the place I dropped you last night?" She looked a little too hopeful.

"I am not going to have a conversation like this out in the middle of the street, Aggie."

"But the two of us together in there. Alone. It is not at all proper."

"Proper?" Devin cocked an eyebrow. "Truly? You are going to try that ploy? Maybe pulling up together at your uncle's residence would be more proper?"

Aggie growled, turning from him, then started to climb down. "Fine. But whatever you may think of me at this moment—outside of this, outside of my current outfit—I am nothing but a respectable lady, and I would like it to remain that way."

"Duly noted." Devin followed her down.

She went into the carriage first, pushing her hood off her head as she sat, arms crossed over her chest. Even in the dim light coming from the outside carriage lantern, her glare was obvious.

"What is that?" Aggie pointed at Devin's upper arm as he moved in front of her.

He sat and Aggie scampered across the coach to sit next to him.

"Your coat—the tear?" Aggie reached out to touch a hole in the dark cloth.

Devin looked down at his arm, surprised. He hadn't really noticed it in the commotion.

Without waiting for him, Aggie pulled his overcoat down past his shoulder to inspect his black jacket. It, too, was torn. Her fingers went over the tear.

"It is wet. Take off your coat and jacket." She didn't wait for him to comply, just started to peel off his layers.

Devin allowed her, in silence, to pull off his overcoat. His only motion was to lean forward as Aggie's hands moved up his body to remove the jacket. She took care in how she laid both items next to her, then pushed her own sleeves up past her elbows.

Jacket gone, she returned her attention back to his arm. "Damn, it sliced you." She pulled a leg up under herself, turning fully to him, her nose nearly touching the wound. Devin could see blood staining his white linen shirt around the tear in the cloth.

"Does it hurt?" She tugged at the hole in the fabric, trying to see under it.

Devin shrugged.

She looked up at him, worry mixed with hesitation in her eyes. "Shrugging means it hurts, you realize. Would you mind if I ripped your shirt a bit more so I could see the wound?"

Devin gave her a perplexed look. And she was the one worried about properness? "I would rather you not tatter my clothes."

"But it is already ruined. I cannot tell how deep the slice is until the shirt is off the wound."

"True. But the whole shirt can just come off, you realize."

Her bottom lip slipped under her front teeth in obvious moral struggle. Devin kept an innocent look on his face as he watched, amusement growing, as she worked up the nerve to allow his shirt to come off. She moved from him and made a long, silent production of lighting the interior lantern.

"Maybe I should just remove it?" Devin's eyebrow cocked helpfully.

It took Aggie another minute to decide.

"Yes, please do so. I am not looking to become a harlot, mind you, but you are injured because of me." The dim carriage light did little to mask the color that was quickly flushing her face on the few sootless areas. She shifted her eyes from Devin to the far upper corner of the coach.

Devin took that as his cue to get on with the shirt removal. He did so slowly, prolonging Aggie's obvious embarrassment, intentionally bumping her several times as he struggled out of his waistcoat, braces, and linen shirt.

He cleared his throat.

Aggie didn't turn back.

He cleared it again with a little more insistence.

Aggie abruptly swung her head back, her eyes locking onto Devin's bare arm. She reached out to softly touch the wound. Much of the blood about the gash was dried, falling from her touch. A good sign. She prodded about the wound, pulling the skin slightly.

"It, ah," she cleared her throat, "it should be fine. The knife did not slice very deep at all. Just have your man wash it thoroughly when you arrive home." She offered a weak smile, her head still next to his arm, still staring intently at the wound, eyes refusing to veer.

"Are you positive it did not go too deep?" Devin shifted his weight to investigate himself, effectively positioning his chest directly in front of Aggie's face.

He held in a laugh when she froze, hands in mid-air, staring at his naked chest. Her head tilted downward, and Devin could see she wasn't closing her eyes against the show in front of her.

Her breathing had all but stopped, and Devin wasn't so convinced she truly wanted to avoid becoming a harlot. He shifted in his trousers that were quickly becoming a little tight. He wasn't going to get to his questions if she kept looking at him like that.

"Aggie, dear—"

Aggie's head shot straight up, knocking her forehead into Devin's chin and jamming his teeth together.

"Oh no, your grace." Her hand reached out to touch the side of his jawbone. "I am so sorry, I..." Her voice trailed off as her gaze fell down to his chest once more.

"Yes?" Devin prodded.

Aggie jumped again, this time to the opposite bench. Her hand went in front of her mouth, clearly mortified at her own gawking. Eyes darting to the side window, she looked like she was either planning on crawling out of it, or hoping another knife would come flying into the coach to put her out of her humiliation.

Devin rubbed his twanging jaw, contemplating her, waiting for her.

She took a deep breath, hand dropping from her lips.

"Could you please put your shirt back on?" Her voice turned meek as words tumbled together. "As the wound is not deep, or life-threatening, it is not at all proper for us…for you…to be… well, without enough clothes on, with…ahem, the two of us being here alone…"

Devin saw it took amazing restraint, but Aggie finally made her mouth close.

He nodded, very serious. "Yes, Aggie, you are quite right. This is not at all proper." He put his shirt on, his movements not impeded at all by the small wound.

"Good, I am glad you agree." Her agreement didn't stop her eyes from searching out the last glimpse of his chest disappearing beneath the once crisp shirt. Then her look flew down to her lap. "And I apologize about the wound. It should have been mine."

"Aggie, look at me."

Her eyes lifted.

"No, it should not have been. Not yours."

Her gaze slipped back down to her hands. "I am sorry. I honestly regret your injury. That you have been hurt because of me."

Devin hadn't given the scratch a second thought, but he could tell Aggie was plagued with guilt over the injury. He couldn't let an opportunity like that slide away.

"If you truly are apologetic, I think you could prove your regret by calling me Devin."

"Your grace, that is too intimate."

"And where your hands just were, was not?"

Eyes to the carriage ceiling, Aggie sighed, buying a moment. "Your name, your grace. If I use it, it makes promises of future encounters. I am hoping we end these very soon."

"I am sitting here, wound in my shoulder, bloody because of the situation you put me in, and you are going to deny me simplicity in conversation?"

"Fine, your grace. Devin." She gave a beaten-but-not-out smile, which quickly disappeared with her next words. "But if you are going to use your wound as leverage against me, I would like to remind you that you put yourself in this situation tonight. I did not invite you into this carriage. That was your own doing."

Devin sighed. "We are back to that then?"

"We are." Aggie crossed her arms.

They stared at each other for an extended moment, will against will.

"Aggie, whether you will admit it to yourself or not, you need my help. You are foolishly putting yourself in harm's way. It is not necessary. These men can easily and efficiently be disposed of in a more discrete manner."

He leaned forward, his forearms resting upon his knees as he pinned Aggie under his best intimidating glare. It buckled the strongest of men, and he didn't care if it scared her. He needed to inspire the direness of the situation to her.

"Aggie, the harm you would do to your family, if you were injured or killed, far outweighs any sense of satisfaction that may be achieved when these men are brought to justice. You need to believe me on that one. You have been reckless in going about this entire mess. And you need to acknowledge the fact that you are no match for ruthless men such as these."

Aggie took a deep breath as her eyes closed and her head shook slowly. He hadn't scared her in the slightest.

She looked at him, tears fighting on the brim of her soot-lined eyes.

"I do not think you understand how easy it would be for me to just accept your help, your grace…to pass this responsibility off." She looked down and began to play with a corner of her overcoat that had landed in her lap. "I dream of being able to do that. I dream of having my simple life in the country back. I am so tired, and I just wish sometimes that someone would come along and tell me everything is going to be alright. That they would take care of me. So I could crawl into bed and pretend none of this ever happened. That I don't have to worry. That I am safe. That my family is safe. I wish my father were alive. I wish my brother was back. "

Green eyes lifted to meet grey ones.

"But they are not. Which is exactly why I cannot pass responsibility. Only I can guarantee those things to myself."

She looked away.

"And if I fail, there is no one to blame but me." An awkward chuckle left her lips. "I will be dead, but that is a much better fate than having someone else die because of me and my cowardice to my responsibility."

"This is not a game they play, Aggie. This is your life. You dying is not all right."

"I know you think I am stupid—an idiot for doing all this on my own. That I have no idea what they could really do to me. But I do…" Her voice caught as her eyes closed off a memory.

Devin waited.

The corners of her closed eyes crinkled in pain. "I do know. I know very well."

Her hand moved off her lap, slipping under the edge of her cloak. Devin saw her fingers slip onto her bare left forearm.

A vile rage rose into his throat.

"The scar?"

Her hand gripped tight over the pink line of scar tissue, as her head tilted back to rest on the seat cushion, eyes still not opening. Her voice so soft, Devin had to lean forward to hear her as her words floated to the ceiling.

"I have no illusions about pain or death, Devin. I know this isn't a game. I know the raw brutality…what failure feels like. The pain of blood. Of knife in skin."

Devin's imagination went wild. And the picture he conjured in his mind of Aggie at the mercy of the cutthroats—it was all he could do to remain in the carriage instead of out on the dark street, tracking down the bastards, and sending them not just to death, but slow, tortured, mangled death.

"It is why I will not be responsible for involving an innocent in what I must do to save my own life. Your injury tonight is just a reminder of that," Aggie said, her words slow and measured. "I am the only one responsible for me. For my family. Even after last night, you are still an innocent in this. I cannot add more injuries, or heaven forbid, your death, onto my conscience. I am fine. I will be fine. Truly."

She opened her eyes and looked at him. Pleading through pain. "Please, Devin. Please just walk away. I am begging you. Please. Walk away."

Silent, Devin moved forward, eyes locked on hers. He slid his hand under her cloak sleeve, gently prying her fingers from the scar and pulling her arm out from the depths of the fabric. The tips of his fingers slid up the scar, then back down. His eyes didn't lose contact.

"I am not going anywhere, Aggie."

"Please…"

"No." His fingers slid up her arm again. "This is despicable—unacceptable. Those bastards will not harm you again."

Silence settled in the coach. Devin stared at Aggie, waiting. She fidgeted, looking everywhere but at him, knowing she had revealed too much, offered up too much vulnerability.

He didn't let her arm go from his grasp.

After a few minutes, she finally looked directly at him. "What is in this for you? Honesty, please. Why do you want to help me? I thank God for your help last night. It was above the duty of a stranger. But why help me now?"

"Honestly?"

"Please."

"You intrigue me, Lady Augustine. You drive a hack. Can shoot a man dead with perfect aim. Hours later you create the perfect persona of a young lady of the ton. You wear breeches quite well. If there is anyone like you, I have yet to meet her. Although I am already well convinced you are one-of-a-kind. But all of that is minor, next to the fact that this," he rubbed her arm, producing goose bumps under the pads of his fingertips, "this whole threat upon your life is just plain wrong. What it has forced you to do. It hits at my core. A core I had not even suspected I had."

She tried to pull her arm from his grasp. No success. "But what you will want in return…I am afraid I do not think I can give you what you want, Devin. I may be unconventional—"

"May be?"

"Fine, I am unconventional, but circumstances demand it of me. I am mostly very conventional. Truly. What you want in return for your assistance…"

The earlier blush returned to her face.

"You do not need to fret, Lady Augustine. I demand nothing of you. Nothing except acceptance of my help." He let the side of his mouth slip up. "Although I do grow weary over bickering about my involvement in your situation. That you could free me of."

Her mouth opened, and she looked for a moment like she was going to continue to resist. Her mouth closed, and she looked down at his hand on her arm. "Nothing from me?" Her eyes moved up to his. "Can I believe that?"

"Have I given you any reason not to trust me? Aside from stalking you and finding a way into the carriage, of course."

"No. I do not suppose you have. Fine. I will stop my resistance."

She slid from under his arm and stood to exit the carriage. A step, and she froze, her eyes captured by the knife embedded in the side of the wine-velvet cushion. A shaking gasp invaded her body.

With trembling hand, she reached out slowly and touched the previously unnoticed trinket hanging from the knife. Blood splattered and half dug into the cushion, a pretty peach reticule hung from the blade.

"What is that?"

Aggie's hand jerked away from the knife. Devin had to strain to hear her.

"I gave it to him."

Her hand went back to the reticule.

"Who?"

"Tommy…my help, my runner's apprentice. I gave it to him tonight." Aggie choked the words out, hand gripping the bloody reticule.

"My God. Look at this. What would they have done to him? He is so young. Why?" She took a deep breath, controlling the panic. "He has to be okay. He is smart, he will be okay. He has to be."

She collapsed onto the bench, eyes closed, voice wispy. "They are too close. They know my horse, my carriage. Your arm. Tommy. This is too much blood." She opened her eyes and ripped the purse from the knife, gripping it tightly in her hand.

Head hung, Aggie stood and stepped out of the carriage, not waiting for Devin to reply.

Devin followed her. "Aggie, yes, they know." He notched his voice into gentle, or at least what he hoped was gentle, as he grabbed her hand to help her up to the driver's perch.

He vaulted up beside her and grabbed the reins, sending her horse forward. "After last night, they know exactly what you have been doing, and who you are pretending to be. You cannot deny it. So this charade is now finished. You will go home, leave these men to me, and cease putting yourself in needless danger night after night."

Turning onto a main thoroughfare, he couldn't hold in a sigh, shaking his head. "Clearly the men in your life have had a hard time saying 'no' to you, Aggie, which is why you now find yourself in your current state. Make no mistake. I have no such reservations. The only thing you should be hearing right now is 'no.' The biggest no you have ever heard in your life, ringing in your ears. You are stopping this nonsense."

Devin hoped her head-down silence, meant that maybe, just maybe, she was actually listening to him.

"I understand. I can see that panic drove you to this point. But your panic needs to stop. Your planning. Your scheming. All of it needs to stop. I will take care of the remaining men, and I will condone no more of your late-night sneak-outs."

Her hands tightened in her lap. Devin could feel her whole body recoil next to his. But she didn't look up. Didn't challenge.

"If I find you out again, Aggie, I will drag you to your aunt and uncle's home. They will be told what is going on and what you have been doing. They might forgive you for such a transgression, or they might not. Either way, they will not forget. And I will have them put you under lock and key until I resolve this situation."

At the alley a block away from Aggie's townhouse, Devin slowed the hack. Aggie slipped off the perch before Devin stopped the wheels, and she started to walk stoically, gait stiff, past the courtyards behind the houses.

He didn't like the complete avoidance. She was either completely humiliated, or planning something. He didn't like where his strongest suspicion took him.

"Aggie," he said, voice loud but low. She stopped, but didn't turn around to him. "I expect to see you at the Appleton party this evening, per your previous commitment."

A silent nod, and she moved forward, disappearing into her house.

No. He didn't like at all what he suspected.

CHAPTER 7

Warm night air filtered in through the tall window she stood next to, and Aggie leaned slightly to the breeze. If it weren't for the whiffs of air, she would have passed out long ago from the combination of no sleep and the stuffy crowd. The party twinkled, music filtering through the crowd and chandeliers casting a warm, glowing quality above the sea of lightly colored gowns and contrasting dark colors.

Aunt Beatrix stood by her side, talking endlessly with her friends about which of the men present were rakes, scoundrels, gold-diggers, or solid husband material.

Aggie couldn't count the number of times her aunt, or one of her aunt's friends, turned to her, and with sly confidence, berated her for whatever social sin they believed Aggie was committing at a particular moment—stand straighter, bigger smile, flutter the fan, too many blinks, smaller smile. Each of the ladies surrounding her was convinced introductions would roll in if Aggie just tried a bit harder.

Introductions and requests to land on her dance card petered in, and Aggie danced a few sets, but whenever another dance or more conversation was requested of her, she always politely made excuses to get back to her aunt.

Each time, Aggie could see the disappointment in Aunt Beatrix's face as she made her way back to her aunt's side. It was like this at every soirée. And although Aggie appeared to be continually scanning the attendees of the party, she was not looking for interesting, marriageable men—she was looking for one man.

One evil face. The one face she had to find. The one face that would grant her peace. Even if the duke found the other two bastards and disposed of them, she would not be at peace. Devin didn't know about the fifth man. The one Aggie was desperate to find. Their leader.

He was the one that had put the final bullet into her father.

A familiar pang rang across her left arm. The one that had cut her.

He was too well-dressed, talked too much in the cadence of a gentleman for him not to be part of society. She was positive if she searched hard enough, she would find the man.

Party after party, ball after ball, she scoured. But she had yet to find him. And until she did, she had to continue putting on a false front at these parties—with at least enough pleasantness to ensure the invitations kept coming.

Her initial certainty that society would be the best place to find the man who killed her father was beginning to wane. But his ego and wardrobe still had her convinced he would show up in society eventually. Aggie just prayed he would appear soon— either in society or given away by one of his thugs.

A young man, blond hair just barely hanging out of his eyes, approached her at that moment, flanked by Aggie's aunt, who was wearing a cat-caught-mouse grin on her face. Introductions to Lord Ferrington were made, and Aggie politely allowed herself to be led to the dance floor.

Not two turns in, Aggie was astonished by Lord Ferrington's pretentiousness. Her aunt must be getting desperate if this was the best that could now be produced. Aggie bit her lip as he swept her through the crowd, trying to remain agreeable, docile, and dumb. It was an easy enough task, and afforded her a nice round of face searching.

Dance over, Aggie escaped the Baron and made her way back through the throng to her aunt. Her aunt started in before Aggie's feet stopped.

"Aggie, honey, I see you have dissuaded yet another. I do not know how you manage to do it so quickly. I had to pull upon all my guile to capture Lord Ferrington as it was. You are putting them away faster than I can take them in, dear," her aunt said good-naturedly. "Now, far be it for me—of all people—to be pushy about such matters, but maybe you should give some of these men a chance?"

"Yes, maybe I should," Aggie said, noncommittal.

"It is dreadfully warm in here." Aunt Beatrix flipped open her fan and fluttered it around her round face. "Now dear, do not be coy with your aunt. I watched you that entire dance with Lord Ferrington and you did not say but two words. I believe I even saw you openly biting your lip. Your lip! I do not care how odious a comment that man made—and yes, I am sure he made several—your mother taught you better than to bite your lip in the middle of a ballroom."

"Biting the lip was a bit much, was it not?"

"I am afraid so, dear." Beatrix smiled warmly at her niece. "Now, we both know how charming you can be when you set your mind to it, so maybe you would like to try it one of these nights?"

The hope in her aunt's voice sent a pang of guilt through Aggie. As if she didn't have enough to feel guilty about. Tommy, the duke, now she couldn't even properly paste a smile on her face for her aunt. Blast it, she needed to get some sleep. She was near to being a walking corpse.

Even in reprimanding, her aunt was more than kind to her, and Aggie knew she had done little to deserve it. She forced a bright smile. "You are right Aunt Beatrix, I should try harder. You have been amazing at securing all of these introductions. Thank you for being so understanding."

Her aunt smiled in satisfaction and turned to join in on the conversation of her friends. Aggie was relieved it had been that easy. Usually her aunt went on for a bit longer.

Aggie took a sip of champagne. She just had to make it through a few months and then she could get back to the plan for the rest of her life. Live at Clapinshire. Take care of her mother. Marry off Lizzy. Be content.

All she had to do was participate in the season and find her father's killers. That was all.

At least the social functions placated her aunt and uncle, so they could at least believe they tried their best to get her a husband. Aggie knew her aunt would never forgive herself if she felt she hadn't done all she could to find Aggie a suitable husband—Beatrix had lived through the pain of spinsterhood until she met Howard. But Aggie hoped that after this season, her aunt would turn her attentions to grooming Lizzie into a darling debutante.

The evening wore on, and Aggie scanned the room, watching the balcony above as new arrivals were continually announced and descending down the half-circular, green marble staircase. The crush was thicker than normal, and Aggie couldn't shake the feeling that if she didn't look at every present person's face, she would miss him. That one man who could end her torment. The man who murdered her father.

The pit in her stomach expanded. The pit of failure. If she could just see a bit more, hear a bit more, search a bit more, she would find him. Two were down, but three still remained. And they knew all about her. Time was critical now.

A flash of Lizzie and her mother home alone without her seized Aggie. She would have to put more guards on the house first thing tomorrow. Had she been thinking straight today, she would have already done so. But by the time she got in, scrubbed every bit of stubborn soot from her skin, found Tommy, rounded up a doctor for him, stayed with his mother and his baby sister for the afternoon, stopped by the stables to make sure the duke had deposited Sunshine appropriately, and made her way home to ready for the party, she was exhausted. Sleep hadn't been an option.

How dare the duke demand her presence here tonight? She could be at home, tucked into bed. Yes, he had assisted her—killed for her, if she was honest about it. Yes, he gave blood for her. Yes, he claimed he wanted to help her. But did that really give him control over her whereabouts?

Yet here she was.

Aggie cringed at the list. It actually was a generous tally in the duke's favor.

Aunt Beatrix nudged her in the side, head tilted to the left. "Apparently, your latest dissuasion was not as successful as you hoped."

Aggie ripped her eyes off the crowd and looked left, only to see Lord Ferrington moving through the crowd, his determined eyes locked on Aggie.

She swallowed a sigh and produced a polite smile. Her aunt deserved it.

~ ~ ~

Devin was in a foul mood. The search that day for the two remaining bastards was worthless. And not only had he not taken care of the men threatening Aggie, when he arrived at the Appleton party, he walked in to find Aggie immersed in conversation with Lord Ferrington. He did not like the man. Though he barely knew him, he knew of him. The baron was a bloodsucker.

Across the wide room, Killian extracted himself from a circle of men and joined Devin, handing him a glass of Madeira.

"My men have had no luck. Have you found out anything else?" Devin didn't bother with pleasantries after the day Killian and he had. Even though he had a slew of investigators after the two men, he and Killian had spent most of the day visiting the lowest of the low holes trying to find the two bastards.

Devin wasn't stupid enough to enter those holes without Killian watching his back. Although they ferreted out those that knew of the band of four, now two—notorious in their own right—they weren't to be found in any of the places people guessed. The two were hiding. And hiding meant planning.

"No," Killian said. "And I visited some of Vivienne's most sketchy connections. No luck."

Devin nodded. Killian's red-headed mistress had a rather colorful past, and she was always one to make sure she had plenty of favors to cash–in around London. "I am beginning to wonder if they are not alone. The continued attacks, they do not make sense. If we learned anything today, it was that these men are brutal, but simple idiots. Why continue after her? Why continue unless someone was prodding them. Someone who had something to lose."

"Could very well be," Killian said. "You know the best person to explore that theory with is across the room. She probably knows much more than she has let on."

"Do you think?"

"I do not trust. So yes, I do think so."

Devin sighed. "Thank you for your assistance."

"Happy to help. Even if it was for naught today. It is a nice change for me to help you, not the reverse."

Killian's eyes followed Devin's glaze. "Are you going to tell her we did not find them?"

Devin took a sip of the wine he had yet to lift. "Yes. She needs to be ready for anything, since I cannot be constantly by her side."

A smirk ran across Killian's face. "There is a way you can be by her side, you know."

Devin's glare shot to his friend. A look feared by many, it did nothing to the smirk still set firmly on Killian's face.

"Why would you go there? Again?" He shifted his look back to Aggie.

"Aside from the obvious duty to produce an heir, one, your eyes have not left her since you came in. Even just now, you could not afford to look away from her to me for more than a second."

"She is better looking than you."

"Ego be-dammed, I will give you that." Killian took a long swallow from his glass. "And two, you look like you want to crush Ferrington."

"She has spent far too long with the man. The gossips love fresh meat, and she is very near to being served up. Where the hell is her aunt? She should be cutting the conversation."

Killian gave a courtesy look around, smirk not moved.

"What good is a chaperone that does not know how to chaperone?"

"Seems her lack of a proper chaperone has been quite convenient for her," Killian said, "and for you, thus far."

Devin's eyes flickered to Killian, then back to Aggie. Granted, Aggie appeared to be just barely concealing a face of boredom over the conversation, but Killian was right. The sight of the two of them sent slivers of unnatural—yes, he would have to admit it—jealousy, down his spine.

He didn't really care to explore it, but he had begun to think of Aggie as his. Yes, he wanted her in his bed. But this was beyond a simple bedroom rendezvous. He was afraid he had actually begun to care about her well-being.

Then there was the matter of her innocence. After the obvious embarrassment Aggie displayed the previous night when Devin was shirtless, he was beginning to question his earlier conclusion about her experience with men. Was it possible, as bold as she was, that she was not experienced in the bedroom?

Devin's cool gaze pierced into the back of Ferrington's head. Jealousy was new to him, and he didn't particularly enjoy it. But to interrupt Aggie's conversation would only create an unnecessary stir throughout the party.

At this point, he didn't want to start raising questions about his association with Aggie.

"You should think about putting the demons to rest, Devin." Killian's voice interrupted his thoughts. "Move on. Live a real life. Who they were, is not who you are."

Devin's gaze swung sharply, eyes cutting into Killian. He contemplated for a moment punching him, disregarding the fact they were in the middle of a party.

"That is the advice that you, of all people, are going to give me?"

"My situation is different."

"Demons are demons, Killian. Put down yours and I'll put down mine."

Killian shrugged and stepped away to work the room. Devin shook his head. He knew his friend was no more willing to let go of the past than he was.

With a sigh, Devin moved to the entrance of the silver drawing room, swirling the glass of Madeira in his hand, leaning against a pillar and chatting disinterestedly with several men for a stretch. He seethed the entire time.

He tried to keep his eyes off her, but Ferrington continued to leer at the swell of her breasts rising out of her elegant yellow dress—too much skin for an unmarried woman. Killian was right. He did want to bust that leer off of Ferrington's face. Enough.

His eyes seared into Aggie's Ferrington-directed gaze, willing her to look at him.

As if on cue, she glanced in his direction, not in the least startled by his demanding stare. Devin gave a nod toward the French doors nearest Aggie, and was not disappointed when Aggie slightly inclined her head in response.

~ ~ ~

She had felt his eyes follow her most of the night, and she was grateful when the duke finally nodded her to the line of French doors open to the evening air. She had been monopolized by Lord Ferrington much too long tonight. Why had her aunt not cut this short? She would have extracted herself much earlier, but Ferrington required little from her in way of conversation. As long as she nodded her head, he would talk, and she was free to search the faces in the crush.

At the duke's motion, she excused herself to get some fresh air on the terrace, politely declining his offer to join her, and quickly slipped through the crowd toward the beckoning breeze.

Stepping onto the terrace, she walked past one of the open sets of white-paned French doors, trying to locate the duke. Inside, at the far end of the ballroom, she caught a glimpse of Devin's head moving past dancers. A couple passed in front of her, leaving her stretch of the terrace empty. When she located the duke again, he had stopped to talk to another man.

It wasn't until Devin moved toward the French doors that Aggie caught the side profile of the man he had been talking to.

She froze, her head slowly shaking in disbelief.

The man turned and disappeared into the crowd.

It couldn't have been. Not after all her time here in London. Not after all the searching she had done. No. Their leader would not just happen to show up.

Going to her toes, she searched the room again. Nothing. She ran along the travertine terrace to the next set of doors, searching.

She didn't see the duke step onto the terrace behind her. By the time she turned from the ballroom, he was leaning on the sculpted stone railing that ran along the drop of the terrace, his dark hair curled about his neck and crisp cravat, looking out into the night as though in a deep thought.

Taking a deep breath to shake what she was sure her imagination just manifested, Aggie started toward Devin, passing by a door that led into the drawing room. She caught the slightest glimpse of the man again.

She stopped and took a half-step into the drawing room, frantic eyes searching, but the man wasn't there. It had to have been her imagination. The leader that instigated her father's murder and tried to kill her was not here. He couldn't be. It had to be a cruel illusion her exhausted mind played on her. It had to be.

Her eyes gave one more fruitless search into the throng of people. No. It was impossible. Her father's murderer could not have just walked right by her. Could not have just talked to the Devin.

She saw nothing.

She turned back toward the duke, only to find him assessing her with a questioning look on his face. It took her a moment to realize both of her hands were clenched into tight fists. The slim fan in her right hand had cracked in half.

Unclenching her fists and taking a calming breath, Aggie casually stepped toward him, her light skirt swishing in the gentle night breeze. She looked behind her to make sure they were still alone.

She stopped several steps away from him, making sure to keep a bit of distance. As proved last night, she seemed to become nothing but an idiot when they were in close proximity. Aggie turned, resting her palms on the railing, leaning forward to gaze at the dark sky.

"Who was that?" Devin asked, his eyes not leaving her face.

Aggie gave a slight cough. "Who was what?"

"The person you were just searching for in the drawing room. The one who obviously just scared you to death." His stare continued to bore into her features.

"Scared me?"

"You're shaking."

Aggie whipped her arms across her ribcage, standing straight and tightening her body. She hadn't realized.

"Really, your grace, it was no one. I thought I saw someone I knew, but I didn't. I was mistaken. It happens sometimes, what with the many people milling about and all," Aggie said lightly, her gaze continuing to avert from his look. She shifted her eyes to stare at the perfectly symmetrical shrubbery below.

"All right then, who was it you thought you saw?"

Aggie turned toward him, catching his gaze, and realized her mistake. She doubted she could lie directly into his steely eyes. So she looked over his shoulder. "Really, Devin, it was, or would have been, no one of consequence."

She saw out of the corner of her eye the suspicion on his face grow. But he went silent. They stood for a few moments before he spoke again.

"Walk with me?"

"Yes." She answered too quickly, with too much enthusiasm, but didn't care. She was just grateful he dropped the matter.

She glanced around once more to make sure no errant eyes saw them, and then walked with him down the set of stairs at the end of the terrace. They strolled in silence. Turning along the walk adjacent to the gardens, Aggie was thankful for the quiet moments to compose herself. Her insides were still a torrential maelstrom after who she just thought she saw.

"Ferrington was certainly holding your attention."

Aggie blinked twice in surprise, not immediately understanding the changed subject, or his tone, for she had long since dismissed Lord Ferrington from her mind.

"Yes, well, my usual polite exit lines were not working, and I was having a devil of a time coming up with anything new." She looked up at him. "I am sure you can imagine my mind has been on other matters tonight."

Devin nodded, a satisfied look on his face. He pointed at a turn into the gardens. Even though she would never enter sequestered gardens like these with the opposite sex—their tall evergreen hedges, thick arbors of trailing roses, and dark corners could so easily ruin a young lady—Aggie thought she saw the tiniest wince as Devin raised his injured arm. Sudden guilt outweighed her natural avoidance of this type of garden, and she let him steer her inward.

"How is the cut? Healing?" Aggie asked, scolding herself at her rudeness to have not inquired about it right away.

"A dull ache, nothing more."

Aggie nodded, relieved.

"Your boy, Tommy, is he okay?"

The guilt on Aggie's face multiplied. "Yes, I saw him today. He was badly beaten, but he will be fine. I have a very good doctor looking after him. I never realized how young he was to have the responsibility I put on him. I was so very wrong about that. I just never thought…" Her eyes shifted downward as guilt tears brimmed on her lashes. Tommy's face had been bloodied and mangled. Another person hurt by her actions. Her exhaustion did nothing to help her control her emotions.

Devin stopped and Aggie took a few steps past him before stopping herself. The cool of the evening pooled between the thick hedges where they stood. They were deep in the gardens now. Aggie's gloved hands went to her upper arms, rubbing them against the chill.

"Aggie, do you not realize how young you are to have such responsibility on your shoulders?"

Not turning back to him, she tilted her head upward, looking at the stars, and a memory rush of young naïveté hit her. She was now so very far from those days of innocence. "I am not so young. Fate did not give me the luxury of choice in the matter."

Right behind her, his sudden heat blanketed her bare
shoulders before he spoke again.

"But you have a choice now." His voice was low in her ear.

She spun to him, and immediately regretted it when she saw
the look on his face. A predator sensing weakness, he moved even
closer. She stepped backward, looking for space, only to move
herself into a small arbor, offset from the path, with three sides of
thick climbing roses. She hadn't even noticed it was there.

Not allowing a successful retreat, Devin slid in front of her,
his wide shoulders cornering her in the alcove.

Aggie's eyes darted around him, but before a muscle could
spring, he leaned in, breath hot on her bare neck as his fingers slid
across the line at the tip of her shoulder.

"Tell me who you saw back there in the party, Aggie."

Her breathing stopped, along with her body. So he hadn't
dropped it. Damn. Why could she not move away from this man?
She was usually quite good at thwarting unwanted suitors. This
was when she needed to run, and she couldn't even make her toes
twitch.

"It was no one. A mistake."

"Your eyes were panicked." His lips were close, brushing her
neck just below her ear as he spoke. Words had never been softer
from him. "You need to let it go, Aggie. Let it go. Whatever fear
just stabbed you, give it to me. Tell me. I will take of care it. Who
was it?"

His lips landed fully on her neck, expanding the gentle graze.
Her body betrayed the last little part of her mind that screamed
at her to run, and she leaned into him. The caress of his lips drew
her in, willing her body to mold into him as his arm slipped low
around her back.

"I am just so tired, Devin." He felt so good. So hard against
her. So big, like he could wrap her in a cocoon and she would
never have to come out. Exhaustion wore on her, and she couldn't
muster any defense against him.

"So tell me. Tell me and I will take care of it."

Her head tilted against her will, giving him better access to the line of skin he gently devoured. All thoughts left her mind, but still he prodded.

"Tell me."

She didn't know if she still stood, or if he held her up. All sensation, except for where his mouth met her neck, disappeared.

"Give it to me, Aggie. Tell me."

"The fifth." The words left her mouth only because she didn't want him to stop. Didn't want the complete void of everything except the pleasure on her skin to disappear. It was one little moment in time. But a moment where she didn't think. Didn't remember. Didn't hate. Wasn't scared. He had her.

"The fifth what?" The whisper barely reached her ears.

"A fifth man. Their leader."

The lips stopped. "There's another? A leader? And you just thought you saw him? Here?"

His mouth hadn't moved from her neck, so she couldn't see the thunderclouds in his eyes, but she could hear them. It cleared her senses, and she abruptly stepped back from him.

He straightened.

She wasn't wrong about the thunderclouds. Two jabs from the climbing roses poked into her shoulder. Thorns behind her. A seething Devin in front of her. She wasn't sure which was worse.

"His clothes. How he talked—carried himself. He is of money—peerage, maybe—I do not know. I have been searching every ballroom and every party for him, and nothing."

"Hell and damnation, Aggie. Why did you not tell me? This is pretty damn important information. I thought there were only the four." He ran his hand across the back of his neck. "Blast it. I have been going about this all wrong if there's a moneyed leader. Hell—and now you think you saw him here?"

"It was only a glimpse, Devin. I was wrong. My mind is playing tricks, I am so tired. I am sure it was not he. I do not know what I saw."

His jaw worked back and forth, the hard line throbbing—a stark contradiction from the gentleness on her neck just a moment ago.

Aggie looked up at him, not sure what to do. And she probably needed to get back to the party before her aunt started to worry about her whereabouts.

"The two. They were not found," Devin stated simply. "Not today."

Aggie closed her eyes, fighting the lump in her throat. She hadn't wanted to ask. If she avoided it, she could hide from reality just a little longer. Keep hope alive for a few extra minutes. But there it was.

Choice dissolved once more. After what they did to Tommy, this had to end tonight. No more would be injured on her account.

Aggie fought the fatigue making her brain swim. Now was not the time to buckle. She had to wake up and steel herself. Latch onto those last few tattered shreds of courage.

Sudden lips on hers made her jump, for she hadn't seen Devin move down on her. His arms went around her, pulling her body away from the thorns and into him.

His lips, hard, yet gentle, parted, and he teased her mouth open, deepening the kiss. His tongue slipped into her, sending a shot down her spine and waking up something deep in her core.

In her gut she knew exactly what he was doing. Making her forget. Taking her pain and her worry. Creating belief that she would be beyond threats. She leaned into him, wanting all of that, and more, if only for a few seconds.

He pulled up slightly, lips still wispy on hers. "They will be found tonight, Aggie. All three of them. I guarantee it."

Her eyes slivered open, and her breath caught at the raw conviction she saw in Devin's hard features. His hand at the small of her back pressed, contouring her body even harder into his. The other hand moved up to her neck, tilting her head slightly as he closed the air between them again.

She wanted this. She wanted to believe him. Wanted him to take care of everything. She opened her mouth wider to his onslaught, taking him. Her tongue flickered with his as a hot flood rushed through her body.

But her mind didn't stop.

It wasn't enough.

As much as she wanted to, she couldn't avoid her own responsibility. She couldn't trust him. Even as she reveled in the fire running up and down her body from his kiss, his body encapsulating hers, her mind started to churn again.

She had been weak. And then what had she done? She had entrusted a total stranger to do what she should have finished.

Yes, they would be found tonight.

But Devin wasn't guaranteeing it. She was.

~ ~ ~

"Augustine Christopherson."

The shrill words cut through the night air, making Devin inwardly jump.

Outwardly, he calmly pulled up from Aggie, noting that the words hadn't broken through the haze she was in. Eyes closed, cheeks flushed, lips cherry raw and plump from the deluge he had just put them through.

He tried to delicately slide the right strap of her dress back into place, covering her exposed breast. He didn't think Aggie even knew where his hand had been, she was so engrossed.

He hid his smile before removing his arm from her waist, and stepped out of the arbor. She swayed slightly at the loss of support, then caught herself, eyes flying open, realizing what had just happened.

Aggie's aunt and uncle both heaved, rage blustering. Her aunt whipped out a hand, stomping the few steps into the arbor, and yanked Aggie from the alcove. Protective mama bear, she shoved Aggie behind her and her husband.

Both aunt and uncle had their hands on their hips as they squared off against Devin.

"I will not have my niece ruined by the likes of you, your grace. What exactly are your intentions, here?" Her uncle's face was beet red, anger only allowing halting words to make it out.

Devin raised an eyebrow. "Intentions?"

He knew damn well what the uncle insinuated, the ruin that could become of his niece, and under his watch. But Devin also didn't like being cornered over a wandering hand and one entirely too lusty a kiss.

Taller than her aunt, Aggie's eyes went wide above the feathers from the cap in the plump woman's hair. Aggie shook her head, silently mouthing the word "no" with vigor. Telling him to somehow get them both out of this situation.

She looked petrified. She didn't want him. Wasn't looking to be trapped.

The aunt poked her husband.

"Dunway. This is unacceptable. My niece is above reproach, and you have just tattered her possibilities for a suitable husband."

Aggie's eyes flittered over her shoulder at the main house, then back to Devin. Still petrified. Why was she looking at him like that? A thousand chits in her place would be glorying in the success of the trap just concocted. Scandal attached to him or not, his station allowed a wide berth in what a cunning social climber would overlook.

Unless this wasn't a trap. Unless she actually didn't want anything to do with him.

Devin's gut gave the slightest cringe. She probably didn't even know what she just did, but after the carnal kiss they had just shared, it was clear. A woman like Aggie needed to be in a man's bed. His bed. It was sacrilege for her not to be.

Too beautiful, too passionate, and too spirited not to be enjoyed as the good lord clearly intended. She was created for wanton pleasure, whether she knew it or not. She was created for a man that knew what to with her body. One that would not shy away from the challenge of manipulating her skin, her limbs, her senses, and make her scream in pleasure. A man like him.

Her uncle railed at him, really working himself into it. Devin didn't hear a word of it. He was too busy trying to calm his throbbing member and staring at the girl still shaking her head no.

In all of their encounters, in all of the times he should have seen fear on her face, it lacked. Yet there she stood, attempting to shrink into nothingness behind her relatives, even though at average height, she was a head taller than her uncle, two heads over her aunt.

She looked terrified at the very thought of becoming bound in any real way to him. It rankled Devin's pride, and he knew, at that moment, he should just walk away. Just like she had asked over and over.

Walk away and be done with this girl, her blustering uncle, and the mess she was embroiled in. He could do that. His title, his money, allowed it of him.

But his feet refused to move.

Her uncle continued his rant, but Devin's eyes remained firmly on the trapped rabbit behind him, her eyes darting about, looking for some other escape as she slowly realized he wasn't going to help her get out of this. He wasn't going to smooth this over.

Devin watched her fear escalate and hid the sudden smile that attempted to line his lips. This wasn't simple. Not simple at all.

But for the first time in his life, simple didn't hold quite the allure it usually did. There was something about complicated that suddenly seemed fitting.

Killian was right when he had said it was time for Devin to produce an heir. And Devin would have a blasted fine time producing one with Aggie.

He adjusted his stance.

Even if she came with complications. Even if she was currently desperate to erase him from her sight.

Her uncle trailed off, having spewed the last of the imaginable threats he could conjure. Devin smiled first at Aggie's aunt, then her uncle.

"Let me assure you, my intentions to your niece are honorable. I apologize for my momentary loss of control." He looked pointedly at her uncle. "I am sure you can remember a time when you met your lovely bride, that you were also overwhelmed?" Devin hoped he remembered right from the reports that theirs was a love match and not a marriage of convenience.

"Yes, well, that may be." He sputtered, looking at his wife. "But those were different times."

"Not so different." Devin interrupted him, not wanting him to launch into another rant. "I will call on your residence tomorrow to begin the official courtship, assuming Lady Augustine is available and that it is acceptable? We will be properly chaperoned there? It will be best to maintain proper sequence."

If it was possible, Aggie's eyes grew even wider.

"What? Yes, fine. It is," Aggie's uncle said, his reinvigorated tirade unexpectedly halted.

"What? No." Aggie's head shook. "You cannot truly mean to—"

"Hush, Augustine." Aggie's aunt looked sharply over her shoulder at her niece. "You will be silent, and let your uncle handle this matter. He is trying to save your reputation, my dear."

Aggie's jaw remained askew at the reprimand.

Devin had to hide another smile.

"Yes, well then, tomorrow." Aggie's uncle turned to the women. "Let us get back to the party. Your grace."

Devin tilted his head at the group.

He waited an appropriate minute before trailing after the three back into the party. By the time they had reached the French doors in front of him, Aggie's jaw had reattached itself, and he had to admire her graceful poise under such circumstance as she glided back into the crush.

Devin re-entered the house through the drawing room. Unfortunately, several matronly women immediately accosted him, hoping to make introductions between him and some eligible daughters. His reputation should have kept them all at bay, but it was amazing how much some mothers were able to overlook when it came to marrying their daughters off to rich, titled men.

But as talking to—no, kissing—Aggie had put him into an unusually polite mood, Devin put up with their babble. One half hour passed by before he was able to excuse himself to prepare for the late supper.

It was halfway through the first course when Devin realized Aggie was not eating like she should have been. She was, as far as he could tell, no longer even at the party. Nor were her aunt or uncle.

Damn—where could she be?

It dawned on him in a lightning bolt. She hadn't taken his kiss for the mere pleasure. She had done it to throw him off course.

She had gone after the killers once more.

And she had at least an hour-and-a-half on him.

The stir that Devin caused as he strode out of the meal mid-course was quite exciting for the guests, who were left to revel in their speculations on his abrupt, and entirely impolite, exit.

CHAPTER 8

Aggie's teeth gnashed on her tongue, biting back the scream exploding in her throat. Arms pinned to her sides, the man crushed her from behind, her ribs jabbing painfully into her lungs. She had to save her breath if she was going to escape this man.

Damn. The plan had been working. She had stolen a hack from an inebriated driver lying in a stupor beside his coach. She had tucked a handful of guinea coins under the man's coat for usage of the carriage and horse, and then started her search. That had been the easy part, obtaining an unidentifiable hack to drive.

She made it past Charing Cross, deep into the east side. Soon enough, she had come across the last two of the four as they stumbled out into the street leaving the Black Fin. It was too easy. And she should have known then.

She followed them, invisible, for about ten blocks. They stumbled into an alley. Using the coach to block the street-side of the alley, she stopped, her fortune too good that it was a dead-end alley. She should have known then.

It was time to end the whole miserable affair. They were beyond drunk, and she was certain she could get one of them to talk, to tell her how to find their leader.

Pulling out two pistols, she set them on her gloves next to her feet. She pulled two more, one for each hand, and cocked them. Aggie took several panting breaths in a fight against fear. They both had their backs to her. She had to do it now or she was not going to get another chance.

She stood, pulling the reins tight and putting them under her boot.

"Which one of you wants to die, and which one wants to tell me who hired you to kill my father?" A voice that sounded nothing like hers came from her mouth.

They both spun, fumbling, reaching into their clothes.

"I would stop, if I were you."

They both froze, glaring up at her.

"I think you both know I have no problems with aim or pulling the trigger. So which one of you wants to tell me who hired you?"

The toothless lanky one sneered at her. "You sound desperate, lass."

Aggie evened her aim. "I am. So I will not hesitate to put a bullet in you."

The short bald one on the right pulled a pistol from his jacket, arm rising at Aggie. No hesitation, she shot him through the heart, his arm dropping, along with his body, just before his pistol fired.

The horse jumped at the shots, and Aggie lost her balance. She caught herself on the bench, dropping the used pistol and switching the live pistol to her right hand.

Standing back up, she took aim at the leg of the taller man just as he bungled with his own pistol. Her last chance. She had to get him to talk.

"I am going to blow your leg off if you don't drop it right now."

The man glanced at the body next to him, then back up to her. Slowly, his hand lifted in surrender and he bent to set the pistol on the ground.

Aggie breathed her first breath since stopping the carriage.

Just when the tip of the man's pistol touched the ground, he looked up at her. His sneer was back.

She should have known then.

In the next instant, she was ripped backward, jerked off her perch, pistol falling from her hand.

A satisfied grunt echoed in her ear as an iron grip wrapped around her. A brutal hand tore the hood and cap from her head.

Another grunt. Both arms wrapped around her, strangling her air.

Aggie kicked, tried to move her arms against the clamp—it did nothing to stop the man from dragging her around the horse and into the alley.

She twisted, trying to see her attacker, but turning her head was impossible.

He stopped, and hot, sticky breath went into her ear. "I will, of course, pleasure myself before your fate is executed, my lady. You do remember how I pleasure myself, do you not?"

She recognized the voice instantly. The leader. Flashes of his silver blade cutting into her flesh flooded her mind.

She squeezed her eyes shut against the memory. Against the terror.

Her toes not touching the ground, he shifted her body, crushing down even harder. It was in that moment she had to swallow her own scream.

Full panic hit Aggie. She opened her eyes to see the other thug staggering toward her.

She was nothing without her pistols. Even if she freed herself from the leader's grip, she would somehow need to escape the drunk too.

But she had to try.

She twisted as violently as she could and kicked at his shins the best she could in her hampered position. Vile laughter was the only response.

"Still trying? Maybe this will kill your fight." He shifted again, setting one hand free, and then shoved it under her cloak, groping. Finding her breast, he squeezed and twisted, sending Aggie into writhing pain.

The thug stumbled closer.

Aggie froze, overcome with the bile that shot up from her stomach. Please. Not two of them at once. A brutal hand twisted her skin. Waves of pain followed by waves of pain.

Laughter rang in her ear. Aggie tried to suck breath into her crushed lungs, gathering the last of her energy to try to fight one last time, when she noticed out of the corner of her eye the bastard in front of her dropping soundlessly to the ground.

A dark figure with a gleaming, blood-stained knife, stepped over the now inert body.

She was thrown, and the last thing she saw before her head hit the brick wall and blackness swallowed her, were familiar grey eyes.

Grey eyes rushing toward her in a desperate effort to stop her fall.

Grey eyes flooded with rage.

~ ~ ~

"Hell, Aggie." Devin got to her just as she hit the ground.

He glanced over his shoulder, only to see the cloaked figure disappear around the coach. Running footsteps echoed down the street.

On his knees beside her, Devin gently tilted Aggie's face toward him. Blood ran along her temple from a gash. Her eyes closed, she wasn't moving.

Devin put his ear to her chest. Her breathing, although raspy, was close to normal. Shaking her slightly—as gently as he could, considering the anger he just barely had control over—he attempted to prod her awake.

He looked out past the coach into the street again.

There was nothing that would give him more satisfaction than to go after that damn bastard and give him a death he would beg for.

But Aggie was unconscious. And he would not leave her alone.

His only option was to hope that she would be able to describe the man when she woke. That bastard had to be the fifth one Aggie talked about. The leader.

Devin would destroy him. Aggie would have peace. He would make certain of it.

He moved one foot for balance and slipped his arms under her. Picking her up gently, he took care not to jostle her too much.

Bunching up her hood under her head for support, he laid her on the floor of the hack. He didn't want her to roll off the seat as they moved.

Closing the door, he turned and leapt to the driver's perch, setting the horse quickly in the only direction he could.

~ ~ ~

The pounding on the front door rudely awakened Howard and Beatrix Rutland.

Howard, disgruntled at his interrupted sleep, decided to take the pleasure of a good tongue lashing at the intruder, away from the butler and do it himself.

"Of all the most inconsiderate," Howard muttered as he pulled open the front door while tying his robe. The sight that greeted him jolted him awake. "What the hell...?"

Devin strode into the front hallway, an unconscious Aggie secure in his arms.

"Aggie! Dear God—is she okay?"

Devin nodded in the affirmative.

The two men stared at each other. Howard with a perturbed look. Devin with an expressionless face. Devin waited for Aggie's uncle to come to his conclusions.

"You know what this means, Dunway?" Howard asked several moments later.

"Yes, I do."

"Well then, get my niece up to the spare bedroom, two doors down on the left." Howard's thumb gently rubbed across Aggie's forehead, both bloody and dirty with soot. His fingers stopped at the open gash.

His voice softened. "What the hell happened? She will be fine, will she not?"

"Yes, it is just a minor cut. But I will send a doctor as soon as I leave here."

"Do I want to know what happened?"

"No."

Devin turned from Aggie's uncle and carried her up the stairs to the spare bedroom. He laid her on the bed, removed her cloak and boots, and pulled the covers of the bed around her.

Stepping back, he paused a moment, looking down at her soot-lined face. His eyes paused at her forehead, crinkled hard, even in sleep. Pain—physical or emotional? Either way, it didn't disappear from her with unconsciousness. Devin's gut hardened.

Instinct made him lean back in, and he laid a gentle kiss on her forehead before striding back down the stairs into the foyer.

"How long will it take?" Howard's face glowered an angry red after having several minutes to work himself up.

"One day."

Howard nodded. "Well then, I will be expecting you tomorrow at eleven, Dunway."

"Make it ten," Devin replied. Hand on the door, he stopped. "If the doctor is worried or she does not awaken today, let me know. And under no circumstance are you to let her out of this house."

Devin disappeared out the door into the morning's first rays.

CHAPTER 9

"Aggie, sweetheart, wake up, honey."

The gentle prodding voice of Aunt Beatrix, coupled with the jostling of her arm, pulled Aggie out of the deep abyss.

"Aggie, honey, you must get up if we are to be ready." Aunt Beatrix continued her gentle demands.

Aggie turned over onto her stomach in bed, one bare arm flopping down the side of the bed. Her head sank deep into the feather pillow, and she fought consciousness to regain the cavernous sleep she was just lost in.

Then her head started to pound.

Skull near exploding, she sat up, swaying with grogginess.

Why her aunt would be at her townhouse, prodding her awake, was beyond Aggie at the moment. But wait. She squinted through her pounding forehead, scanning her surroundings.

She wasn't at her townhouse. She was at her aunt and uncle's home.

Befuddled, she found focus on her aunt, sitting on the edge of the bed. The pain sent nausea to her stomach, and she raised her hand to her forehead to touch the origin of the painful shards. Fingers slid across a scab that ran just past her hairline, and her eyes opened wide, bewildered. Aunt Beatrix smiled at her sympathetically, patted her hand, and dabbed a tear off the edge of her own eye.

"Aunt Bea, why…" Aggie's raspy voice broke off as fuzzy shreds of nothing floating through her mind. She didn't even know what to ask in her groggy state.

Eyes growing wider as moments passed, Aggie demanded in a low whisper, "Aunt Bea, how long have I been asleep?"

"Oh, dear, it has been a day and a night," Aunt Beatrix said. "You woke up yesterday, do you not remember?" She waved her hand. "It was only for a short while, though. You arrived here about six yesterday morn. Giving us quite a fright, I might add. But no need to worry. It is now only nine in the morning, and you still have plenty of time, sweetheart."

"Time?" Aggie asked. The throbbing in her brain ruined any chance she had to follow Aunt Beatrix's scattered talk.

"Why yes, time to get properly attired for the wedding," Beatrix said, rising from the edge of the bed. She walked across the room to fetch a light cream gown with a low-fitted bodice, embroidered by French lace and complete with a flowing train.

"I had the maid try to wash that dreadful black stuff off your face, but she just made it worse. And you shoved her away. None too politely. So you need to wash it yourself, it is quite smeared, my dear. Unfortunately, there is no time for a bath. I would prefer that there be time, but I have to listen to Howard. It is what it is." She laid the dress at the end of the bed. "Put this on, and I shall be back with a maid in a few moments to do your hair. It was certainly lucky that I had bought this dress for your birthday on our last trip to France."

Birthday. France. Bath. Did she say wedding? Aggie fought the sway as a feeling of dread twinged into the corners of her mind. Why would her brain not work? "What is going on, Aunt Bea?"

Aunt Beatrix gave her an odd smile, then scooted out of the room without so much as a glance back at Aggie. No answer to her question.

The feeling of impending doom grew. But at least her headache had moved from vibrating sharp pangs into her body, to a persistent pounding located mostly in her mind.

Not able to make her brain function, much less grasp what her aunt prattled on about, Aggie decided to follow the simple instructions Aunt Beatrix had left her with. Wash her face.

Aggie pulled herself out of bed, each movement sending painful shards through the thumping in her head. She wore a shift that wasn't hers—when had that happened?

Both hands clasped onto her head to hold it still, she trudged over to the basin with tepid water and looked at herself in the silver encased mirror poised above.

Alarm shot through her. She looked freakishly terrible. No
wonder her aunt looked at her with such worry.

The dark soot on her face had smudged and expanded, her
hair could not have been in more disarray, and was that dried
blood trailing down her cheek?

What the hell had happened to her?

As much as she tried to get a solid thought in her head,
she couldn't grasp onto anything. Sighing at her own blasted
ignorance, she dunked the washcloth into the bowl.

Face scrubbed raw, she walked over to the gown her aunt
had left for her to wear. Why her aunt would have her wear such
a gown at nine in the morning was beyond her muddled mind's
comprehension. Shaking her head, she put on the dress. Simple
instructions. Hold onto those.

Sitting heavy onto the settee, she closed her eyes, attempting
to get her mind in working order again. She followed back
through the darkness. She was at the ball. The Samuelson ball—
no, the Appleton party. Inside, then out. She smelled roses. Then
Devin. Oh God, Devin. He kissed her. A flush rushed her cheeks.
He kissed her hard.

Then what?

Her aunt and uncle. Hell.

She hit a big black wall of no memories. Nothing after that.

A knock on the door made her jump. Without a reply from
Aggie, her aunt bustled in with ribbons, maid in tow.

Aunt Beatrix pulled Aggie to her feet, turning her and
starting up the long line of buttons in the back of Aggie's silk
gown. The maid started working on the tangled blond ends of her
hair.

Buttons done, her aunt steered her to the stool before the
little mahogany vanity to sit. She started to untangle the other
side of Aggie's hair. For having an excruciating headache, neither
the maid, nor her aunt afforded much gentleness as they worked
through the snarls. Frenzied, even. Aggie turned her head and
caught sight of a clock atop the corner bureau. Ten minutes to
ten.

"Aggie, honey, your uncle has yet to share the full story with me, but frankly, I am not sure I actually care to know how you showed up on our doorstep yesterday morning."

Aggie tried to concentrate on her aunt's chattering, but the explosions in her head still commanded more attention.

The maid finished plaiting Aggie's hair, and went on to twist in the ribbons.

"I guess I would prefer to remain ignorant about the whole ordeal. Especially since you are alive and healthy. I do not need my imagination running away without me." Aunt Beatrix tugged a lock of hair, re-igniting the aching through Aggie's skull. "And even though your uncle and I had this goal in mind, we had hoped to go about these activities in a more proper way—mind you, we are not about to argue with the situation, after all, lemons and lemonade, dear."

Aunt Beatrix followed the maid around Aggie's head, tucking and twisting strands to her liking, deftly creating beauty. "Your mother will not be privy to the details of when and how you showed up on our doorstep yesterday—not that she could even comprehend it, poor dear."

"Details?" Aggie interrupted. Why would her aunt need to hide details? Aggie tilted her head to her aunt. "What details, and why would they upset my mother?"

"Oh dear, you do not recall anything of arriving here?"

Aggie shook her head. The maid stepped away and left the room.

Her aunt clasped her hands in front of her ample bosom. "Truly? Nothing at all?"

The feeling of dread from earlier intensified in Aggie's gut. "Aunt Bea, what happened?"

"Well, dear…" Aunt Beatrix hedged, playing with a rogue strand of hair along Aggie's forehead. "As I said earlier, I do not know why or how the Duke of Dunway came about bringing you to our doorstep—"

"Dev—his grace brought me here?"

Realization filtered through Aggie's headache. No, it couldn't be. It wouldn't be possible. There was no need. And why the hell couldn't she remember anything?

"Aunt Bea." Aggie's voice punctuated her words as dread stiffened every pore in her body. "Just whose wedding will I be attending today?"

Aunt Beatrix's sympathetic smile was all the answer Aggie needed.

~ ~ ~

The coach had just made it outside of the city limits.

Devin looked across the carriage at his new wife, only to catch a rabbit-trapped-in-steel-claws look, and inwardly winced. He was not a brute dragging his woman off by the hair, but he felt every bit of it.

He knew she didn't want this. Hell—it was him. He wanted this. He wanted her. And he had made it happen. He wasn't forced into this marriage. He could have taken her to her home, called a doctor, and walked away.

Sure, she might have been ruined—but he couldn't do that to her. Not after all she had suffered. He wanted her, enough to make this happen—anyway it needed to.

He had hoped Aggie's aunt would have let him have a few moments alone with her before the wedding to explain the situation calmly. He knew Aggie would need the rational explanation, but her aunt was ferocious about keeping the wedding, if not the engagement, proper.

Avoiding the petrified set to her face, his eyes swept over Aggie. Before they left she had changed into a traveling ensemble, with a deep purple jacket fitted close to her body, accentuating her curves. He had not allowed her time to change her hair, so it was still bundled atop her head with ribbons intertwined, but now a jaunty little matching hat sat half atop the bundle. Soft honey wisps curled about her neck, and Devin's thoughts meandered to brushing them aside when he got the chance to enjoy her sweet skin again. To actually make it downward along the gentle slope, clothes not hindering progression to the tips of her breasts.

Devin shifted slightly. Damn, he wanted her. All the more so when she didn't have charcoal smeared on her cheeks, a drunkard's smell about her, and men's breeches on. But maybe the breeches could make an occasional appearance—they did curve around her buttocks nicely.

He pulled his eyes off her and busied himself with plucking nonexistent lint off his pants. Had he known he would be anticipating bedding Aggie with this intensity, he might have thought twice about immediately leaving for Stonewell. An afternoon in his bedroom would have wiped the panicked look from her face, he would have made sure of that. But leaving for his main country estate was the safest choice.

He wanted his new wife completely out of danger, and the best place for that to happen was at Stonewell. His own selfish lusting would have to wait. At least until tonight.

Aggie took a deep breath, and his eyes shifted upward on her body. Not exactly a sigh, but it noticeably raised her chest. Damn enticing. Devin stretched out a leg and exhaled silently. It was going to be a long ride.

He knew he was going to have to make this sudden marriage right for her, though, before he touched her. He wanted her willing, open. Not performing a duty.

For himself, he had decided Killian's jammering-on about heirs maybe did have some merit. As bonus, it would shut his friend up. Although Devin generally disliked the thought of having a wife—mistresses were far simpler to manage—he did enjoy children, and Aggie could provide him with that.

As for settling on a wife, Aggie was a fine choice. He knew she was as honorable as a woman could get, and that life with her didn't contain the threat of ever being boring. Plus, he admitted to himself, he was becoming somewhat fond of the nymph. Not to mention he felt an inescapable need to keep her safe.

But how to convince her the marriage was a good choice? She would benefit tremendously from the marriage. She would be protected, her family would be protected, she would have more comfort and money than she could ever desire, and, she could come and go as she pleased.

No. Devin corrected himself. She couldn't come and go as she pleased. Her safety depended on it for now, and when the threat was removed…well, it would be better for their future children if she refrained from gallivanting about.

Regardless, she would be content. If he explained it to her, he was confident her posture would not reflect the defeat of a person sentenced to the gallows. He looked out the carriage window, searching for a way to start.

"I am sorry."

Devin's startled eyes darted to Aggie. Did he really just hear that? "What was that?"

"I am sorry, and please do not make me say it again," Aggie whispered, her gaze directed at her white-gloved, clasped hands.

Devin still didn't believe his ears.

"I know that marriage was the last thing you wanted. I know that it was my own idiocy and, well…stubbornness that got us into this situation." Her eyes stayed down. "I have just been alone for so long, with so much to handle. I did not know how to accept your help. I wanted to trust you, truly, but it was so hard, and I could not. Not after…I should have gone about things differently. So I apologize."

Devin brightened. She was finally straightening out her misguided notions. "Aggie, I—"

"But," she interrupted, "I do not apologize for trying to protect myself or my mother and sister. I did what was necessary, and no matter how much you disapprove of my methods, something had to be done and I was the only one who could do it."

Of course not. There was no straightening. She felt bad about the outcome, but still believed what she was doing was unavoidable.

Devin's mouth drew into a tight line, but he nodded. He liked the apology enough to let the other comment slide. He despised the situations she continued to put herself in, but their marriage effectively ended any chance she had of repeating her actions. Truth told, he understood why she did it. Panic, and the need to control one's own fate—for good or bad, drove her.

"It is not right."

She glanced up at him. "What?"

"That you had to handle this by yourself—and not just because you are a woman. Because you deserve better."

"I do?" Her eyebrows pulled together, questioning. "Really, Devin, what do you know of me? I could be an ogre of a woman. Why did you marry me? We have only known each other for a few days. You did not need to bring me to my uncle's home the other night. You could have walked away. I would have been fine."

"I do not walk away from honor, Aggie. I married you because it was the only way to save you from yourself. And quite a bit more convenient than chasing you all over London."

Devin leaned forward, elbows resting on his knees, hands clasped. "Plus, truthfully, Aggie, I like you. And I don't like a lot of people. Am I wrong in that you don't find me too terrible as well?"

She bit her lip, hesitating as she stared at him. "You are not wrong. But that is no reason to marry me."

"Would you rather I had done the dishonorable thing and dumped you unconscious at your back door?"

"I was unconscious?"

"Do you not remember?"

"No. The last thing I remember is leaving the party. My aunt and uncle were not pleased with me after finding us in the gardens."

"Understandable. Your uncle clearly had never expected such wanton behavior from you." Devin didn't bother to hide the smile that crossed his face, remembering how her body had slid into his, throaty moans escaping her.

A flush touched her cheeks, but she didn't back away from his comment. "As unfortunate as the garden ended, I must admit I did enjoy it." She stopped, suddenly embarrassed.

"Did I just say that out loud?" Her hand flew to cover her mouth. "I am wanton. I am sorry, I am sure that is not what you are expecting in a wife. My sense of demureness has deserted me—I am afraid I have been in some undesirable areas these past months where propriety is nonexistent. My own lines of what is and is not respectable have wavered as a result."

Devin laughed. He couldn't have imagined a better reaction from her. His hands moved forward, grabbing her knees through the plum folds of her skirts. "Stop. You never have to worry about properness with me, Aggie. I like that you are not reserved around me. I like that the front you put on wavers. I like that you are not afraid to admit what you like, what you want. I would be disappointed if you decided to change just because we married."

"Truly?"

"Truly. I want you, Aggie, and I want you with whatever thoughts—wanton or not—are running through your mind. I never want you to curb yourself around me."

The side of her mouth lifted, a slow smile radiating across her face as she nodded in response.

Devin sat back, leaning on the cushions, studying her. God, she was beautiful when she smiled. And her forehead. It wasn't in the least scrunched. It was the first time he remembered seeing her without worry lines. Her face was at ease, and Devin had done that. He suddenly felt inordinately proud of himself.

His eyes paused at a lock of hair that had been artfully curled down to cover the healing gash on her left temple. A shot of anger rolled through his chest.

"How is your head?"

Her hand flew up, flitting with the hair in front of the wound. "It was beyond horrible this morning but does not pain too terribly anymore. What happened? How did I get it?"

"When I found you, you had already taken down one of them." Devin swallowed hard against the rage that overtook him at just remembering the scene.

"I had?"

He cleared his throat. "Yes, but one was advancing on you. The other had you, and he threw you at the wall. You hit it. Hard."

Her hand moved down from her temple. "Two of them… that meant the leader."

Devin nodded. "Yes. Most likely." He clamped down on his next words.

He knew he had to interrogate her about the fifth man, the leader. He and Killian had uncovered very little about who he was in the past day, and Aggie was the key to any new leads on finding him. But he couldn't start the hundreds of questions he needed to ask her. Not at that moment.

She looked peaceful, for a change, and though the worry lines hinted at re-appearing across her forehead, he could stop them if he just held his questions. Tonight. He would ask her tonight.

"I had hoped to hide it, the cut, from my sister this morning, but she has uncanny skills of observation. She saw it."

"You sat with her for some time this morning after the wedding."

"Yes, thank you for the time with her. She was quite worried about me. She is still so young and has lost so much." Aggie smiled at him. "She did think you very handsome. Though possibly a bit too tall."

"Too tall?"

"Yes, she wondered how I would stop my neck from hurting at looking up at you."

"Really?"

"She is nine." Aggie shrugged. "And you must look like a giant to her. But again, remember, she thought you at least a dashing giant."

"It is too bad your mother was too ill to come to the wedding." Devin watched with interest the lightning quick change in Aggie's demeanor at mention of her mother. As much as her eyes glowed when talking of her sister, they became equally guarded at mention of her mother.

"Yes, I missed her. But I did talk to her when we stopped by our house to pack a few things."

"Is your mother often ill?"

"She…"

Aggie's voice trailed off, and Devin could see her searching for the right words.

"People get sick, Aggie. It is okay to talk about it."

"Yes. It is just that she is…physically fine. It is her mind. After father died, she shut herself off, both emotionally and physically, from the world…from us. She has not said a coherent sentence in the past year."

Devin's eyes narrowed. "Which has left you to take care of everything, including your sister."

"Please, no, Devin. I did not want to tell you, because I did not want that look on your face. Please do not judge her. She is my mother, and I love her dearly."

Devin tilted his head, startled. He should have guessed her fierce loyalty would rear. "I apologize. I meant no disrespect."

"Thank you for understanding." A bright smile slipped onto her face to cover whatever she harbored. "Do you plan on us being at Stonewell for long? Or will we be back to London soon?"

"It depends." A perfect opening to pepper Aggie with questions about her assailants, but Devin resisted. Normal conversation with Aggie was delightful. Plus, she admitted he was handsome—or at least didn't argue with her sister's assessment. Something he rather enjoyed. "Why?"

"My sister and mother. I know they will be fine with my aunt and uncle, but I am hoping they may join us at Stonewell if we will be there for an extended period. I am still responsible for them, and I know my aunt and uncle had hoped to get back to their travels soon. After an appropriate time period, and with your approval, of course."

"If that would make you happy, and ease your worry, then of course they may join us."

The smile Aggie rewarded him with beamed so brightly, Devin's breath caught.

He had no idea that could even happen.

CHAPTER 10

Out the carriage window, the hazy sun fell behind distant trees, and Aggie stared at the orange glow through cracked eyes, trying to right her mind after waking. That she had fallen asleep in the jostling carriage was evidence of her continued exhaustion. It had taken a hard jolt, knocking her head clear through the cushion to the wood frame, to wake her.

She concentrated on the bobbing, fiery orb.

Carriage. Countryside. Marriage. Devin.

The avalanche of the morning's events swept her mind and shocked her upright, eyes wide as she remembered Devin sitting across from her. A slight smile tilted the right side of his face, now slightly darkened with evening stubble.

The swing of the carriage slowed, and the last of Aggie's grogginess disappeared.

"Are we stopping?" She leaned forward to search their surroundings, relaxing as she realized they were turning to enter a stately drive.

Aggie moved closer to the carriage window to gain a new vantage as the wheels crunched over granite gravel. After a few minutes, wide-open space appeared. Flat, immaculate lawns rolled in all directions from an enormous, grey brick home. Double wings disappeared behind the main hall, and Aggie could see the late-sun glimmer on a glass dome protruding from the roof above the entrance. By its elaborateness and proximity to London, the home was obviously used not only for entertaining, but for impressing as well.

"This is Lord Southfork's home?" Aggie asked. Devin had mentioned earlier they would be spending the night at his friend's home.

"Yes, but Killian will not be here, nor any other guests at the moment. Just us," Devin said as the carriage came to a gentle stop in front of the arched double mahogany doors. The footman let the stairs down and Devin exited, extending his hand to assist Aggie.

"That is regrettable. I would have liked to have been properly introduced to Lord Southfork." Aggie stepped out of the carriage, still looking up at the magnificent home. "From what I have gathered, he is a true friend to you."

Aggie looked over to her new husband, only to see a pained expression cross his face.

"Oh, I am sorry, I must be wrong about Lord Southfork?"

"Aggie, dearest," Devin's voice was gentle—too gentle—as he guided her up the marble stairs, "you were introduced to him."

Aggie stopped on the top step, staring blankly at Devin. She searched her mind for an introduction with the man, but nothing appeared. She shook her head.

"At our wedding this morning."

"What?" A horrified look crept across her face. "Really?"

Devin nodded.

"No. I…blazes…I do not remember meeting him." Frozen in mortification, she looked at Devin, voice turning meek. "Was I horribly rude to him? I am afraid I was not contained enough to be polite this morning."

"Not to fear. You were a complete lady. I was surprised myself at how composed you were."

"You, my grace, are a liar." Aggie chuckled, leaning in and grabbing his arm. "Now tell me what I really did."

"If you must know, you stared right through him as though he were invisible. Said nothing. Not even a nod. All told, you did not even look up at him, just his chest. Then you shuffled away."

"No." She leaned away, face falling, but her fingers stayed on Devin's arm, gripping. "I could not have done such a thing."

"Yes, you could, and you did." Devin shrugged with a wicked smile. "It made me laugh, though. His face was priceless. Killian takes great pride in his charm with the ladies. So it was nice to see my new wife is immune to his allure."

"Your enjoyment aside, rudeness is not how I wanted to conduct myself with such a respected friend of yours."

"No need for mortification, Aggie. Killian can be far from respectable. You will recall he is privy to the whole situation, so I am positive he was not offended."

Aggie dropped her hand from his arm, taking a step to the door. "I can see that, in your own way, you are trying your best to soften this for me, but I am going to be mortified nonetheless."

Devin didn't let her escape, and grabbed her hand, resetting it back onto his forearm. "Fine, you can remain mortified, but you will have plenty of chances to rectify your poor showing today and make friends with Killian in the future. Already in your favor, he is a big fan of your hackney skills."

Devin flashed her another wicked smile, and Aggie didn't bother to suppress a groan as he pulled her in through the doors.

Her eyes swept across the grand three-story entry. Built to impress with its glass dome above, it did its job well. "Lord Southfork's home is beautiful. Have you two been friends for many years? Where did you meet him?"

Devin guided Aggie deeper into the house, past the grand curving staircase. "The war. We were both there, in the thick of it, for different reasons, but at the core, it was the same reason."

"Which was?"

"To disappear. And at first we hated each other for a long time."

Aggie stopped and looked up at Devin. "Hated each other? Really? I never would have guessed. I have heard nothing but respect in your voice when you talk of him. What changed?"

"He saved my life. Twice. The first time was an accident." A half-smile crossed his face. "The second time was on purpose. After that, I had little choice but to make him my friend. One of the smartest things I ever did."

~ ~ ~

Courtesy of orders sent ahead by Killian, a small dinner awaited them. As she savored a tender morsel of duck, Aggie determined Killian had very high demands of the wine and food served in his home.

Devin had wanted to eat right away, so she hadn't bothered to change out of her travelling dress. But she did have just enough time before the meal to pull the ribbons and some of the pins out of her hair, and that alone had lessened the headache that still floated from spot to spot on her skull.

Another bite of duck melting on her tongue, she looked above the low candlelight at her husband.

Husband. She kept saying that to herself, but it was still hard to believe.

Days ago, she was tucking pistols into her cloak, roaming the streets of London, dirty and tired, and looking to kill—but somehow, she had ended up here, without thought or plan.

Here, sitting across from a man that she not only liked, but was also quickly becoming overly attached to.

Her chest tightened at the thought. Even though in her gut, she unequivocally trusted him, her mind had not caught up to her core. She still couldn't quite place his intentions or his actions—mostly because she had spent the past year afraid and suspicious of everything, and it was hard to cut off those brutally learned emotions.

Her breath caught as his grey eyes met hers. They were so sharp, like a hawk's, and she wondered if he really knew all that was going on in her mind, or if he just looked that way. His was not the sweet handsome that fills little girls' dreams. Not at all. His was a hard handsome—cutting cheekbones, dangerous jawline, muscles that were not in the slightest soft.

Lethal. That's what he was. She had seen that more than once. And he didn't show the slightest reservation in being so. A lethalness that should, by all rights, scare her. But it didn't. It only made her feel safe. Even when he kissed her.

But then his hawk eyes moved off of her and he appeared to be avoiding her eyes. He seemed to be waffling about something he wanted to say, mouth opening and closing.

"What is it?" she asked.

"What?"

"You have something you either want to ask, or want to tell me."

His eyebrow rose, and his fork went down. "That obvious?"

"Just a guess. I have not seen you look like this before." She smiled, teasing. "You do not tend to hesitate when it comes to making demands on me."

The smile was not returned; instead, Devin looked down at his plate, then pushed it forward away from him. He looked up at her, grey eyes holding no hint of amusement.

"Aggie, about the other night, did you see the man who attacked you?" His voice stayed very even, and a flicker of panic went down Aggie's spine, turned into her body, and settled in her gut.

Aggie's duck-skewered fork paused mid-air.

"Devin, you killed that man."

"No, I mean the man who was holding you."

"Why would you ask?"

Devin's mouth pulled back in a tight, silent line.

"Why…" Her fork clattered to her plate. "You don't mean… No…You mean that man is still…alive?"

Devin nodded.

Aggie's hands went to the edge of the table, gripping, holding her upright as her chest clamped down and breathing stopped. "I thought…I mean I had…I believed you had killed…He is still alive?"

Aggie could feel her face begin to sag as the blood rushed out of it. She fought to take in breath, her lungs only allowing short, tight gasps to enter. No. He had to be dead.

"Aggie, I am sorry. I thought you knew. I should have guessed, you were so relaxed today. He threw you against the brick and ran off, and I could not leave you, so he escaped."

"And you have not found him?" The best Aggie could produce was a cracking whisper.

"No. Every lead has been exhausted. You hold the only clues. I did not want to have to bring him up. I actually want you to never have to think of him again, but I have to know everything that you know of him."

"Damn." In an instant, the clamp on her breath blew, and Aggie jerked to her feet, pushing away from the table. "Damn to hell and back. So stupid. I should have known. I should have thought. Stupid."

She stalked to the edge of the room, pacing the dark wood floors in front of the fireplace, arms clasped tight around her belly. "It only makes sense. Of course he is still alive. I am so stupid. What was I thinking? I never should have let you help. Never should have gotten involved. Stupid and weak."

Her right arm swung wide as she spun on her heel, her fist coming back and hitting her upper arm. "Why did I do that? Weak. What was I thinking? Such idiocy. This never should have happened. I should have finished what I set out to do and not let anything stop me."

Eyes on the floor, her fist continued to pummel her own arm. "I am such an idiot to have let this happen. Damn. Weak. So damn weak and now he is still out there and—hell—my sister." Panic swelled her voice. Her eyes flew up. "Devin, I have to get back to London. My family—"

Devin stood, voice hard, hand up to stop her. "No. They are well-protected. No one is coming or going from your uncle's home until the fifth man has been disposed of. There has been no indication that these men want anything to do with your mother and sister, and as long as you are alive, this fifth man seems to want you for some reason. They have had plenty of opportunities to get to your mother or sister, but have not. I have talked to every man you hired. He wants you, Aggie. You. And the best place to protect you is at Stonewell. The best place to protect them is at your aunt and uncle's. That is what will happen. I will not argue this, Aggie."

Aggie's eyes narrowed at him, and then she spun away, stomping into a pace again. "God, I am so stupid. Stupid, stupid. I let my guard down—so stupid weak—and now everyone is in danger again. I had the best damn plan and then I veered and now everything is lost. Lost because I am too damn weak to stand up and do what needed to be done. I—"

Devin's finger's gripped her arm from behind, yanking her to a stop and spinning her around.

Aggie gasped. He seethed, jaw throbbing, eyes furious. She had never seen such anger directed at her.

"Stop it." The words hissed from his tight lips.

"No. You don't know how this feels." Aggie jerked her arm from his grasp, feet moving backward. "I am stupid. I let my guard down. And hell. I didn't even pack my pistols. Stupid. I left them under the bed. My damn pistols. Stupid. What was I thinking? I never should have let go. I cannot believe I let you talk me into it. A few kind words from you and I became an idiot."

Her freedom from his grasp only lasted a moment. Both shoulders were instantly clasped under his hands, stopping her from backing away.

"No. You will stop right now." He leaned down, his face in hers. "If you are to be angry, be angry at me, not yourself. Never yourself."

She tried to jerk away again, but couldn't escape the iron grasp. "Fine."

Her hands into fists, she went at his chest. "How about this—I trusted you. I didn't want to, but I did. You convinced me I could trust you, and now I cannot even find him—they were the key and they are dead—I don't know how else to get to him. He knows everything—everything—about me and I know nothing. Because of you and your promises and I was stupid because I wanted to believe you and—"

The kiss came down on her hard, ravaging her mouth, sending words back into the depths of her raging panic. She fought it, arms still pushing at him, knowing what he was doing. She couldn't let him take away her rage, it was the only thing keeping her from curling up into a panicked, quivering ball on the floor.

His hands slid from her shoulders, one going up, burying into the deep hair at the nape of her neck, the other to the small of her back. Pressing her body into his, he gave her no angle to escape, no angle to breathe against his onslaught.

The rage. She couldn't let it go. She couldn't dare.

Devin's mouth opened on hers, nudging her lips apart, his tongue easing into her. A whimper escaped her, and Devin pounced, pressing her body even harder into his, tilting her head for better access.

His lips left her mouth, moving along her jaw and down her neck. Aggie dragged air into her chest, and Devin's wine-mingled woodsy scent filled her head. Against every instinct, the rage in her chest started to scatter, replaced with not the panic she was so afraid of, but a fire, a need, deep in her core that sent shivers to all her limbs. A fire fighting to consume her.

Hands shaking, her fists unwound as she flattened her palms on his chest, the feeling in her fingertips disappearing. As her legs started to buckle, he turned their bodies, mouth still on her neck, and walked her backward until the edge of the table hit her backside just below his palm. His hand slid down under her, and he lifted, setting her on the table.

He pulled back, and Aggie cracked her eyes open, the red rage in her mind now mixed with the blackness his touch brought. The anger that had burned in his grey eyes had been replaced by an entirely different intensity.

Breath ragged, but voice still brutal, his left hand went along her neck, thumb under her chin. "You are angry at me. Me alone, Aggie. Do you understand?"

Aggie could feel her head nod without conscious thought of making it do so.

"Good."

He came at her even harder, his mouth assaulting furiously, forcing hers into opening. Aggie didn't notice when he pushed her legs apart, settling himself into her. Yanking her bottom forward, his hardness pressed insistently into her belly. Before she could react, tongue met tongue, and Aggie's leg kicked up, wrapping around his thigh, desperate for something solid to grab onto.

Sudden cool air touched her back, and it filtered into her mind that her jacket was gone and the buttons on her dress were popping behind her. Hazy, she pulled back from Devin's mouth, and he instantly invaded her neck again.

Her hands went to the back of his head, curling into his dark hair as she fought to get words out.

"The servants…they…"

"Doors are closed. They will not bother us." His words heated her neck as his hand came from her back and went down to the leg wrapped around him, pushing up the plum skirt.

"But—"

"No. They value their jobs. They will not enter."

His mouth trailed from her neck, down the front of her chest. Fabric ripped as air hit her nipple, then the warm wet of his mouth enclosed on her. Shocked, gasping, Aggie jerked, but Devin had her locked in place, hand on her bare back. In the next breath, teeth played with delicate skin just as his fingers found her core under her skirts.

Aggie lurched, the touch foreign, then had to concentrate on breathing as his fingers plied her folds, diving into her, pulling, teasing her into hard throbbing.

Her fingernails dug into his shoulders, and she realized she was half naked and he still had his coat on. Skin. She needed his skin.

She pushed his jacket down, effectively locking his arms until he growled and pulled back from her, shaking off the jacket. Cravat, waistcoat and shirt disappeared, and before he could move in on her again, Aggie spread her hands onto his chest, stopping him, wanting to take in the skin, the tight muscles.

She wouldn't have done this a day ago, but now, now she could. She had every right, and she was going to use being a bride to her advantage. She had wanted to know what he felt like since the she saw him shirtless. Palms flat on his boiling skin, she ran her hands across his chest, down his belly, around and up his back, drawing him in.

Without thought, her lips went to his chest, kissing, tongue slipping out to taste the salt of his skin. Devin groaned.

Aggie looked up to see him grimacing. "Is this not all right?"

"Hell, yes, it is all right."

His hand dove back under her skirts, deep into her, while the other gripped the hair at the back of her neck, forcing her backwards and down onto the long table. He descended onto her lips again, fire in his tongue, thrusting in and out, as he pushed her fully onto the table. Both of her legs wrapped around him.

Mouth hovering above hers, he steadied, even as she strained to pull him back down to encompass her again.

"Your anger. All of it, Aggie. I want it now."

At his words, Aggie unleashed and leaned up from the table to meet his mouth, taking in his tongue, then biting his lip as her fingernails raked across his back. She thought she tasted blood, but couldn't be sure, and honestly didn't care. She needed whatever he was doing to her. Whatever he was demanding of her.

He pushed her dress, short stays, and shift up over her head, shoving it off the table as his mouth took her nipple into his teeth once more.

Aggie's nails streaked down his back, and she realized he had lost his buckskin breeches without the slightest notice from her. Her fingertips curled over the curve of his backside, and she was rewarded by his hand moving in her folds even faster, manipulating her with speed. Aggie's hips thrust, uncontrolled, both for and against the agony he created in her core.

Her right hand flew from his back, over her head, flattening on the table in search of something hard to hold onto against the onslaught. The first scream built instantly, and she gripped, clawing at the table until it unleashed, burning fire mixed with pleading.

More screams erupted, and at the instant she didn't know what would win, pleasure or pain, an explosion tore through her body, and Devin ripped into her, thrusting hard, spiraling the pleasure even deeper into her body.

Aggie thought she heard a guttural "Hell" in her ear as he filled her again and again, but she could think of nothing except the black exploding chasm her mind had become. Devin's muscles suddenly tightened under her grip, and in the next instant, she could feel him swell and explode deep within her.

Their chests warred with each other, both heaving for breath, and then Devin slipped a hand under the small of her back and flipped them, him flat on the table, still deep inside of her draped body.

Aggie buried her face in his chest, still tasting the saltiness of his skin, still gasping for breath. Both of his hands went deep into her hair, and his thumbs slid along her jaw, lifting her slightly as he tilted her face to his. Worry etched his eyes as he searched her face.

"Hell, Aggie. I did not know. I was terribly wrong. Are you okay?"

"Okay? Yes. Is there something wrong?" She could only afford a murmur against her ragged breath.

"No. Your virginity. I should not have—" He sighed. "That should have been slow. Gentle."

"What was wrong with that?" She propped her chin on the crook in the middle of his chest, licking her lips, now plump and red. "Should I have not felt that? Did I do something wrong? Are there rules I do not know about?"

"Are you in pain?"

"No." She shifted her hips slightly on him. "Ouch. Yes."

His hands went to her hips, stilling her.

"I did not know that was part of it. So there are rules."

Devin laughed, low and thick, rumbling her on his chest. "No. No rules. At least not as far as I am concerned. You may come up with some along the way, though."

Aggie's eyes widened, but a smile played on her lips. "You are looking pretty wicked right now. I can only imagine what is in your mind."

Devin shrugged and his fingers moved along the back of her neck, kneading the muscles. "You will be sore for a while, but after that passes, any sort of pain from now on is by choice."

"Even more wicked-looking, you are." She reached up and touched the small cut she just noticed on his lip. "Sorry about that."

He snatched her finger in-between his teeth, making her jump. Closing his mouth around it, he sucked, tongue caressing the tip.

Aggie's breath caught. How could one little move so instantly light up her core?

He let her finger slip from his mouth, and she slid it down his chin onto his chest, trailing circles along his collarbone.

"I always wondered."

"Wondered what?"

"What went on in all those brothels."

Devin sputtered. "Brothels?"

"Well, yes, I mean, I knew what went on inside of them, but I really did not know. And I was quite curious every time I dropped a gentleman off at one—and believe me, that was a lot. Brothels have to be the most common destination among men. I probably now know the location of every brothel in London."

His hand went through her hair, caressing the long strands that had freed themselves from her upsweep. "That makes you a very dangerous woman."

"Maybe so." She smiled, contemplating the thought. "I will have you know I was propositioned several times by the ladies when I was driving."

He laughed. "And you got out of those invitations how?"

"Best I could, silently and with my head down. I just wanted you to know I am wanted in many circles."

"I will keep that in mind."

Aggie twirled her fingers on his chest. "Regardless, I always tried to imagine what was going on inside of them."

"And how far did you get?"

"Pretty far, I would say. I did grow up in the country, after all, so have seen animals mate. But I never really knew. And now that I do…"

"Now that you do—what is the verdict?"

"Well, now that I do…wow."

Devin's chest shook with a laugh and Aggie's head bobbed up and down on it.

"Leave it to you to know all about brothels, everything except for what actually goes on inside the rooms. But I can tell you on good authority that what goes on inside those establishments is not even a shadow of the good we just experienced."

She craned her neck to look at him. "Really? On good authority you say?"

"Don't ask."

"I will not."

"Just trust that what we did is on a completely different level—one I didn't know existed."

Wary, she looked at him, trying to decide whether to believe him. He hadn't lied to her yet, as far as she knew. "Well then, that is good to know."

Her head heavy, she let it fall back down onto his chest.

His fingertips were gentle up and down her spine. "Aggie, if I had known, I would have waited until we got to Stonewell. This was sudden, I know, and I should have let you have more time to get used to the idea of losing your virginity—"

Her head snapped up. "You did not think I was a virgin?"

Devin shrugged in apology. "You did not catch that earlier? I was not sure, and I leaned on the side of experienced—how we met, you must admit, was a bit unconventional. So I assumed. I should not have."

"And you were okay with me not being a virgin? I am surprised."

"I wanted you. I want you. I do not really care how."

She smiled. "This is the fun part of marriage, isn't it?"

"Apparently, yes. I honestly had never dared hope I would get this lucky in the marital bed."

Her hand slid up, caressing his jaw. "Except we are not in a bed. Maybe you will be less lucky once we are in one."

His eyebrow cocked at her. "Now who is wicked? Let us get upstairs to a bath."

CHAPTER 11

Devin slid down into the warm water between Aggie's naked back and the side of the fat copper tub, soap and washcloth in hand.

She didn't pull away as he settled his legs around her, but did look over her shoulder at him. "You are in the bathtub with me. Naked."

Her voice even, Devin wasn't sure if she was delighted or appalled. He brushed the wet ends of tendrils along her neck. "Did you expect I would dare let your nudity out of my sight?"

Aggie's arm went up, arching backward to wrap her fingers along his neck, while the back of her head snuggled below his collarbone just above the water line. "You are not one to let go of something once you have it, are you?"

"That one is true, my duchess." Devin scrubbed the washcloth and soap together, then slipped it across the front of Aggie's body, down between her breasts, passing her stomach, and diving into the depths of her.

At the touch, she immediately clamped her thighs and jerked away, sending a thick wave of water splashing over the far end of the tub. He grabbed her arm before she could escape from his legs.

"You are not going shy on me now, are you?"

She stopped movement. "Yes. I guess. Instinct. I am sorry. This. Naked with you. It is just so new and you do not need to…I can do it myself."

"Of course you can, but I want to. I now have access to every nook of you, and I intend to use that privilege." He tugged on her arm, and resistance gone, she let him spin her back into her snug place between his legs. Devin dove again with the washcloth and she only gave a minor twitch as the fabric went down past her belly to gently clean the area he had ravaged earlier. "Clean up after the messes you make. That was the one lesson from my father I actually took to."

"Only one lesson took?"

"I am sure there were more, but they were beyond me." Devin shrugged. "That particular lesson only took because I watched him spend his whole life cleaning up the mess he made."

"What mess was that?"

Devin stiffened. "I apologize. I was misleading when I brought up my father. I do not intend to continue talk of him."

No reply. Aggie tensed in response to his rigid muscles. Devin swore to himself. He wanted her pliable, not on-guard, not silent.

"Trust me, Aggs, when I say that talk of my father is not worth our time. Especially when we are naked in a warm tub."

She relaxed slightly against him. "You have other plans for us?" He could hear the smile in her voice.

"I do, but I have some business to take care of first."

Aggie's right arm floated along the break of the water, methodically swirling little ripples. "I imagine you are a busy man, but what business do you need attend to?"

"You. Our conversation downstairs. We have to talk about the fifth man. The leader."

Her hand froze mid-circle. "We do?"

Devin's chest tightened at how quickly her voice shriveled. It infuriated him to have to ask her anything, but he had to. "Yes. I would rather not speak of him ever again, but we need to."

He set the washcloth down on the wide teak ledge that encased the tub. "But first you need to turn around." Gently, he grabbed her upper arms and spun her until she faced him.

"Why?" Her eyes were locked onto his chest. "I was fine where I was."

"I need to see your face to know if you are telling me the truth."

Scared green eyes flipped to enraged as her look jerked to his face. "Truth? I take offense—when have I ever lied to you?"

"You have omitted important details in the past. That, you cannot deny. And that is what I am guarding against."

Crossing her arms below her breasts, Aggie shoved back in the water until her back hit the opposite end of the tub. "Fine. Ask. I will be sure to include as many details as I can."

Devin stared at Aggie's taut face. He wished he didn't have to ask Aggie about the man, and he wouldn't if he had even the slightest clue as to who this fifth man was, why he was involved, or how he could find the bastard. But he had nothing. Dead ends all around.

In the dark alley, Devin had not gotten the slightest look at him. He'd had a hood deep over his face, and Devin was too preoccupied by Aggie flying at the wall. Asking Aggie was his only choice. She had gone through enough, but she was his only link to the bastard.

"The leader—he is the key to this mess. I need to know exactly why he wants you dead. You said you witnessed something that marked you for disposal. What was it? When did this start? The real story."

Almost instantly, Aggie's crossed arms softened, her whole body eased into calm, and a controlled mask slipped onto her face as her eyes went to the water in front of her. That she suddenly gained control of every nuance in her body was telling.

Devin braced himself.

"It started a year ago, the moment I saw my father murdered by these men." Her voice sat above the water, eerily even, not a flicker of emotion breaking through.

Shock sent Devin's eyes wide. He had no idea she witnessed her father's murder. He also realized he had neglected to ask her days ago what the terrible incident was that she had witnessed.

Outrage sent waves through his body, threatening to take him over, but he stifled it for Aggie's sake.

"Aggs, what happened?"

Aggie looked up, startled. "You are not angry with me for not telling you sooner?"

He shook his head. "Tell me."

Her eyes moved back down, fixating on the water. "We were traveling into London, Papa and I. We were at the bottom of a hill, through a line of woods. We had been through there a thousand times. Shots stopped our carriage. They killed our driver and footman immediately. I do not even know why Papa was carrying so many pistols that day. He rarely did. But he put one into my hand, and took the other two. He told me to run and hide in the woods. Then he jumped out. I pleaded with him not to go. He knew I was an excellent shot. He knew I could have helped. But he jumped."

Her voice stayed incredibly flat.

"Three bullets went into him before he could even raise his arms. He died in front of me."

"Aggs—"

Her palm, but not her eyes, came up, stopping him. Devin went silent.

"I jumped from the carriage to go to him. That is when I saw them all. The four surrounded me, and their leader stayed back on his horse, partway up the hill. None of them had bothered to cover their faces. And the leader…" Her voice gave the slightest quiver as she closed her eyes. "He had the most evil eyes."

She fell silent.

Devin paused, exhaling his held breath. "How did you escape?"

"I didn't. I did nothing. I did not even grab the pistol when I jumped from the carriage. Worthless."

Devin could see under the water her hands had balled into tight fists, straining against her upper arms.

"The carriage that came over the crest of the hill was the only thing that saved me. They disappeared into the woods."

Aggie took a deep breath, her chest rising above the water.

It grated him to have to continue, but Devin steeled himself. "Had your father acted strangely before your trip? Was there any reason he should have been afraid? Business deal gone bad, maybe?"

Eyes still closed, Aggie shook her head. "No. But I knew very little of his business dealings. Jason had always been by his side with the investments. I have been lost in all his paperwork."

"Was the leader with the other men on the other occasions they tried to kill you?"

"Not the first time, but the second time he was there. After they came to our house, I decided to go after them." Aggie opened her eyes and gave a sad half-smile to Devin. "And that, you know all about."

"Did you see anything at all that would identify him? A unique button, watch, pin—anything?"

She shook her head.

Devin stared at Aggie. She had told the entire story with as much emotion as reading a stagecoach schedule. Not even the slightest glimmer of a tear showed in her eyes.

"Aggie, have you ever grieved for you father?"

Hard resolve flickered into her green eyes. "No, and I will not until my family is safe, justice has been served, and death is not coming for me."

Devin moved forward in the water, his hands searching for her knees that had curled into her body. He needed to wrap her into such a cocoon of safety that she would never have to think these thoughts or visit these memories again.

"There is no need for you to worry about this last man, Aggie. I will take care of it," Devin said as he squeezed her knees, letting every drop of raw determination reverberate in his words.

The calm gone, her body had shifted into a tight coil, and something deep and grave that Devin couldn't identify invaded her face at his words.

"Devin, there is one other thing you need to know. What I did in London, how I went after the four—I did it with a lack of fear. I was afraid for my family, but not for me. Nothing could ever compare to the fear I felt the day my father was murdered. So facing the four killers didn't frighten me."

Aggie paused, and Devin could see she had to choke the last words out.

"But Devin, this fifth man, the leader…I am afraid." She drew a quivering breath, her rigid body shaking, sending rippling waves along the water. "And I am so tired of being afraid."

The sheer vulnerability she let escape in that second rammed into his chest. Hell. He had failed her. Failed her by not killing that bastard. And now she was terrified.

Details. He needed damn details to find the leader. But he also needed Aggie not to look like she did right now. Now was not the time to push—details could wait. Now was the time to remove that tension from her. He had to. She needed to be safe. Needed to feel safe. Mere vows were not enough.

His hands left her legs, and he reached around her, drawing her body into his. She let him, and the shaking lessened, but didn't cease. She needed more.

A hand on her back, he clasped her harder into him. His mouth went to her ear, voice gentle. "I cannot take away the fear, Aggs, not in this moment. But I can make you forget. Let me do that."

Heartbeats passed. Then her forehead rubbed against his chest in the smallest nod.

"Good…good. Just concentrate on my touch. My hands on you." Devin slipped his fingers up her spine to her neck and tilted her head. "My mouth on you."

He started lightly behind her ear, lips taking in the wet beads, and slowly moved downward along her slick skin. She responded immediately, her shoulder leaning into his chest even as she opened her neck more fully to him. A heated moan rose from her throat just as the shaking yielded to his touch.

She untangled the hold she had on herself, her hands moving to grip his solid arms, digging into the straining muscles.

He had her now. And he wasn't about to let go.

Devin moved to her mouth, tongue touching hers, and it was all he could do to not push her back against the tub and take her, but it was too soon. She would still be sore. He squashed his own throbbing need and concentrated on moving his fingers along her skin, bringing to life nerves that begged to be unleashed.

It was fire, and she was quick to reciprocate, fingers dancing along his body, tongue thrusting back at his. His fingers went into her hair and he pulled her head to the side, gaining access to his next attack on her neck.

Low, guttural groans escaped from deep within Aggie's chest, and both of her legs found their way to wrapping around Devin's waist.

Aggie's hands went about his neck, burying into dark hair. "Yes. Please. Take it away. Please…" Her voice trailed off as her legs clamped and her hips moved forward.

Her body, so tight when he first grabbed her, was now as pliable as a rag doll. Only her legs and her hands strained, but that was only to get her body closer to his. It was what Devin had wanted to accomplish. And now he wanted her to have more.

He trailed his thumb slowly in a line from her neck to the slope of her breasts, letting the nerves prick the skin. He moved downward, caressing her right nipple, twirling it between his fingers. It only prompted her to tilt her head back further, opening all the more to him.

His lips found her neck again as he pushed her body backward to the edge of the tub. Reaching it, he slipped his hands under her thighs and lifted her, setting her on the lip of the tub, her weight carried by the wide teak ledge.

Hazy confusion set across Aggie's face. "What? We are stopping?"

"No." Devin gave her a lascivious smile. "No, we have only just started."

"What?"

Devin grabbed her knees, pushing her legs apart. Her hands dropped behind her, holding herself upright on the ledge.

He bent to her inner thigh, her skin dripping, and began to taste, to tease his way up her leg.

"Oh, God…" One hand pushed at his shoulders. "Devin, this…"

Devin didn't look up, and he kept his lips on her thigh. "Let me do this, Aggs. Just close your eyes and concentrate on my touch."

His fingers preceded his mouth to her core, readying her, and when he reached her to begin to taste, he heard an audible gulp. Lips not leaving her, he glanced up just in time to see her head tilt back, trembling. He pulled her left leg inward, draping it over his shoulder.

"Hell, Devin." Aggie's palms slipped on the wood, and she clunked down hard onto her elbows.

Hand still manipulating, Devin pulled up, chuckling. The clunk hadn't stopped her writhing. The heel of her foot dug into his back, demanding, bringing him into her again. Devin obliged.

Faster, he attacked, hungry for the screams she failed to control. Her other leg came over his shoulder, and Aggie jerked up, hands diving into his hair. Half for support, half begging, she clutched him.

He continued his onslaught, both tongue and fingers searching the deepest parts of her. Faster and faster he plied her, hard against her struggle for relief, until her body seized, thrusting against him, scream at her lips.

She collapsed on him.

Devin wrapped his hands up Aggie's back and pulled her down into the water. He moved backward to lean against the wall of the tub, Aggie limp atop him.

He tightened his arm across her back, and she snuggled closer with a sigh. Every trace of rigidness had disappeared from her body. Devin congratulated himself on achieving that. And if he had to keep her constantly in bed—or bath—to keep her from worry, well, there were worse fates.

Minutes skimmed by, and sure she had fallen asleep, Devin untangled his fingers from her hair and started to move.

"That was…" Her voice, purring into his chest, surprised him.

"Yes?"

She propped her chin on the center of his chest to look up at him. "Amazing. Can I do that to you?"

Devin laughed. "You can do anything you want to me, Aggs." He brushed a lock of hair from her forehead. "But not right now. Right now I am carrying you over to bed before you pass out on me and we are stuck in here."

~ ~ ~

The screams sent him running up the stairs. Sleep had eluded him, so he had left Aggie in bed and gone down to Killian's study. He wanted to go over one of the initial reports he had on activities of the band of four.

There had to be something he was missing about their connection to the leader. Maybe he had to go further back in history with them. Where they came from, how they knew each other. He had already made plans to send one of the extra guards he had hired to accompany them, back into London with more direct instructions for his team of five runners. They were still investigating, attempting to find the leader. They were smart, and probably already digging into pasts, but Devin wasn't leaving it up to assumption.

The screams, screeching, blood-curdling, in a pitch like nothing he had ever heard before, shot him out of the carved wooden chair and sprinting up the stairs.

Wearing only pants and wishing he had a knife in hand, he busted into the room he always used at Killian's home, battle-cocked to fight whoever was attacking Aggie.

Searching the dark corners of the room, Devin saw no movement. Frantic, he focused on Aggie in the stream of moonlight coming through the open window, only to see her still in bed, still lying down, still screeching. A chill went to his bones as he watched her writhe, sheets flying.

Rushing to her, he hoped against hope she wasn't injured. Damn his idiocy in leaving her alone. Untangling her limbs from the sheets, he caught her face in full-out scream, eyes closed, and realized she was asleep.

He clamped down on her shoulders, pinning her to the bed. The screams got louder and she pitched violently, trying to free herself from his hands.

"Aggie. Wake up. Wake up." Devin's face hovered over hers. He wasn't sure she could hear him through her own shrieking.

"Aggie. Stop. You're safe. Aggie. Wake up."

A quick gasp of air, and Aggie's eyes flew open as she jerked up against his hold.

Panic flooded her face, then confusion, then she collapsed back into the bed, panting, as her face fell. "I was screaming, wasn't I?"

"Like someone had cut your arm off."

Devin thought he saw her cringe at his words, but then she closed her eyes, tilting her head back up against the pillow.

"I am so embarrassed that you saw that." She opened her eyes to look at him. "I am sorry I woke you up."

"I wasn't asleep, I was downstairs. No apologizing. Now tell me."

"Tell you what?"

"Tell me what is going on in your mind."

She closed her eyes again, shaking her head, wedging it deeper into the pillow. "I dream. I cannot control my dreams when I am overly tired."

"You are not going to tell me, are you?"

"No." She said quickly, jumping on the option he inadvertently offered up.

Devin sighed and removed his hands from her shoulders. He pulled the sheet over her. "Fine. Back to sleep for you. But I am asking again in the morning."

Standing, the surprise hand gripping his wrist stopped his exit. He looked down at her, only to see remnants of her earlier terrorized face still etched around her eyes. She hid it well. She always hid it well, but Devin was starting to see right through the mask she usually held in place.

"I hoped…can you stay? Please? You here…I fell asleep so easily before."

Devin's chest tightened. Hell yes, he could stay.

He dropped his pants and slid under the sheet next to Aggie, fitting her body solidly into his. Pushing her hair back, she put her ear on his chest and heaved a breath.

Within a minute she was back asleep.

CHAPTER 12

On the bed, Aggie laid a fresh chemise, stays, stockings, a pleated shirt, and a deep wine colored traveling skirt and jacket that she knew warmed the color of her face. The military-styled braided accents and sleek lines would accent her shape, and for that, she was grateful. After what Devin had done to her body last night—things she had never imagined possible—she wasn't above keeping a constant reminder of her curves in front of him. She would let him have free rein on her body at any time he saw fit. And she hoped he would see fit a lot.

Not bothering with a maid, she dressed, and found she couldn't deny the haunting emptiness in the spot where she usually strapped a pistol to her thigh. She silently chastised herself again for letting her guard down. She would just have to ask Devin for a pistol once they got to Stonewell, despite the fact she guessed it would irk his pride. Pricked pride or not, she knew the best person to protect herself, was herself.

"After you fell back asleep, you said 'panther' in your sleep," Devin said as he sat on the edge of the bed to pull on his Hessians. "It was better than the screaming, but strange. Why 'panther?'"

Aggie stopped mid-motion in packing her bag and turned to him. "I did?"

"Yes. It was oddest thing a woman has ever said in bed with me."

Aggie laughed. "I do not know if I want to hear what the second oddest thing was. But I guess 'panther' is odd. It is actually nothing—give me a chance to dig this out." She turned back to her bag, hands diving deep into the contents. Pulling out a dark blue ball of cloth, she unwrapped the edges of the fabric to reveal the only trinket she insisted on bringing with her everywhere, a wooden sculpture of a panther, no bigger than her hand. "My brother sent it."

She couldn't help her light mood from swinging to mournful as she held up the black wood piece for Devin. "Jason was always sending items home from his travels for the crown. This is the last thing he sent. A few days after we received it, we got word that he was missing. Most thought he was dead. Father did not believe it though, and neither did mother, although that was when she started to withdraw. But father never found any evidence either way, save for the fact that he believed the panther was sent after the date Jason went missing."

"How would he know that?"

"Father hired several investigators," Aggie sat heavily on the bed next to Devin, "and they traced the panther back to a courier who was supposedly given it two days after Jason was reported missing."

"Do you believe he is alive? I think our discussion the other day about your brother fits into that 'omitting information' arena."

Aggie looked down at the panther. "I do. I have to. Until I have proof that he is not, I will believe he is alive. I have been doing everything I can to try to hold the estate together until he returns. Including—" Aggie cut herself off.

"Good try," Devin said. "You need to finish that sentence."

Aggie sighed. She may as well tell him, because the man was going to figure it out soon enough anyway. "Jason has been gone for so long—years—and the solicitors were beginning to question whether he is alive. No matter how much I insisted on his good health, they kept pressuring me. So I manufactured a message from him several months ago as proof that he is still alive."

Devin smiled, and Aggie wasn't sure if that was a good sign or not.

"How did you do that?"

"I arranged to have a letter come in on a ship from the continent. Jason and I were very close, and I am pretty good at forging his handwriting." She shrugged. "It quelled the swell of questions that were beginning to surface. At least for now. People get antsy when a title is involved."

Devin's hand went lightly on her arm. "Do you truly believe he is alive, or are you pretending because it is easier than the alternative?"

Aggie eyed him. She didn't like the probing. Didn't like having to question her own faith that Jason was alive. She looked away, staring out the window at the light of the morning brightening the trees. "Honestly, I am not sure. I would like to be, but he has just been away so long. If he is alive, I am certain he would have contacted us by now. Especially if he knew about father and..." Her voice trailed, cut off by her own fears.

If Jason was alive and knew about the danger his family was in, he would have been back. Aggie was sure of it. But he didn't know. That was the only explanation. That was the only reason he would stay away.

She ran her fingers over the smooth backbone of the panther. "One of the last things my father said to me was to keep the panther with me always—I guess to keep the hope of Jason alive. So the panther stays with me. It keeps me optimistic, as it is my only link to the hope that he is okay."

"Can I see it?"

Devin took the offered sculpture, turning it back and forth in his hands, studying it. "It certainly is an exquisite piece. The craftsmanship is of very high quality."

Devin handed the panther back to Aggie.

Her finger ran along the front outstretched leg of the cat. "Yes, Jason always did have an eye for fine craftsmanship."

She stood, turning from Devin, and carefully rewrapped it. Jason had to be alive, she repeated in her head. He just had to be.

Devin stood and Aggie turned to him.

"Before we go, Devin, there is something else as long as we are talking about Jason and the estate."

"Tell me."

He crossed his arms across his chest, and Aggie swallowed. She wondered if he always had to brace himself when she was about to talk. But then, he was the one that said he didn't like her omitting information.

"I do not want to burden you more than I already have, but I have a favor to ask. Will you help me with the dealings of the estate? I don't want to lose anything before Jason returns, and I fear I am doing just that. Father never included me in any discussions about the estate, and why would he? So I have tried, but I know I have been making a mess of things."

Aggie smirked up at her husband as his stance relaxed. "Plus, I am sure Jason would have settled a more-than-generous dowry on me, and I can still make that happen. The hasty wedding did not exactly leave any time to discuss such important details."

Devin mirrored her smirk. "The last thing I need is your money, Aggie. You are what I wanted, nothing more. That said, I would be happy to help in any way you need me to."

Relief visibly went through her body as she exhaled. "Thank you. You have no idea how that would alleviate my worries. I will just be happy if the entire estate is not lost by the time Jason returns."

~ ~ ~

Aggie looked across the carriage at Devin. He was watching her, grey eyes hovering, as usual, and she found it both comforting, and suddenly, slightly unnerving.

Unnerving because she wanted to love this man.

Hell.

She probably already did.

She had been denying herself that truth for the entire first half of the day. It was too soon for something as fanciful as love, she kept telling herself. She wasn't ready for this. She wasn't safe. And she had only known him for a few days.

A few days that felt like forever.

He had no reason to help her that first night, yet he had. He willingly took on her problems. The problems of a stranger. And then he didn't let her disappear. Time and again, he showed up. And that told Aggie all she needed to know about his character.

She denied him repeatedly, denied his help, but he didn't listen and refused to cave to the demands of her pride. Instead, he simply took care of her. Took her burdens. Took her worries. Put her first. He wasn't just a man. He was a force. A force she was no match to resist.

Her eyes moved across his wide shoulders, settling on his chest, and the memory of her mouth on his skin, gasping for breath, flashed in her mind. He was also a force that could twist her body into incomprehensible pleasure. How could she not be falling in love with him?

Why was she fighting it? He was her husband. What more could she need? Had she become so jaded over the past year she had no room for love? Or was it that she didn't want him hurt? If she still wasn't safe, that meant he wasn't safe. The thought settled into her chest, and she didn't like the weight it added to her breath.

"The worry lines on your forehead." Devin's voice startled her. "They were not there a moment ago. Is something wrong?"

Aggie pasted a smile on her face. "No. Absolutely nothing. Just an errant thread of thought."

Devin's eyebrow arched, and Aggie could see him start to question her. She wasn't about to share her current thoughts with him. Not yet.

"Truly. Nothing of concern." Aggie searched her mind. "Stonewell. Tell me about it. You grew up there, correct?"

"I did."

Aggie waited, but those were the only words he spoke. "That is all you are going to share?"

He shrugged. "Why don't you tell me about your childhood?"

Aggie's face lit up. "Happily, but only if you reciprocate and tell me about your own."

Devin sighed. "I would rather not."

"Well then, I would rather not either." Aggie crossed her arms and looked out the window at white sheep dotting the greenery.

Several moments passed in silence.

"Fine. Deal." Devin looked none too pleased at the manipulation.

"Excellent." Aggie smiled and held out her gloved hand for Devin to shake. He paused, but then grabbed her fingers. Aggie saw the slightest smirk pass on his face as he shook her hand.

"Okay. Where do I start?" Aggie tapped her finger on the fold in the fabric of her maroon skirt. Her eyes glowed as memories filtered to the front of her mind. "I had a happy childhood. Occasionally we spent time in London, or at one of the other estates, but those times were infrequent. Mother rarely wanted to leave our country estate, Clapinshire. But you probably know all of that about me already, don't you?" Aggie had gathered that Devin knew much more about her than she knew of him.

"I have done some research, yes." Devin shrugged.

"Then I shall talk about my brother. Jason and I were extremely close. We were two years apart in age, and I idolized him. He always had time to explain things to me, why frogs ate flies, how to build a boat that wouldn't sink, how not to get stuck to one's knees in mud—all the terribly important things."

Aggie paused for a moment and gazed out the window. Memories of mucky, wet, wonderful days put a soft smile on her lips. "We used to play in the woods and creek for hours and hours at a time, fishing, building platforms in the trees, playing hide-and-seek. Fun and more fun. Days that disappeared into everything and nothing. Father was gone at times, but whenever he came back from London, he would bring us little gifts. My favorite was a bow and arrow set—"

"Your father gave you a bow and arrow?"

Aggie chuckled. "Not exactly. Hiders-rights won out. I constantly stole it from Jason, and I had three fantastic hiding spots for it. Jason got tired of looking for it. Papa got tired of hearing him complain about it. So he eventually purchased another set for Jason."

"Brat," Devin said with a smile.

"Yes, well, I got what I wanted." Aggie smiled and shrugged her shoulders. She wasn't going to argue the point. She had been a brat. "Anyway, I became quite good. I always enjoyed shooting at targets and I loved to challenge Jason to contests. It took me half-of-a-year of practice, but the day I beat him was the day he refused to compete with me anymore."

"I don't blame him. And that your parents encouraged the behavior—double the brat."

"Yes. And I have not even gotten to the pistol part yet."

"Pistol? Do I want to hear this part of the story?"

"You did ask about my childhood."

"Fine, tell me, and we will prove the point that ignorance is bliss."

Aggie's hands settled into her lap as she smiled. "Jason was humiliated when I beat him—although he continued to dispute the outcome of that contest. So he dropped the bow and convinced father it was time to become skilled in shooting firearms. It gave Jason the perfect chance to flaunt something that only he was allowed to do, for he knew that our father would never let me touch a pistol."

"And rightfully so."

"Yes, well the bugger took away all my fun. He started to spend all his time practicing his aim and cleaning his pistol. I lost my playmate…and then when he wanted to leave me behind, all he had to do was tell mother or father that he was going off to practice shooting, and that it would not be safe for me to come along. So I was resigned to sit inside. My mother would inevitably corner me with her needlepoint and make me practice it." Aggie cringed.

"I take it you do not enjoy the needlepoint?"

"I think it does not enjoy me. I am terrible at it. While I am glad for the experience, it is best for both my fingertips and the thread that I resist taking needle to cloth."

"So you must have escaped you mother's watch?"

"I did. I was so very jealous of Jason and his pistol, on top of being irritated that I no longer had anyone to show off to or to compete with."

Devin's forehead wrinkled in trepidation. "You turned to a life of crime again, didn't you?"

"Yes." Aggie nodded. "The only way I could humiliate my brother again—which was my main objective, of course—was to also become an expert with the gun. Knowing that my brother and father would never let me near a pistol, I secretly constructed a practice area, far into the woods, where I could sneak off with one of the pistols my father rarely used, and practice my shot."

Aggie paused, hedging. "Now if I tell you the rest of this, you must promise not to laugh at me, for you must remember that I was young, and possibly a bit impetuous."

"And you are not the slightest bit impetuous now?"

She raised an eyebrow to glower at him. "Possibly. But I have also managed to survive. So I will accept that flaw."

Devin chuckled. "As that is true—best you keep that flaw, then. Please, continue."

She tilted her head at him, not sure his words qualified as a promise.

"Please. I would like to hear how this story ends."

"All right. It was a sunny day, right in the middle of the afternoon, and I snuck into my father's study and took one of the oldest pistols—thinking, of course, that it would be the least missed one. I took off into the woods and set up my little target at the practice field." Aggie smiled to herself. "I was so proud, grinning ear to ear. I think I was even humming. But having only observed in bits and pieces what Jason actually did with his pistol, I loaded the bullet and gun powder, not, of course, knowing at all what I was really doing…"

A deep groan coupled with Devin's cringing face. "What did you hit?"

"My foot." Aggie closed her eyes, not wanting to see Devin's reaction.

Silence.

She cracked her eyelids.

He held a tight smile, but no laughter escaped. It looked like it took immense effort.

Aggie's eyes opened fully.

"Laugh now?" Devin squeaked out.

"Yes, fine, laugh, get it over with." Aggie sighed, shaking her head, laughing at herself. It was hard not to with Devin's rumble filling the coach.

"So, bullet in your foot, what happened?"

"I screeched like a fox, and it turned out my secret practice grounds were closer to the house than I had figured, for within a few moments, my brother and father came busting through the woods and took me home."

"How did your foot fare?"

"I was lucky. The bullet went right through my foot—I did not lose any toes—and I just have the scars on the top and bottom of my foot as remembrance."

"But that does not explain how you became the excellent shot you did," Devin said. "You should still be shooting yourself in the foot every time you pick up a pistol."

Aggie gave a wicked smile. "That was the true beauty of what my plan turned into. It was epic in its failure, but plans can change for the better. And I was smart enough to recognize when mine did. After my foot healed, my father decided it was safer to teach me the proper way with a pistol, than to risk having my other foot marred. He knew how stubborn I was—"

"Am."

"We really are taking a tour of my flaws, aren't we?" Aggie shrugged. "But again—alive, so I will take it. Regardless, once I received proper instruction with the shooting of a pistol, I became quite good."

"Better than your brother?"

Aggie smirked. "He was humiliated once or twice more. But I think he was proud of me, even though he would never admit it."

"After we reach Stonewell and settle in, I shall be sure to challenge you to a shooting contest of our own."

Tilting her head at him, she chuckled with competitive gleam in her eye. "I would be delighted to take you up on that challenge."

Devin's eyes twinkled from her story. His eyes were still dangerous, but when he smiled they had a light in them that

Aggie couldn't look away from. Her breath actually caught at the raw shining power that emanated from him.

Even though she was still in danger, at that moment, she felt lighter than she had in years. She was actually smiling, and she couldn't remember the last time a true, heartfelt smile had crossed her face. A smile that wasn't fake. Wasn't pasted on to soothe others. A smile just because she was in a moment of happiness.

Aggie forced herself to turn from his gaze. If he could do that to her, what else could he do? The thought was absolutely terrifying. The last time she was truly happy was when Jason was still home and her father was alive. Her heart hurt at the thought. She didn't think she could go through loss like that again without breaking like her mother had.

The carriage slowed.

Aggie perked up, looking out the window. "Are we stopping?"

"Yes, we are well within my main lands now, so I thought you could use a short stop to refresh yourself. My men have checked the area. There is a brook along the border of these woods." Devin leaned forward and pointed to the thick of trees they pulled up next to. "We are only about two hours to my home, but it has been a long day so far, and we should take a moment to enjoy the sun."

"This seems a bit too convenient." Aggie's eyes narrowed into suspicion. "You would not be trying to get out of our little bargain about talking about your childhood, would you? Because stalling will not work with me. I rarely forget things, and I am not about to forget our bargain."

"The thought never crossed my mind. You, my dear Augustine, have a very suspicious mind."

"My suspicious mind has been quite useful, so I will not let it rest just yet."

The carriage came to a full stop, steps were pulled, and Devin exited and then assisted Aggie. Foot on the step, her hand ensconced in his, he grabbed her about the waist and gently lifted her and placed her on the ground. Feet firm, she turned in his arm to peer up at him, surprised by his spontaneous, affectionate motion. She hadn't expected it from him.

He smiled at her, but the smile almost immediately disappeared as a frown crossed his face and creased his forehead. It threw Aggie, and she stepped backward, loosening his hold on her. Had she done something wrong?

She looked over her shoulder at the water at the bottom of the slight embankment, trying to hide the disappointment that she knew was obvious on her face. "I would like a few moments to freshen up at the stream," she said, not bothering to turn back to Devin with the words.

She stopped along the edge of the woods, sliding down the green mossy bank, and paused at a large boulder. Kneeling, she dipped her handkerchief into the gurgling stream to soak it. She pressed the cool cloth to her eyes and mouth, chiding herself for running so quickly when Devin's demeanor suddenly changed.

He had suddenly looked fierce, and all she could think of was to escape from whatever had darkened his face. She didn't know why the sudden change, but she should have held her ground and found out. She let herself be intimidated, and she hated the feeling. In the future, she would never run away as she had just done. Never.

Sitting back on the bank, Aggie looked up at the sky. The sun had moved behind fluffy clouds, but it was pleasantly warm, warm enough to dip her toes into the cool water for just a moment. Hiking her skirt up, she unlaced her tall traveling boots, untied her stockings, and scooted down to the water. Big toes in first to test the waters, she slowly slipped the rest of her feet into the brook.

Enjoying the soothing sounds of the bubbling water, and the earthy smell of the adjacent woods, she unbuttoned her traveling jacket to let the air breeze to her white pleated shirt. She leaned back upon the mossy embankment, arms crossed above her head, and relaxed her body, trying to regain some sort of control over her thoughts and emotions that had been running rampant over the past days. The clouds moved past the sun and she closed her eyes to the bright rays.

All of it simmered together in one big pot of emotional stew—almost being killed, Devin saving her, marriage, the leader being killed then not killed, the beautiful things Devin had done to her body last night, the ease of being with him, actual laughter—it was no wonder she ran from him when his mood changed. She could barely keep her own emotions level, much less worry about—

Two jarring blasts of pistol shots tore through the air and ripped her upright.

She rolled, hands fumbling under her skirts for her pistol strapped to her thigh. Damn. Empty leg. She didn't have it with her. On her stomach, searching the road, she moved up the bank, fear seizing her. Highwaymen? Was Devin okay? Two more shots blasted. Moss flew into the air next to her head, and Aggie realized the shots were aimed at her.

Aggie flipped onto her back, scanning the thick of trees across the stream. By the quick succession of the pistol shots, there was either one assailant with several guns, or more than one person shooting at her. Not seeing a glimpse of a pistol in the trees opposite her, she started to flip as two more shots sent tufts of moss to the sky. Her shoulder twinged as she fell hard on it, then she scurried up the bank.

Out of nowhere, steel arms clasped around her waist, lifting her straight up. Aggie twisted as violently as she could, arms swinging out at the person who grabbed her. She felt her fist slam into a face, but he didn't drop her. Petrified, she squirmed, trying to escape the tight arms that were squeezing the breath out of her.

"Aggie, enough." Devin's harsh whisper reached her ears as he moved them into the relative safety of the woods, trees blocking them from the opposing bank. Aggie calmed.

"Devin, let me down. I can walk on my own."

"You have no shoes on." He kept his pace, weaving through the trees back to the carriage. From her hanging position, Aggie could see Devin's outriders, blades and guns in hands, splashing across the stream.

Devin walked past the carriage to two of the outriders' horses. "We can cut the remaining trip in more than half by horseback, but no sidesaddle. Are you okay with that?" He set her down on the grassy side of the road, carriage between her and the woods.

"I will be." Aggie numbly nodded as Devin raised the stirrups on one of the saddles.

"Good."

Three shots came from the woods and Aggie jumped. Back to her in an instant, Devin plucked her from the grass and set her on the smaller of the two black horses, snugging her bare feet into the stirrups. He vaulted onto his horse and swung his head around.

"It is time for us to take leave. Are you okay? Ready?"

Aggie nodded, silenced by his complete, calm control of the situation and her own lack of awareness next to the stream.

What had she been thinking? Lying on the bank—a huge target—and not paying any attention to her surroundings or possible threats. She had abandoned all of her own defenses, and had put not only herself in danger, but Devin as well. He was extremely adept at showing up anytime she was in mortal danger, and that put him at risk.

Aggie swallowed hard against the thought of Devin getting hurt, or worse, and gripped the reins, putting her head down as he took off at a manic pace. Her horse followed his without question, so Aggie only had to concentrate on holding on.

No words were spoken, more because of the hard riding than anything else. After a half hour of flesh-bruising riding, Devin slowed the horses, pulling his steed in line next to Aggie's.

"We are now only about twenty minutes away," he said, looking over at her. Devin stared at her hard, brow wrinkled. "Aggie, are you sure you're okay?"

Aggie nodded, hoping she was hiding the fact that she knew she wasn't okay. Her left arm had been of no use to her during the brutal ride thus far. She couldn't feel anything on her arm or hand.

But she also knew they needed to get to the safety of Stonewell before she could do anything about the numbness. She guessed a bullet had grazed her arm, but couldn't be sure, and didn't want to investigate the problem while Devin was riding next to her. She had to wait until Stonewell.

"Down the road another couple of minutes is the lane for Stonewell, and then it is another ten minutes up the drive to the main building," Devin said, and stepped his horse in front of Aggie's once more. His concentration was on scanning the road, so Aggie took the moment to check her shoulder under her hair that had come loose.

No blood was on the outside of her jacket, but there seemed to be a small tear. She gave slack to the reins in her right hand and slipped her fingers under her jacket, only to feel warm, sticky liquid, and then the hole it was coming from.

She pulled her hand from her jacket and looked down at it in horror. It was soaked in blood. She looked up at Devin's back, a couple of paces in front of her. Right beyond him, huge brick columns framed a wide black iron gate.

"Devin, we're safe now, right?"

"Yes." He looked over her his shoulder at her. Shock flooded his face. "Hell, Aggs."

A whisper was all she could afford.

"Catch me."

CHAPTER 13

Devin was to her before her hand dropped the reins. He pulled her onto his horse and ran his hands over her passed-out body, desperate to find the source of the blood that covered her hand.

Ripping back her jacket, terror seized him when he saw her blood-soaked shoulder and the bullet hole through her white shirt. Swearing, Devin set his horse into full gallop and got to the main house in minutes, praying that Aggie had passed out enough that the jolting wasn't too agonizing.

Aggie in his arms, he dismounted and burst through the front door.

"Thompson. Where the hell are you? Thompson."

Devin's steward appeared at the back of the deep entry, rushing forward. "Your grace—my God."

Devin almost ran Thompson over at the base of the sweeping stairs. "Get Christianson."

"Immediately, your grace." Thompson turned and retreated to the back of the house.

"And wet cloths," Devin yelled as he tore up the stairs three at a time.

Setting her gently on his bed, Devin pulled the knife secured at his waist and cut through her jacket, shirt, and chemise, ripping it away from the wound. Her shoulder bare, he wiped the mess of blood and found the bullet had gone into her shoulder, just above her heart. He lifted her, scanning the back of her shoulder. The bullet had not passed through.

"Damn." He swallowed hard at the horrible pain Aggie was about to have to go through.

"Devin." Aggie's eyes cracked open with her whisper. "I am sorry I got you involved. I—"

"Hush. Save your strength." Devin considered for a moment not telling her what was going to happen. But as much as he knew of her, she would hate not knowing the full truth even more.

"Aggs…" He gently brushed back the hair on her forehead. "The bullet didn't go cleanly through your shoulder. The doctor is going to have to dig it out."

"Okay." She closed her eyes.

Devin hedged, not sure she fully understood what this would mean. "Aggs, this is going to be extremely painful."

She didn't open her eyes, but did drag in a deep breath. "Stay? Please?"

Devin had to lean in to hear the words.

His hand went to her cheek. "I will be by your side throughout."

Aggie nodded, then slipped into unconsciousness once more. Thompson delivered the wet cloths, and Devin cleared as much blood as he could.

Ten silent minutes passed. Ten agonizing minutes that Devin could look nowhere but at the rise and fall of Aggie's chest, his breath held at each slice of time there was no movement.

Doctor Christianson entered the room, winded, and set his bag down. "What happened?"

"A bullet is in her shoulder." Devin moved the cloth soaking up the blood from the hole.

"Is she aware of the upcoming pain?" Christianson asked.

"Yes, but I am praying she will remain unconscious, or at least pass out quickly once you start."

"I can give her laudanum."

Devin looked sharply at the doctor. "You will do no such thing."

"It will help, your grace."

"You will do no such thing." Devin's voice left no room to argue.

"But—"

"Leave it, Christianson."

A hand gripped his wrist. Devin looked down at Aggie, swearing in his mind that she was awake.

"No. Devin, please. Give it to me."

"You can make it through this without, Aggie. You can."

"No." She started to pull herself up.

"You need to hold her down," Christianson said.

Aggie's eyes swung to the doctor. Scalpel, tweezers and probe in his hands, he moved to the bed.

Desperate eyes locked onto Devin. "No. Devin. Please don't do this to me." She grabbed his shirt with her good hand, pulling, pleading. "You don't know. Oh my God. You don't know. Please don't let him."

Tears flooded her face.

Tapping all his will, Devin tore her wrist away from his chest and pushed her down onto the bed, steel in his words. "You can do this, Aggie. Don't look at him. Don't look at his hands. Look at me."

"My grace, we need to stop the bleeding."

Devin moved onto the bed, throwing his leg over Aggie's and clamping his arm across her shaking chest. It didn't stop her begging.

"Devin, please no, not this, anything—"

The doctor probed the bullet hole and Aggie thrashed, screaming.

"Hold her still."

Devin moved, settling the length of his weight onto Aggie with his right hand pinning her left arm to the bed. He gripped her chin with his other hand, forcing her face to his, instead of at the scalpel going into her flesh.

It threw Aggie into jerking, tortured screams. Her body molded under his, Devin felt every anguished convulsion as the doctor probed deeper into the wound.

"Move faster, Christianson."

"Just keep her still." The doctor didn't look up.

The screaming stopped for a breath. Then, broken, Aggie managed to form pleading, agonized words.

"Make it stop. Please, Devin. Stop. Why? Why are you doing this to me? Please—oh, God no—why? Please, please make it stop. Please."

Devin had held down writhing soldiers at Waterloo as their legs were sawed off. But that was nothing. Nothing compared to Aggie's convulsions. It ripped him to shreds, like nothing ever had, Aggie pleading for him to stop the pain. He was helpless. All he could do was hold her. He prayed she would pass out, yet she held onto consciousness, wrenching his soul with every word, every tremor of her body.

"Soon, Aggs, soon," he said into her ear as he stroked the hair from her forehead. "I swear it will be over real soon."

"Got it." Christianson stood and dropped the tweezers and bullet onto the table next to the bed. "I just need to sew the wound, and it will be all over, dear child."

"Devin." Aggie thrashed. "Devin, where are you?"

"Right here, Aggs, right here." Devin knew she was out of her mind then and was grateful for it. She still twitched under his crushing weight as the needle went through her skin, but was mostly still.

"That is all. I am done." Christianson wiped the remaining blood from the stitches and put a clean cloth over the wound. "Now just pray the wound does not get infected."

Devin nodded at the doctor, then turned back to Aggie's ear. "It is all over, Aggs, rest now."

An incompressible word, low and guttural, escaped Aggie's throat. Then she passed out.

Devin eased himself off her body and stood up next to the bed.

Doctor Christianson had moved to the basin in the room, scrubbing blood from his hands. He shot Devin a look. "Don't you ever dare try to make me do something like that again. That woman was in unnecessary pain, Dunway. Pain by your choice, not hers, not mine. Yours. Whoever she is, she is not your mother. Unnecessary." Droplets splattered.

Devin didn't look up from Aggie's still form. "She is my wife and her pain is not your concern, Christianson. And you would do well to not mention my mother."

Drying his hands, the doctor walked over and stood next to Devin. He lifted the cloth over the wound. The blood looked to be slowing. He set it back in place.

"I repeat, Dunway, if you ever attempt to make me do something like that again, you can find yourself a new doctor." Christianson's boots thudded hard on the wood floors as he left, but he closed the door gently.

~ ~ ~

Aggie's eyes flew open, and the pain that was ravaging her arm instantly disappeared, replaced by an aching throb in her shoulder.

She closed her eyes, trying to gain lucidity. The pain in her left arm wasn't real. The pain in her left shoulder was. She wondered if she had been screaming, the nightmare more vivid than ever after the doctor's scalpel digging into her.

Deep breaths, and she opened her eyes again. Dark, and she was alone. She could hear heavy rain falling. A lamp on a far bureau held just enough light in its wick that she could make out shapes in the room. The room was enormous, as was the bed. This had to be Devin's room. But where was Devin?

Exhausted just by looking around, Aggie wanted nothing more than to close her eyes again and let sleep overtake her. Nothing more, except to not get lost in the nightmares again.

Devin. He could help.

She took a deep breath and sat up, working hard not to move the left side of her body. Stiffly, she slid her legs off the bed and stood. She had been stripped down; someone had put a clean chemise on her, and a band of cloth was wrapped over her shoulder and the wound. She looked around but didn't see a robe in the low light. Not that she would be able to get it on. So she shuffled over to the lamp, grabbed it, and found the door.

Stepping out along the hallway, she peeked into several rooms as she walked, having to set the lamp on the floor each time she wanted to open a door. After three empty rooms, she gave up on finding Devin on this floor. At the top of the wide stairs, she set the lamp on the floor again, turned up the wick, and took a deep breath. She needed her good hand on the railing if she wasn't going to collapse. The light at the top of the dark stairs would have to be enough.

After an agonizing descent, each step sending waves of pain from the tip of her shoulder into her chest, she rested, leaning against the newel post at the bottom of the stairs. That was when she saw the smallest sliver of light coming from below a door off to her left.

Fighting the dizziness that had set in, she made it to the door and slid the panel open. One lantern on a near wall produced the slightest bit of light, showing the room to be the library. Aggie scanned the room, at first thinking it empty; then she saw the top of a head above a fat chair facing a tall window. Heavy rain beat the glass, rhythmic and chaotic at the same time.

Aggie walked to the chair.

Short glass in hand, empty decanter on the floor, Devin sat, face to the window. Aggie stepped closer, trying to see in the low light if he was sleeping.

"You should be in bed." His eyes stayed down.

Aggie jumped at the sound. She took another step, stopping in front of him. She waited for the sway in her head to stop before she spoke. "I wanted to find you."

"You should not have found me."

"Oh." Aggie wasn't sure what to do with that statement.

He looked up at her. "Aggie, I was wrong. I dragged you into marriage and I should not have." His voice was low, blunt. "Us staying together will only cause you more pain. Pain I will not see you in. We will dissolve the marriage. I will arrange it so there is not the slightest mar on your reputation. You can go on to live your own life. I will hire an impenetrable barrier of guards to get you back to London, and they will surround you until the threat is past."

"What? No." His words a gut punch, she leaned back against the window for support, and instantly regretted it when the cold hit her back. "Dissolve the—I don't understand. I don't want guards. I want to stay with you."

"I cannot protect you, Aggie. Arrogance. Too much arrogance. I thought I could."

"You can. You have done nothing but protect me."

"I cannot. I will fail you. You will die. You need to go."

"What? No. I am fine. I will be fine. No." Aggie shook her head against the confusion muddling her brain. How could he really mean this?

"Yes. When you have healed enough to travel, you will go back to London."

"Devin, I don't know what you are talking about. I am safe. I need to stay." Heaven help her, she was too tired to let pride stop her words. "Please, just let me stay with you, Devin. I want you. I want to be here. I will be safe."

He hadn't moved a muscle. Done nothing but tilt his head to look at her. His eyes went down, avoiding her completely.

"Leave. Go back to bed, Aggie."

Aggie recognized them as final words, and her breath caught in her chest. Stomach twisting, her pride manifested, and she pushed off from the window with her right hand.

Dizziness hit immediately, but Aggie moved her feet, fighting through it. She walked to the entrance, surprising herself by managing to stay upright.

She paused at the door, fingers going to the dark wood of the frame for support. She leaned her forehead on the wood, closing her eyes to stop the spinning. A few breaths to regain her balance, and then without control, words came from her mouth.

"I just don't understand. I was stupid being by the woods. I should not have let my guard down. I am sorry. I really just came down here to ask…" She took a deep breath to both stay upright and to stop the sudden swell of tears that threatened. "To ask you to sleep with me. I woke up screaming just now. But last night, when you were with me, I slept. Real sleep. Sleep that didn't turn me inside out. And I am so tired. You may not think you can protect me, Devin, but my dreams know different."

She pushed her head off the wood, hand slipping to her side. "That was all. I am sorry to bother you."

There was no response. Head down, Aggie stepped into the hallway, concentrating on moving one foot in front of the other. Was Devin really done with her? Just like that? He got what he wanted, and now he was done?

She proved to be too much trouble. Wasn't worth the effort. That he had even helped her to begin with was a miracle. Why should she have expected the miracle to continue?

Stopping at the bottom of the stairs, she heaved a breath, trying to calm herself, trying to calm the pain shooting through her shoulder with each step she took.

Damn. Stupid. She had let it all go. Her responsibility. Her courage. She let it go. And that was the worst mistake. She was always the best one to protect herself, and then she let him. She got weak. Started to depend on him. And in the process, she let the fire that was keeping her alive, wane.

No more. She had to steel herself, because she was on her own again.

But first, she had to sit down. She wasn't going to make it up the stairs at the moment.

Aggie let herself sink to the second stair, thudding on the wood. She exhaled. Sitting was good. Lying would be even better.

It would just be for a moment, just until she could get up and tackle the stairs. She leaned down on her side across the step, ignoring the pain the movement caused. Using her right arm as a pillow, she propped her back on the stair tread behind her. Blackness hit, and she welcomed it.

Not sure how long she had been asleep, Aggie suddenly felt the sensation of being lifted. She cracked her eyes. Everything was still dark. But now she was moving up the stairs through no effort of her own.

She turned her head upward. Devin's eyes were on her, but in the dark, she couldn't see what was in them.

She offered a weak smile. Maybe he wasn't done. Not done at all.

She drifted back into darkness. Darkness that was safe. Darkness that held no dreams.

CHAPTER 14

Aggie opened her eyes slowly, not quite sure where she was, or what had transpired. Then the pain hit, and her eyes flew open. She was greeted with darkness.

In Devin's bed, she turned her head to see the room. The last thing she remembered was falling asleep on the stairs. Wait. Devin carried her upstairs.

"You are awake." Devin's gruff voice reached from the side of the bed.

Head still deep in the pillow, she looked toward the sound of his voice, her eyes beginning to adjust to the darkness.

"You are here."

"Yes."

His hand moved off her leg. She hadn't noticed it was on there until the cold absence of its removal. Aggie pushed herself up onto her good elbow.

"Does this mean you have reconsidered?"

"I was hoping you would forget about our conversation in the library."

"I am not about to forget something so important. Devin, have you reconsidered?"

"It is your choice, Aggie. If you would like to go back to London, I will make sure you are untouchable."

"My choice?"

Devin nodded.

"Then I choose here. Here with you. I am safest with you. There is not a part of me that doubts it."

Devin slid back in his chair, straightening. "Thank you for your confidence. I do not deserve it."

Aggie slumped back down into the soft bed, but she used her right hand to fluff the pillow to keep her head up as she kept her eyes on Devin. "I am not even going to argue that point, as it is a ridiculous statement."

"Not ridiculous as I see it."

Aggie's voice turned soft in its sincerity. "Then you need to re-look, Devin. You have done nothing but earn my complete confidence. My very life—you are the only one I trust with it."

He gave a weary shrug. He wasn't going to believe her.

"Did your men find who was shooting at me?"

"They did. There were two." Devin's eyes turned dark. "Hired. Neither one was of the same build as the leader."

"But can you be sure? You said you didn't see the leader's face, so maybe one of them—"

"I saw their bodies myself, Aggie. Both were skinny and short. The leader was tall, burly. He wasn't there."

"And they are dead? Did they say anything, have any clues with them?"

Devin shook his head. "They were dead before any information could be extracted. Both had nothing except for guns and bullets on their bodies. I am sorry it did not turn into a lead."

Aggie closed her eyes, inhaling a deep breath. Not another dead end. She was so sick of not being able to find the bastard. She just wanted to be able to stop thinking, stop worrying about him at every corner.

After a moment, she opened her eyes and looked around the room. "Why is it so dark in here?"

Devin looked up at the windows. "I had not noticed."

He stood from the bedside and went to open the thick blue velvet drapes. Sunlight streamed into the dark room full force. The room was huge, and in even in the light, dark. Dark browns, blacks and blues surrounded her—a dark cherry valet in the corner, a matching writing desk, wardrobe, and two sitting chairs dotted the room. The bed she was in was wide, framed by a lush, mahogany four-post bed. A man's room. A man who felt extremely comfortable in the shadows.

"How long have I been asleep?" Aggie asked, the fog in her mind beginning to lift.

"Since falling asleep on the stairs?"

"I did, didn't I? I was only planning on resting for a moment."

"Yes, and you actually looked comfortable. You slept through yesterday and last night."

Aggie watched him look out the window. The sunlight revealed an unshaven, haggard-looking Devin. "When was the last time you slept?"

A slight smile raised the corners of his hard mouth. "About the same amount of time." He walked back to the bed and sat down by Aggie's legs.

Devin stared at her with a peculiar look on his face, a strange mix of relief, anger, and happiness, mixed in with something odd she couldn't quite name. She wasn't quite sure how to react to it.

"I have sequestered Doctor Christianson in the guest quarters. He has been in every other hour to check on your progress, and he will be pleased to see you are awake. Are you hungry?"

"Thirsty." Aggie reached over to touch the bandage wrapped around her shoulder. It was tight and clean. "Have you seen it? Is it infected?"

"I have. It looks good, and you have not had much of a fever." Devin stood from the bed with a satisfied nod. "I will send the doctor in to check on you. Your eyes look bright, but I want you to stay in this bed for the next few days. I imagine Christianson will agree with me, so don't try to convince him otherwise."

"You think I will not listen to you?"

"I think you will think you are ready to move long before you actually are. Be patient. I want you healed. The doctor says you should be up and around within the next couple days. At which time, I will introduce you to the staff and show you about Stonewell."

Aggie's teeth kept her tongue in place. There wasn't much room to argue, and her slight poking at her shoulder had stung. Plus, unprovoked, he had just offered to show her about Stonewell. She might actually get some information from him about his life and childhood. She wanted to know Devin. Not just because he was her husband, because she liked him—liked him in the moments that weren't filled with drama. Maybe she could hurry it a bit.

She sat up. "If Doctor Christianson checks the wound and says I am healing fine, perhaps we could start my introductions to Stonewell this afternoon? I am feeling much better." She offered up what she hoped was a beguiling smile.

Devin laughed. "Good try, but no chance. That will not work on me, and it will not work on Christianson. You will rest today, and rest well. That is an order."

Aggie leaned back into the soft bed, giving a sigh, then grimaced as pain shot through her shoulder.

"See, you need the rest." He walked to the door. "When you can make a simple movement like that without agony crossing your face, you will be free."

Aggie groaned as Devin exited. His chuckle echoed back from the hallway.

Would nothing get by that man?

~ ~ ~

Apparently, no.

Four times throughout the rest of the day, Aggie tried to escape the bed. Each time, Devin, exerting a peculiar sixth sense as to her whereabouts, caught her either with toe perched on the hallway floor trying to exit the room, or within two steps of the monstrous bed. Each time she was sternly ordered back to bed.

Devin did take his dinner with Aggie in his room, and by the curious looks of the servants bringing in the food, table and chairs, Aggie guessed it was out of the norm for the household.

Nonetheless, she was ecstatic at having his company, for he was being more than pleasant to her. Which was more than welcome after their encounter in the library. Aggie still didn't know what to make of his demand that they split. But as he had said no more on the matter, she hoped desperately it was just drunken ramblings and their conversation in the morning was the end of the matter.

The next day was a repeat of the first, save for one exception. If Aggie promised to stop trying to escape the bed, Devin would allow Aggie out of the room to visit the library and to pick out some readings to pass time. She gladly snatched up the deal. Boredom was the entire reason she was trying to sneak out.

At her first step into the vast room, Aggie gasped at what she hadn't seen before in the dark. From floor to the two-story ceiling, all neatly arranged in mahogany bookcases, were thousands of books. No knickknacks or trinkets filling in empty spaces—there were no empty spaces to fill. This was a serious collection.

Fat books, skinny books, new books, old books, and really, really old books that looked like they were going to fall apart if she breathed on them. Awestruck, but beaming at the wonder of it, she almost skipped into the center of the library. Which she would have done, had her shoulder allowed. Devin followed her, amusement plain on his face.

"I take it by your reaction you enjoy a good read?"

Aggie laughed. "Yes, I adore reading. Growing up, if I was not outside with Jason, I was inside with a book. How in the world did you amass a collection so large?"

Devin pointed high into the shelves where it looked like a good portion of the ancient texts were grouped. "My ancestors were enthusiastic proponents of the written word. This collection has been growing for hundreds of years."

"Have you contributed many to the collection?" Aggie spun in a circle, taking in the scores of volumes about her.

"Too many, I am afraid. It is a weakness."

"I am glad to finally have a flaw of yours flaunted." She swept her hand around her. "Although I would hardly call this a flaw."

"It is a flaw in that we have run out of space. At this point, I am afraid I am faced with either going through the volumes, and putting some of them into storage, or knocking out a wall and expanding the library into the next room."

"Knock the wall out."

Devin laughed. "No question about it?"

"None."

Aggie took in the enormity of the room once more. "Where do I even begin?"

"Follow me." Devin walked across the room over three dark-hued Oriental rugs with deep reds splashing into haunting greens, blues, and blacks in intricate patterns. "I had the collection cleaned and reorganized five years ago. It had become a slight nightmare with each generation having differing methods in categorization."

He stopped at the far right back corner of the library and pointed to a section at the very bottom of the bookcase, one column wide and three rows high. "This was my mother's section. I am sure you will find something entertaining here."

Devin stepped back to let Aggie have a look. Aggie moved forward, tightening her pale green robe at her waist, and bent gingerly to her knees in front of the section.

Aggie scanned the titles. Curiosity piqued as she contemplated the rows.

"What was your mother like, Devin?" Aggie asked after a few moments, not turning around. It wasn't an answer, but what she was seeing before her was giving her a possible clue as to why Devin had never spoken about his parents.

"She was a mother."

Aggie looked over her shoulder up at Devin. His answer was curt. Too curt.

"Yes, but what was she like as a person?"

He stiffened. "I did not really know her well enough to answer that question."

"But you must have known a little bit about her. Was she happy? Sad? Content? Bitter? You must have been able to discern that much."

"No."

"But surely—"

"Aggie, it is time for you to get back to bed, so either pick out some books, or you will just have to lie there bored."

Aggie glanced at the books in front of her, then back to Devin, ready for combat. But the look she saw on his face stopped her cold. Harsh. Murderous. The same look that surfaced just before he slit the throat of one of her attackers.

She wasn't afraid of the look. But she wasn't about to make it worse, either. As much as it irked her to bow to his refusal to speak of his family, she also knew that his face just told her more about his mother, than he would ever actually speak.

She was not going to let it go, not in the long term. But in that moment, she had to let it go. She hadn't regained enough strength yet to fight what his face had already manifested.

But at some point, she was going to find out why he was such an expert at avoiding conversation about his family.

Aggie turned back to his mother's section of the bookcase. As much as she enjoyed a good romantic novel in the line of Edgeworth or Scott, the few titles she recognized in this section were too risqué for her. They were the type of titles whispered about in the corners of drawing rooms—glorifying prostitution, torture, murder, debauchery. Aggie could only guess the few titles she had heard of were indicative of the rest of the section.

Aggie randomly grabbed a thin one with a red spine and tucked it into her arm, not even looking at the title, and then stood to move onto other sections of the library.

"Is that all you want?" Devin asked, nodding to the one book Aggie held in her arm.

Her face crinkled. Did he really believe she would limit herself? Close-by, she spied a brass plate attached to the front of a shelf that said "Modern Philosophy" on it. Aggie brushed passed Devin to move along the wall, taking in all the brass plates and scanning titles. She passed by several sub-categories of philosophy, then on to history, mathematics, geography, poetry, engineering, and she was only a fourth of the way around the room.

She pulled from several sections as she went, balancing the books in her good arm. When it became awkward to both pull books and hold them in her arm, she went over to the gleaming rosewood desk and set the stack down.

"Done?" Devin walked over to the desk, flipping through her selections.

Not answering, Aggie had already moved to a new section of the wall, poking through an area on the Tudor reign. Grabbing a few more titles, she went back to the desk and added them to the stack.

Devin half-sat on the desk, waiting for her. "Done now?"

"Yes, for now, this will do." She slid the stack to the edge of the desk and started to struggle to get them into her good arm.

"It is a nice selection." Devin slipped his arm between Aggie and the stack, sweeping them up. He offered his other arm to her.

Aggie took it and he led them out of the room. She looked back at the walls of books, not hiding her sadness at having to leave the room. "I may come back down later this afternoon? A short trip—not too strenuous?"

Devin looked at the books in his arms and shook his head. "If you wish."

CHAPTER 15

Sunlight streamed in through the tall windows, and Aggie sat up the instant her eyes opened. It had been a week of her bed captivity, and Doctor Christianson had given her the okay for activity today. She had immediately made Devin promise her the tour of Stonewell first thing in the morning.

She glanced down at the bed next to her. Empty. He had slept every night with her, hand on her hip, giving her the security that set her mind to calm in her sleep. The last few mornings he had stayed in bed for a while talking about Stonewell, or what he was going to do during the day, but this morning he was gone.

Blasted. He was going to renege on his promise.

Furious that he thought he could keep her in the room another long day, Aggie jumped out of the bed. Landing on the floor jostled her wound, but it didn't stop her as she jerked her robe over her night chemise, muttering to herself about the prevalent injustices from the man she married.

She turned the knob on the door, half-surprised it wasn't locked. At least Devin had the good sense not to imprison her in the room. She peered out into the long hallway, curious. She had only been taken to the library a couple times, had fumbled in the dark the first night, and had no idea where anything else in the house was.

But she would look in every room if need be to find Devin. Her first guess was the study, if she could find it. Bare heels thumping on the wood floors, she stepped into the hall, turning right at the corner to the stairs.

She crashed into the chest of a grey haired, distinguished man, who could only have been Devin's steward, Thompson, if Aggie recalled correctly what Devin had told her about him.

He stepped backward, horrified at running straight into his injured duchess. "I am so sorry, your grace." He managed to maintain a dignified air, even though he now teetered on the top edge of the stairs.

Aggie reached out to grab his arm and pull him forward. She didn't want crippling the house steward to be her first act at Stonewell. But the crash, coupled with the pull, sent sharp pains through her shoulder.

"No, no," Aggie said, gripping her shoulder tenderly as the pain peaked, then ebbed away. "It was my fault. I was at a near run when I turned the corner. You are Thompson?"

Thompson nodded. "I should have been further out in the hall, your grace. Please accept my apologies."

"There was no way you could have seen me coming, Thompson. Truly. I was too fast in my hunt for his grace."

Thompson gave a worried look at her shoulder. "Duchess, if I may be so bold, perhaps I shall have a soothing bath drawn up for you? Once refreshed, I am sure the duke will be pleased to take you on the grand tour of Stonewell. The staff has eagerly awaited your recovery."

Aggie sighed. The temptation of a nice hot bath overrode her immediate need to find Devin and demand her tour. Even if it did mean being stuck in the room a bit longer. She did, after all, want to look her best when she was presented to the staff. "Yes, that does sound nice. But you will find his grace for me?"

"I will do so." With a nod, Thompson turned and went down the stairs.

In the private quarters connecting to Devin's bedroom, the bath was ready in short order. Aggie sank into the steaming liquid, the lavender-scented water invading her pores and soothing her wound. She soaked in the tub, eyes closed, for an extended time. Washing her hair and scrubbing her body was next in line, and just as she finished scrubbing the toes on her left foot, freezing water ran onto her neck and shocked her into scrambling to her feet.

Feet slipping in the copper tub, she whipped around to find Devin, smirk on his face and a pitcher of water in his right hand.

Screeching, Aggie kicked water in his general vicinity. Devin jumped backward out of the spray. Aggie kicked harder, slipping and falling straight down into the tub, sending a splash that did get Devin—and a good portion of the room—wet.

Aggie laughed in victory and splashed some of the little water that was left at Devin.

"Hey, hey, truce, truce," he said, as he made his way closer to the tub, hands up to block what little water he could. "I do not want you to re-injure yourself. And since I am already soaked, how about I join you in your bath? The tub is big enough for two."

Aggie splashed. "Do not even think of stalling anymore. I am getting out of this tub right now, and you are taking me on a tour of this colossal place."

She stood up, dripping. "Will you get me a towel, please?"

"Gladly." Devin snatched a towel from a short table by the fire and strode to Aggie, wrapping the towel around her slowly, kissing her moist neck. He lifted her out of the tub and turned her around.

Those grey eyes. They told her exactly what was on his mind. Aggie took a quick step back to avoid getting sucked into Devin's assault. She was going to get out of these rooms, and making love to Devin would not get her any closer to the outside world.

Sensing defeat, Devin sighed, and went over to his wardrobe to replace the now sopping black pants and simple white shirt he wore. Holding the towel wrapped high on her chest, as un-enticing as she could manage, Aggie walked to her trunk, which had been delivered to Devin's rooms several days ago. She pulled out a practical muslin dress for traipsing about the house and grounds.

After proper introductions to Thompson and the staff, and a rambling tour through the three levels of the south wing, Devin brought her back to the main structure through a low boxwood hedge maze that skirted the outside of the building. Back in the main entry, Devin veered to the right, and Aggie followed into the stone-walled, two-story dining hall.

Aged tapestries half the height of the walls hung in symmetrical increments high along opposing walls. Aggie looked across the enormous hall, noting the void of most furniture.

"That is odd," she said.

"What?"

"The table." Aggie pointed at the disproportionately small table at the end by the immense stone fireplace. A maximum of four people would fit around it, and even at that, elbows would be bumping.

"I put it in after my parents died. I like it better. The true dining sets are brought in when there are formal functions."

He grabbed her shoulders and turned her to one of the long walls. "What you should really be noting in here are the tapestries."

Aggie looked up at the wall, taking in the tapestries past the cursory glance she gave them when they entered. Eyes widened and her mouth slid open.

"What are those?"

"Shall I start on the left?"

Aggie nodded.

"That tapestry was done for my ancestor, the Earl of Fulton. He built the main structure—the main castle and the tapestry were both a gift from King Henry VII, for years of loyal service."

Aggie tried to hold in a smile but didn't succeed. "It is an interesting scene to watch while dining. Was it the King or the earl that liked orgies?"

Devin smirked. "My guess is both. But one does not hide away a gift from the king. One displays it for all to witness. We do tend to seat people according to their sensibilities, and an unmarried woman would never be seated across from it."

"Smart. I am sure you have had a wrinkled nose or two, regardless."

"One or two. It does tend to lead to a split of mostly men on one side of the table and women on the other."

"I can imagine." Aggie looked over her shoulder at the tapestries lining the other side of the wall. "Yes, very docile over there."

She shifted back to the wall in front of her. "Okay, how about the next one." Goat after goat after goat filled the next tapestry over. Nothing but a large stew of goats.

"Yes, the goats. I do not know why, but I have always liked this one. This one is from the third Duke of Dunway. He widowed early, and in grief, took to goats for some reason. By the end of his life, thousands of goats were living inside of Stonewell. That tapestry was his contribution to the collection. Not a likeness of his wife, but of goats. I always wondered if he loved the goats more than the wife that sent him into grief in the first place."

"That next one is creepy." Aggie pointed at the third tapestry in line. The pinched face of a woman with crazy eyes, a half-story tall, was framed by wild black hair. "She looks like a giant witch."

"She was. She lived here at the insistence of the Marchioness of Rivendale. Or at least that was story attached to her. The witch had some extraordinary power over the Marquess and his wife. They had no children, and after all three died—together within a week of each other—the title and land came to my direct ancestors."

They continued down the hall, Devin describing each of the tapestries' history in detail. One gore-filled warfare scene. One depicting childbirth. One a dance between two wart-filled feet.

Aggie found the collection both bizarre and fascinating.

At the end of the hall, she turned to Devin. "I am amazed that you leave them all displayed. They are not at all in common taste."

"I suppose not. But I grew up with them, so they are normal to me. Plus, they are my ancestors, and I respect all of who they were. Even if they tip on the side of peculiar."

Aggie looked at his smiling profile as he looked up at the wall. She wouldn't have guessed, but it turned out her new husband had the ability to be quite amusing. That charm could be a dangerous thing she realized, for when he wanted something, she was not going to be any force not to give it to him. But what would she even want to deny him?

Deep down, she knew she would never want for anything as long as Devin was with her, and above all, she would be protected. He was a man that would let no harm come to his own.

And she was his own.

Devin turned around to face the other wall, sweeping his hand in the general direction. "The rest are all pleasant—or at least within the realm of not producing faints. They also do not have fun stories to accompany them."

"Have you made a contribution to the collection, yet?"

"No." He looked down at her. "I guess it remains to be seen whether I go a little crazy or not."

"Let us hope for not. I like you just like this." She slipped her arm under his. "And I am not looking to add another woman, or goats, into our current arrangement."

"That is excellent news."

Devin started walking back down the length of the room.

"How did you learn all this history? You said your father was not very vocal."

"Thompson taught me most of it. He took it upon himself to learn every detail of the history of the place from my grandmother. Apparently, my father had little interest in history, yet my grandmother thought the history vital to the line. So she imparted as much as she could to Thompson before her death."

Aggie took one more look up at what she had dubbed "the wall of strange" before they exited the hall. "Your lineage is both fascinating, and if I may admit, intimidating."

Devin laughed. "To me, too. Many of them were great people. I have worked very hard to honor the title."

The rest of the tour took them into early evening. Aggie was overwhelmed with the size and history of Stonewell. Devin liked to call it a house. She liked to call it a castle, because that was exactly what it was. Apparently, his ancestors had big personalities and loved drama, so each successive generation attempted to outdo the previous. Hence the rambling wings and rooms for every conceivable occasion.

Aggie discovered that while Devin easily talked of ancestors of past, he never once, aside from in the dining hall, mentioned his father or mother, nor any impact either made on Stonewell.

Twilight approaching, Devin stopped at the door to the room adjoining his.

"This ends our tour for today—your chambers. It has been completely redone." Devin bowed as he opened the door and Aggie entered the rooms. "I hope it is to your liking. If not, you can redirect the staff."

Aggie stepped into the middle of the grand room. The staff had been very busy while she was recovering. Amazing, for she hadn't heard a peep from these rooms. Aggie walked around, breathing in the light scent of lavender. Crisp linens and draperies hung, in shades of violet and creamy yellows, while the shined rosewood furniture added an elegance to counter the soft colors.

She turned to Devin. "It is beautiful."

"You seem to have missed the gift specifically from me in here." He walked over to the rosewood bureau, pointing at a hinged box on top of it.

Head tilted in curiosity, Aggie moved to stand next to him. She pulled open the cover of the box. Inside, a gleaming silver pistol sat tucked into red velvet.

Her eyes flew to Devin. "Truly?"

"My own arrogance got us into trouble the other day. This is my way of apology. If carrying this will set your mind at ease, then my pride needs to step out of the way. I know how good you are with a pistol, and I would be stupid to deny you extra defense."

Wondering smile on her lips, Aggie closed the box. She looked up at him. "Devin, it—all of this—it is perfect. Thank you so much."

She walked over to the bed, her hand trailing on the soft silk covering. "And the bed looks so comfortable."

She gazed at her husband, not bothering to veil her wanton hint.

Devin laughed. "Do not even think that you will get a chance to try it out."

"No?" Aggie's eyebrow arched.

"No." Devin walked to her, his arms enveloping her, and he lifted her far off her feet. She laughed as she wrapped her legs around his waist and he walked across the room.

"Because you will never have need to lie in it." He opened the connecting door between her rooms and his. "There is only one bed that you will sleep in from now on."

She moved her right arm around his neck, her face close to his as she kicked off her silk slippers. "I hope you mean yours, or this will be dreadfully disappointing for me."

Devin's rogue smile was all the answer needed. And he rarely looked rogue. He was a man that knew what he wanted, and took it, so she was flattered to see that he had the ability produce charm for her. Lascivious charm, but she would take it.

"I do not plan on disappointing you." He stopped in the middle of his room, holding her, mouth almost touching her lips. "But I am not taking another step until I verify something. You seemed to have plenty of energy on the tour, but you also like to hide things from me. I am praying you are not overly fatigued."

"Why?"

"Frankly, you have been driving me to madness."

Aggie leaned back as much as his grip allowed. "What? I have? How is that?"

He pulled her tighter, his mouth near hers again. "Night after night, breathing you in. Touching you, but not touching you. Watching your chest rise and fall. I have been damning that wound more than you have. But I will not touch you until you can handle me. Until you can handle all that I want—need to do to your body. Handle every gasp, every tremor, every scream I elicit."

His words settled into her chest, tightening it. Breath slowed. The tightness of her legs around him should have been answer enough, but Aggie wisped her lips onto his, holding back, letting their air mingle. "I am ready. Scream. Tremble. Gasp. Whatever. I can handle it."

Devin started walking before the words finished, cocooning her as they crashed onto the bed. His lips came down on her hard, hungry, demanding all that had been denied him the past week.

He wasted no time in slipping his thumb under the top of her dress and chemise, pushing the fabric down, fingers finding her nipple, teasing it between the pads of his fingers.

Devin's mouth left hers, then snaked downward along her neck, onto her chest, onto her breasts. He caressed the nipple with his tongue, gently at first, then with increasing intensity until it peaked with ripeness.

Aggie arched up into him, her body catching on fire and begging him to take her deeper into his mouth. He chuckled at her response and crossed to her other nipple. He sucked harshly and with greed, as if to drive her to a breaking point. Aggie didn't break, her hands instead diving into the back of his hair, holding him to her, giving him no chance to interrupt the gasps he provoked.

Her core started to ache as the fire spread to her entire body. Reveling in the pleasure he produced, she realized she needed more. Much more. She dragged his head from her nipple, bringing herself up to kiss him.

Her tongue slipped through his lips, skimming his teeth, playing with his warring tongue. She could feel his smile as he bit her lip, taking the swollen skin and making it his own. Every touch on her body was meant to make her his, and she welcomed it.

Devin pushed their bodies back down, burying her deep into the bed. She could tell he still held back, gentle around her wound, but that didn't stop him from thrusting his tongue repeatedly, deeply, into her mouth. At first, she let him overwhelm her with the waves, but she was soon matching his kisses with as much intensity, even more.

The hardness of him pushed into Aggie, straining against his pants and jutting into her thighs. Aggie's hand went down, grabbing him through the fabric, her fingers sliding up and down, pulling him along her thigh.

He lifted from her mouth. "Blasted, Aggs, that is bloody exquisite."

"It would be better without clothes, and I cannot move my left arm enough yet to get you out of yours."

Devin laughed and pulled up, yanking off his shirt and pants. Aggie couldn't hold in the gasp that came at having his naked body over her. Every beautiful morsel of his skin pulsated, muscles tight, ready for her. All of it was hers. She sat up.

"I don't care how you get me out of these layers, just do it now."

The dress was easy. The muslin tore without effort. But after getting a look at her short stays and chemise, he flipped her onto her stomach.

"Damn that I don't have a knife handy." His muttering didn't slow his fingers from working down the laced ribbon, untying the stays, and sliding the chemise up her body. He left the silk stockings, and Aggie could have cared less. She was naked enough.

He slipped his right arm under her waist, pulling her up onto her knees. He kept his arm around her waist, his hand cupping her breast as he held her above the bed. His left hand went down past her belly, fingers slipping deep into the folds, searching and finding the hard nubbin that shocked Aggie out of her skin. He prodded and caressed, teasing her body into a pitching tremble.

"Oh, hell." Her words came jagged between smoldering breaths. "Devin, you need to be in me now. Now."

His hand pulled from her for a moment, and Aggie almost doubled over in torture from his fingers leaving her. But just as quick, he shoved her inner thigh outward, spreading her legs. His fingers were back in her, plunging, reaching deep nerves that exploded at touch. Her body convulsed, near collapsing at the pleasure, but Devin held her upright.

His mouth went to her neck, sucking, just as fingers, slick, moved out of her. He rammed into her, deep, full. Aggie curled over at the bittersweet ferocity, scream escaping as he filled her. His arm latched solid around her body, and he moved her upward, just as he pulled out, only to plunge deep into her again, his grip keeping her solid against the onslaught.

Fingers stroking her pulsating folds, he squeezed and prodded in unison with his thrusts. Aggie's feet wrapped up behind her, locking onto his backside, giving him no chance to escape her body. Frantic, her right arm went up and behind Devin's neck, nails clawing into his skin, demanding satisfaction.

He responded instantly, speeding his thrusts into a pace that notched her closer to the desperate satisfaction she needed. Begging, incoherent screams ripped from her body, and he slammed into her, forcing her body to his fingers as she writhed. Control lost, she hit blinding white light and crashed back into him, her body releasing in core-crushing agony.

She wasn't conscious of his final throes, her body convulsing around him, but the guttural roar in her ear told her he joined her.

Staying in her, Devin collapsed forward, landing half on her body, leaving her wounded shoulder untouched. Chests heaved as both of their bodies continued to spasm. Devin caught his breath first.

"God, Aggs," he said, his warm breath behind her ear. "I never could have waited this full week had I known that was coming."

Aggie laughed, and turned to kiss his bicep that was in front of her face. Salty. "So I was not crazy to want to rush my rest along. I thought as much."

"Maybe, but this means that I am, apparently, the only one that can be trusted to have self-restraint. You needed to heal."

"I did."

Devin jerked up from her body, looking down at her face, sudden worry in his grey eyes. "Tell me I did not hurt you. And if I did—hell—tell me I didn't anyway."

"You did not." Aggie spun in the bed to her back, looking up at him, smile curving her swollen lips. "I think the only hurting you did to me was the exact same hurting I was doing to you."

He chuckled and flopped down onto the bed next to her. "I don't think you know the half of my pain."

"Can we stay like this the rest of the night?"

"Naked?"

"Yes."

"No. You need nourishment for my next ravaging of you. Plus, I am looking forward to finally dining with you at an actual table, as charming as eating in my bedroom has been. Not to mention you will need lots of energy for when we start our grounds tour tomorrow, per your request."

Aggie sat up. "Fine. But let us dress and eat in haste." Her hand slipped across the ridges along his stomach. "I want you back up here, just like this, as quickly as possible."

"That, I can arrange." Devin smiled, grabbing her hand and bringing it to his lips. "I am not about to deny your salaciousness, my dear Aggs."

~ ~

In the darkness, the rain came. And it came with thunder and lightning. It only took a few short minutes for Devin to wake up and leave the bed.

In the library, facing the west window, he had only made it a fourth of the way down the decanter of brandy before he heard soft footsteps padding into the room, the rustle echoing in the cavernous space.

Devin closed his eyes. He hadn't heard her scream. Or had he?

"Did I say something?" Aggie's raspy voice came gently into the room. "Devin, I do not know what I do in my sleep. I know I yell. I cannot control it. If I said something to drive you away, I am sorry. I do not want to bother you, I just came in here…"

"Why? Why did you find me?"

He hadn't looked up at her, and almost thought he scared her off. But then she stepped close to him, her chemise brushing his elbow that rested on the arm of the leather chair.

"Sleep with me. Please."

"What?"

"I was sleeping peacefully, but it…changed. And I woke up and you were gone. I sleep. When you are with me, I sleep. Real sleep. It is amazing. No dreams. No nightmares. Please."

Her hand went to his bare shoulder, her fingers cool on his skin. Devin stared at the glass in his hand, trying to ignore the rain pelting the window in front of him. She really did trust him to keep her safe. Too bad he wasn't worthy of her trust.

Her hand stayed still on him.

No force to ignore her patience, he looked up at her. The one lantern he had lit by the door flickered dim behind her, setting her loose blond hair to ethereal glow.

"On one condition."

"What?"

"You tell me what makes you scream in your sleep."

Her hand jerked off of his skin and she stumbled backward, bending at the waist as though he punched her.

It was a power move he wasn't going to apologize for. He needed to know. And if he had to blackmail her into telling, he would.

Aggie continued her backward shuffle, holding her stomach, shaking her head. "No. I…it is not worth it. I will leave you alone."

Devin shot up, reaching her in two strides and grabbing her wrist, stopping her escape. "You need to tell me, Aggie. Whatever you bear in your sleep, you should not have to do it alone."

"No."

She looked up at him, and the pain in her eyes jolted him. Pain that weighed her soul. Kept her in fear. It burned Devin's determination that she tell him even brighter.

"Aggie, whatever it is. It is time to tell me. I need to know what dreams I am fighting."

He pulled on her wrist, and surprisingly, her feet moved. He led her back to the chair he was sitting in, and nudged her downward. He went to his knees in front of her, hands on her thighs.

He forced his voice soft as he rubbed her legs. "Tell me."

She didn't meet his gaze, and her right hand went to the scar running up her left arm. Devin saw the motion, and his gut hardened.

Of course.

She had never hidden the scar, but she had always hidden how she got the scar.

"Tell me."

"Six months ago…" Her voice caught, and she cleared her throat. "Six months ago, I had gone into town to meet with our solicitor. He is old, so I did not want him to have to make the trip to Clapinshire." Her head stayed down, eyes closed, but her voice held solid. "It took longer than I would have liked, and when we were done, it was dusk when I stepped into the street. My driver had moved my carriage about a block away; the street is narrow there, so that was normal. But my driver was also facing away from me, so he had no chance to see what happened."

Her palm flattened on her scar, and she started to run it up and down the length of her forearm. "They grabbed me, the two of them. It was the leader and that first one I killed in London. They jerked me off the street and dragged me down an alley. Hands over my mouth. My eyes. They pulled me into a building, a room. It was dark and empty. Dirt floor. The last light of day shining through slivers in the wall. One of them shoved a rag into my mouth—wretched filth—filling it, and they pushed me against the wall."

Her head tilted up slightly, but her eyes stayed closed. "I tried. I tried so hard to get free. And then the one I killed pulled me off the wall and slammed me back into it. Punched me. It crushed my air and I could not breathe, and the rag was deep in my throat, choking me. He held me, shoved onto the wall, and when I looked up, the leader was coming at me with a scalpel."

"Aggs—"

She shook her head, holding her hand up to stop him. Devin closed his mouth.

"He grabbed my wrist, pulling it straight up over my head, pinning it to the wall, and then he yanked up. My toes could not touch the ground, so I dangled. He pressed the scalpel into my skin at the wrist, slicing deep until he hit bone. No air, I could not even scream. He twisted the blade in me and then asked me—and it was such a polite asking, like he was not even carving my skin—where the paper was. All I could do was shake my head. I still don't know what he was talking about. So he twisted the blade and ripped it further down my skin."

Her hand on the scar rubbed faster, like she was trying to remove pain that had just resurfaced. "Then he asked me again. I had no answer. He sliced down. Further and slower. Twisting. He asked. No answer. And further down with the blade. By the time the scalpel got to my elbow, I could not even hear him. All I could hear was the pain in my head. Feel the blood that had flowed through my dress to pool along my neck. But then he started yelling. At me, and then he was yelling at the other man. He dropped my arm, and my feet hit ground, and that was when I kneed the other man in the crotch. He crumpled, and it gave me just enough time. I ran. I got out. I do not know how I did it. I got out the door and to the street."

Tears were dropping fully onto Devin's hands on her thighs, but Aggie's eyes remained closed. "That was when I understood the depth of the trouble I was in. And I had to somehow get out of it, even if I understood none of it. That is how I know exactly what he looks like. And that was when the dreams started. Scalpels deep in my body. My father murdered time and again in front of me. That is why I wake up screaming."

Devin forced the rage in his chest to stay there. That they had done this to her. When he found the leader he was going to rip him limb from limb.

God. What he had done to her.

The hell he himself had put her through—he had set Christianson on her with a scalpel, and she had to watch it. It made him sick what he had made her suffer. And for what? His own damn irrational fear?

Devin moved one of his hands behind Aggie's head, gripping her tightly. "Aggs, I am so sorry about Doctor Christianson. I did not know. I would have knocked you out myself had I known."

She tilted her head further up, opening her eyes at him. "It was not your fault. You did not know what I went through."

"I should have by your screaming." Both of his hands went to her cheeks, wiping away the wetness. Then his fingers moved down to her left arm. Her right hand tightened over the scar, so Devin gently wedged his fingers under her palm. Her right hand fell limply into her lap.

He lifted her arm, silent as his thumb followed the raised line, slowly from wrist to elbow, taking in every curve, every bump of the past. He brought the start of the scar on her wrist to his lips for the softest kiss as he looked at her. "I cannot take away the past, Aggs. But God help me, as long as I am with you, I will do everything in my power to banish those dreams."

Aggie rubbed her eyes with the base of her palm. "I do not want to have to depend on you for this. I do not want to burden you. I should be able to control myself. It is just that I have not been this well-rested since my father was killed. It is like I can breathe again. Walk around normally without fighting the cloud in my brain."

"So then you let me continue to help. Accepting me does not make you weak."

She nodded, eyes half-shuttered.

"You do realize this could have made all the difference in trying to find the leader earlier. That they are after something they think you have. Why didn't you tell me this?"

"I am sorry. It is too hard. What he did to me. I am damaged." Her voice cracked. "And I never wanted you to see me damaged."

She closed her eyes and took a quivering breath. Steadied, she opened her eyes to Devin, voice again in control. "So I cannot think of it. Not when I have to keep moving. And I don't know what he wants. What he thinks I have. If I let my mind go there, to what happened, I become nothing. And I cannot protect anyone if I am nothing."

Devin set her arm gently in her lap and cradled her chin. "You understand it is all of you I want, Aggs. All of you, whatever scars may be."

Aggie closed her eyes, exhaling held breath.

His hands went to either side of her face. "Good. Then we will never talk of it again."

CHAPTER 16

"Devin, where—" Aggie grunted from hitting her sidesaddle hard as her horse flew over a stump. "Where are we going?"

Her tongue smacked at the dust she had just sucked in, trying to get the earthy taste out of her mouth. Umph. Another hard jolt. This was ridiculous. "Devin—where?"

Devin looked back and flashed a smile, just as he had done repeatedly over the past hour. She knew he did it to make sure she was keeping up. So smug. She glowered at his back. Him riding high on his enormous black stallion, while she had to hang back in his dust trail because her mare was too skittish around his mount.

He had been irritatingly ambiguous all morning long about their destination. He told her they were to see more of the grounds. That was it. He had even woken her up early and had lunch packed and the horses readied by the time she had completed her morning ablutions.

"Devin." She tried to elevate her voice to a pitch he couldn't ignore. "When are we going to get there?"

The ass. He didn't even turn around. Aggie gritted her teeth. Save for this morning, the last several weeks had been heaven. Her shoulder was healing quickly, and Devin near-doted on her, spending the days showing her about the extensive grounds of Stonewell.

But she still reckoned with the mystery of his childhood. For all the time he spent on the tales of his ancestral home, he continued to be evasive about his childhood. Irksome, for it was a clear reneging on the deal they had made on the trip to Stonewell.

"Damn." Aggie muttered as her left hand slipped on the reins. Her legs clamped hard to the pommels as she tightened her grip with her right hand, easing her left hand back up the leather. Her shoulder wound still made her left arm weak, especially noticeable on this strenuous ride through the northern woods of the estate.

Nice one-month anniversary. Devin probably didn't even realize it had been one month since they were married. To celebrate, she got stuck tasting his trail dirt and being ignored.

Deep into the thick woods, he pulled up on his stallion, stopping in the middle of the main trail, and turned his horse back to her. Aggie looked around as her horse slowed, confused, until she noticed an almost imperceivable path turning off to the right. Her curiosity tripled.

"Devin, for the last time, tell me where we are going."

He laughed. "Careful, my duchess, you are beginning to play the role of the nagging wife."

"Purely a reaction to your unbearable dismissiveness." She smiled sweetly at him.

His smile didn't waver, and he pointed at the nonexistent trail. "We veer here, and the path is complicated by twists and turns. I am not sure what condition it is in further on, so you will need to stay close to me."

"You know very well my horse is not keen on getting close to your beast," Aggie said at his back, but master and horse were already widening the absent path as they dove into the woods.

It took another hour before Devin stopped in a small clearing, and Aggie was grateful. Again and again she almost lost Devin and the trail around a sharp curve, or veered off into an opening that looked like it should be a path, but wasn't. It was a good thing his horse's noise matched its size.

Devin's feet hit the forest floor. "We are here—I was not sure I could find it as easily as that."

Aggie took his hand to dismount. "That was easy?"

She looked down at her riding outfit as she slid off her horse, a beautiful concoction of multiple blues layered over each other, with a fine cut train and a sleek line that pushed up and accentuated her breasts in the best possible fashion. It was now a disaster. The overgrown forest had shredded the delicate fabric, and her skin ached with the multiple scratches.

"And where is here?" Aggie scanned the tall trees surrounding them, and then her eyes settled on Devin.

Enthusiasm poured from him, and Aggie's annoyance evaporated. Wherever they were, Devin's grin indicated it was important. Aggie looked around once more, seeing only shrubbery and trees.

"Ready?" He grabbed her hand, leading her around the horses.

"Maybe?" Aggie nodded her head quizzically. Her husband seemed to be nearing insanity.

"Bend down." At a wall of shrubbery, Devin stepped in front of her and leaned forward, thrusting his hands deep into the branches. Arms disappearing into the twigs, he grunted as he fought the greenery, parting it. A small opening appeared.

"Go on, go through," Devin said.

Aggie leaned down and peeked through the opening. She turned to look at him, her nose almost touching his.

"Just go. Your outfit is already ruined." Devin laughed. "Trust me."

Her eyes lowered to his still-bright smile, and Aggie swallowed a sigh and went to her knees, crawling through the small hole he had made.

Awe hit her the second her head popped out the other side of the hole. Through the bushes, Aggie stood up with mouth agape, dumbstruck.

What surrounded her could only be described as perfection. The thick shrubbery she crawled through stood more than a story tall, in a complete, exacting circle around her. Behind it, a ring of ancient oaks thrust toward the sky. But for some odd reason, the majestic oaks didn't branch inward to cover the circle she stood in. Instead, the only thing she saw above was clear blue sky and sun-rays shining down. The width of the circle was about four horses' lengths, and luscious green grass, long and mounded over, covered the ground.

A small, oddly perfect, utopia.

Aggie tilted her head to the sky, closing her eyes and letting the sun warm her cheeks.

Hands slipped around her waist from behind, and she smiled, leaning into Devin.

"You are forgiven," she said.

"I did not know I needed to be." He nuzzled his cheek onto Aggie's. "What did I do?"

"Drag me out here. Did you not hear me swearing at you the entire time?"

He chuckled. "I did not realize that was directed at me. Or maybe I did, but was choosing to ignore it. Besides, I like it when you swear at me. It usually means I am doing something incredibly sinful to your body. "

"Wanton scoundrel." She turned her head and nipped his neck, laughing, then set her head on his shoulder, eyes taking in the paradise. "This is utterly exquisite. And bizarre. How does it grow like this? Does someone maintain it?"

"No. I have no idea why it grows like this. It just does. I stumbled upon it when I was little, and it has been like this since I knew of it. You have been pestering me about my childhood." His hand swept around them. "So here it is. I spent as much time as possible here in the Circle."

"The Circle? That is what you named it? Your creativity astounds me."

He squeezed her waist, producing a squeal. "I was six when I named it."

"It is a functional name, I will give you that. But do not think I will leave naming our children up to you."

"What? I am much more creative now."

"Really?" Aggie spun in his hold and mock held two imaginary babies, lowering her voice in imitation of Devin. "This one shall be called 'boy,' and this one shall be called 'second boy.'"

Devin rolled his eyes, then pulled Aggie back into him. "Boys you say?"

"I do. But let us not forget about 'first girl' and 'second girl' as well."

His fingers went along her neck, creating goose bumps as he cupped the back of her head. "You give me those children, Aggs, and I will gladly leave all the naming up to you."

Aggie's breath caught hard at his words, at the glint in his grey eyes. The only thing that steadied her was her hands gripping his arms. Was it possible he wanted that as much as she had come to realize that she did? Children. This life. This man. Everything.

"No." He took a decided step away from her. "Before you give me that shameless look, there is more to the Circle, and you are not going to sidetrack me."

The core of her already pulsating, she reluctantly let her hands fall from him. "Fine. But what else could you possible need here? This is perfect just as it is."

"Except when it rains."

Aggie looked around, puzzled. All she saw were fat shrubs and towering trees.

"Over here." Devin took her hand and led her over to the far side of the Circle. "Right here, look," he said, pointing straight ahead.

Perplexed, her eyebrows raised. "I see a shrub."

"Exactly. That is what you are supposed to see." Devin bent down and shoved his arm right into the middle of the greenery.

"Not again."

"Again. But a little cleaner this time." Devin dug around in the thick branches, finding something, and he pushed his arm upward. Near Aggie's feet, an opening appeared in the greenery, just big enough to crawl through.

"Go on in." Devin stood and nudged Aggie.

She looked at him, amazed wonder on her face, then down at the hole, and then back up again at Devin.

"Go on—I don't think it will collapse on you."

"You don't think?" Aggie wrenched an eyebrow at him, then went to her hands and knees and scooted through the opening. Devin followed.

Standing up, Aggie's eyes adjusted from the brightness of the Circle, to the darkness surrounding her. Then she started to laugh. She was in a tiny cabin. Three walls were made of logs—as was the ceiling, and judging by the tweets, a number of birds had taken up residence in the crannies.

The fourth wall was the shrubbery they had just passed through, and it let shreds of light into the room. Dark wood planks made the floor and an upside down drawbridge had created the hole they just went through.

Aggie walked across the room to a small bookcase overflowing with books. Some looked like they had weathered well, others looked fragile. A desk was next to it with a neat stack of paper, and a lantern and matches on it. Even covered with years of dust and dirt, everything was neat and orderly.

Aggie turned to her husband. "Devin, this is fantastic. How long has it been since you were here?"

"I must have been about eleven the last time I was here." A fond smile full of memories danced on Devin's lips.

"Who built it?"

Devin walked about the cabin, inspecting treasures long forgotten, his large form swallowing up the small space. "I did, with Thompson's help."

"Thompson helped?"

"Yes, but not like you are thinking. I stumbled upon the Circle after getting lost trailing my father when he was hunting. I was searching for home, but then I found the clearing and realized I had found something better than home."

Devin went to a side wall and began to crank a round lever. Aggie watched in amazement as the ceiling started to rise and golden rays of light began to peer in. "And that is why the trail here was so complicated—I marked my path when I left that first day, but I was a lost six-year old, so the trail is quite contorted. And then I was always afraid of losing the trail to the Circle if I tried a more direct route. So I never did. Once I knew the trail well enough, I added the branches off the path to sidetrack anyone on it. I was going to be the only one that knew about the Circle."

"Were your parents very worried when you finally got home that first day?"

Devin's face flushed dark for a moment, then he turned from her to secure the lever in place with a latch. Aggie immediately regretted her question.

"No, as a matter of fact. They had both retired to their separate quarters by the time I returned." He picked up a book from the desk and gently blew the dust off it. "Thompson and several of the staff were the only ones out looking for me. And did I ever get a scolding from him when he got back to the house. I was sleeping soundly by then. Thompson came banging into my room, scaring me silly, because he looked a mess and his usual composure was gone. It was one of the few times I ever remember Thompson being openly angry with me."

"Thompson, angry? I do not believe it. He is a pussycat."

"To you, maybe. I don't know how you did it, but you have charmed the haughty nose right off of him. With me he has never hesitated to let me know when he is displeased with me. But that time when I was lost…" Devin shook his head. "That time really got to him."

Aggie smiled, watching Devin clean off books of his youth. "So when did he help you build this?"

"After that first day, I came back here again and again, each time wearing down the path a bit more, bringing my books. It took one long walk back to Stonewell in the rain, for me to decide to build a shelter. And my first attempt was pathetic— twigs and sticks."

He set a few warped books onto the desk. "I spent more and more time here, and then Thompson, being the nosy ass he can be, followed me one day." Devin chuckled. "I was lying under my twigs, reading, when Thompson's head poked through the bushes at me. You can imagine my outrage."

"I can. I have seen it."

"But all he did was 'harrumph' and leave. Said nothing."

Devin moved to a wooden chest with a heavy iron latch, opened it, and pulled out two faded blankets. "For days I stewed about it, but Thompson never said a word. And then one day, I walked into my room and on the middle of my bed was a tiny replica of the Circle. It had miniature trees and shrubs, some moss for the grass in the clearing, and an improved shelter in this spot. It was the neatest thing I had ever seen. The model cabin was as it is now—complete with the opening ceiling and hidden entryway.

And it was built exactly as it was to be life-size, so I could just follow the construction of the miniature."

Devin knelt with the blankets at the wall of shrubbery and crawled back out of the cabin into the Circle. Aggie followed him out.

"He would be horrified if he knew I told you, but he is actually a skilled craftsman and carpenter, although no one knows that about him. His father was a carpenter, and he learned at an early age. But he has kept his skill well-hidden so as to not threaten his position or the respect he demands from the staff."

Standing, Devin shook the mustiness out of one of the blankets and Aggie followed suit with the other.

"He taught me everything late at night in the kitchens using the model, about how to build the cabin correctly. And I honestly do not think he ever came back here."

Devin laid out the blankets on the grass mounds in the middle of the Circle. Then he stripped off his jacket, folding it and setting it on the edge of the closest blanket.

"Devin, that is a wonderful story. I knew I liked Thompson for good reason. Plus, this actually proves you did not just appear one day, full-grown man out of thin air. I was beginning to wonder."

"Good. Will this finally stop your harping on me about my childhood?"

Aggie sat down on one of the blankets and gave the question real thought, then shook her head. "No, probably not, but it may temper me just a bit."

Devin sank to his knees, facing her. "I will just have to keep you quiet other ways then."

Instant predator, he straddled Aggie, moving up her body, forcing her to recline onto the blanket. He hovered over her for a moment, eyes searching her face.

Breath held, Aggie's chest tightened at the glimpse she was seeing of Devin's soul. She had no idea her heart could actually hurt like this when she was with him—physically hurt—a constant crush in her chest that never allowed a full breath to take root.

He came down on her hard, lips meeting lips as though he tried to take her very essence. Then he lightened, the kiss turning long and soft, and curling Aggie's toes against the earth.

Just as Aggie started to work her hands under Devin's shirt, he abruptly stopped and rolled off of her.

Breathless and eyes still closed, it took Aggie a moment before she realized Devin had truly stopped and wasn't rolling back on top of her. Disgruntled, she propped herself up on an elbow, and glared at him as he stretched out on his back.

He chuckled at her distorted face. "Lie back down, Aggs. This is the other thing I used to do out here—"

"Begin to ravage women and then abruptly stop like a lunatic?" Aggie went to her back, her right hand cupped under her head.

"No, you are the first and only woman I have ever had here." He reached out and put a hand on her flat stomach, fingers running over her hip-bone. "And I do intend to take you here in this spot. But first, look up. I just wanted you to experience this as well. I used to lie like this for hours, not moving, soaking in the moist air, staring up at the passing clouds."

Placated, Aggie looked up at the translucent blue sky, and watched as a rolling white cloud meandered by. She was trying to imagine the man next to her as a little boy, lost in the perfect wilderness around him. Time standing still. Nothing to be scared of. Nothing to think about. Devin had no idea how much she needed a place like this.

They stayed on the faded blankets, silent, staring up at the sky for a long period of time. When the passing white clouds stretched out, shifting to grey, Aggie's thoughts followed suit before she could stop them.

"It is one month we have been married." Aggie's voice broke through the noise of trees rustling.

Devin shifted his arm and slid it under Aggie's head, pulling her onto his chest. "Yes. One month." He kissed the top of her head.

"Devin…" Aggie paused, fingers playing on the shirt over his stomach, debating whether to continue. She took a deep breath.

"It has also been almost a month since we have talked about my…problem."

Devin stiffened. Silence.

She winced, knowing she was moving into treacherous waters. But she needed to know. "I have not asked because I believe that you are taking care of it." Aggie turned her head and set her chin on his chest so she could see his face. Not looking at her, he kept his eyes fixated on the sky, line of his jaw flexing.

"I still need to know, Devin. I gave you so few clues, and I know he must be near impossible to find. So I cannot help my worry. I need to know when he is taken care of—if he has not been already. I need to know when I can stop worrying about him and my family…and you."

Devin sat up, and Aggie slipped awkwardly off his chest. "You are worried?"

His voice sent a chill down her spine. She had asked all wrong.

"Devin, I trust you. I do. And this month has shown me—I can almost touch it, touch the life I truly want—because this month has been wonderful. Simple. The two of us. It is simple and beautiful when it is you and I. I have seen what this is like. What life could actually be. I can feel the happiness that could be mine. But it isn't mine. It cannot be. Not with this threat hanging over my head. And I want us more than anything."

Aggie watched the line of his jaw tighten with each passing moment. He stood up, staring at her, hands clenched at his sides, and Aggie could see nothing in his face. His voice had chilled her, but the blank set of his face froze her heart.

"Devin, you need to understand, every time I have let my guard down, every time I stopped—for even a moment—he attacked. And my guard has been down for a month. And that terrifies me."

"Are you saying you don't feel safe?"

Aggie flew to her feet, her hand on his arm. "No—you know that's not why I ask—"

"Because the only reason for you to worry is if you don't feel safe." His arm jerked away and he turned from her.

Lightning quick, Aggie's own ire exploded. "Devin, this man has been terrorizing me for more than a year—and you want me to just stop worrying? He killed my father. He carved a blade through my flesh. He tried to get into my home and do God-knows-what to my mother and sister. My family. The only family I have left. And you want me not to worry? To not ask? To just believe the world is all roses and what?" Her arms swept about. "Perfect little Circles?"

Devin whipped around, icy glare boring into her. "Yes. That is all you should believe, Aggie. That is all you need to know."

"No. Unfair. I have given you a month with not one question on the subject from me—and I, of all people, deserve to know what is going on." Aggie tried to notch her voice into control with little success.

"You don't think I want this? What we have? I have been able to recognize myself again. Little parts of me I thought were lost, are actually still in here." Her palm pounded on her chest. "Happiness, laughter, love. I thought I lost all of that, all of who I was. I have seen glimpses of myself again, not of who I became. What I have done. I have killed people. And what that made me into. So no, of course I would rather live this life, this one—the one where I don't have to be terrified and carry a gun and look over my shoulder."

Her arm swung wild. "But that can never happen. Not until he is dead. Until he is dead or in prison, I am only fooling myself. I cannot be who I was. Protecting myself, my family—it is still my responsibility and getting married didn't change that fact."

"It did change." Devin snatched her flailing wrist mid-air, interrupting her tirade. He leaned in, lethal, inches from her face. "It changed the second you said 'I do.' At that moment you became mine. I am your family."

She tried to jerk away. He gripped her wrist harder.

"You, your problems, and most definitely your responsibilities." He threw her arm down. "I would thank you to remember you are a wife now, duchess. You have no responsibilities. They are mine."

The fury in Devin's eyes stole all words from Aggie's lips.

Silently, he turned from her, bundling up the blankets and going into the cabin. Aggie could hear him cranking the rooftop down. He came back into the Circle, grabbed his jacket, and barreled through the shrubs. Aggie had no choice but to follow.

The returning trip was silent. And painfully long.

CHAPTER 17

Exhausted, both in body and spirit, Aggie crawled alone into the bed in her chambers for the first time. Sheets cold, they did nothing to ward off the chill that had set in when it had started to mist on the way home, soaking her to the bone.

It was dark when they got back to Stonewell. Without word to Devin, she had disappeared into her rooms, changed out of her sopping riding outfit, and knowing the pit in her stomach would not allow food, decided to forego dinner and crawl into bed.

Curling into a ball under the covers, she tried to generate enough heat to stop the shivering. She had just dozed off when thunderous steps came to the door connecting her room to Devin's. The crack of the wood swinging hard into the wall set her upright, her heart violent in her chest.

"You will not leave our bed." Devin stood in the doorway wearing pants but no shirt. In the dim light from his room, Aggie could see his chest heaving. "We are not resolved, but you will not leave our bed. Do you understand."

It was a command, not a question, but Aggie nodded nonetheless. She didn't have the energy to resolve anything either. And as much as she didn't want to admit it, she still ached to be next to him, angry or not.

He left the doorway and disappeared. Aggie flipped back her covers, grabbed her robe, and switched beds. Her sleep was fitful until Devin finally joined her, setting his hand on her waist, his warmth filling the bed. Darkness took her over.

Hours later, a snap crash of thunder woke her. Cold wind and a mist escaping from a brutal rain blew in through the open window next to the bed. Half-conscious, Aggie hopped up, closed the window, and dove back under the warm covers.

Rolling over, she discovered she was alone in the enormous
bed. It surprised her, even in spite of their earlier argument.
Devin was almost always next to her when she opened her eyes.

Aggie stared at the emptiness next to her, then reached her
hand under the covers to feel Devin's side of the bed. It was cold.
He had left the bed a while ago.

Why demand she get into his bed, and then leave? Was he
that upset with her? It didn't make sense.

Was it that he tried, but then couldn't stand to lie next to
her?

At that, Aggie's heart started to thud, slow and painful. His
current bull-headedness aside, she had begun to believe that a
life with him was going to be more than she could have possibly
hoped for. In the deepest corners of her soul, she knew she
loved him. And she had even begun to believe that Devin might
someday love her in return.

She wanted this life with him. Wanted his bed. Wanted to
love him. Wanted him to love her.

And now he had left their bed in the middle of the night.

How often had he done that? How many nights could he not
stand to sleep the whole night with her? He had done it before.
Did he leave every night? How many times had he left their bed?

Aggie knew she was working herself up, but she didn't care.
If he was deserting their bed, she needed to know why. And then
she needed to end it.

She threw the covers off and got up, yanking a robe around
her shoulders. Sliding her feet into a pair of silk slippers, she
walked into the hallway after finding no sign of Devin in his
adjacent rooms.

The lightning flashed at quick intervals, producing enough
light that Aggie didn't bother to light a candle. Checking in
several of the bedrooms along the way, she found nothing and
went down the main staircase. She veered to the library first, since
that was where his was the last time she looked for him in the
middle of the night.

Stepping into the library, a thunder clash hit, making
her jump as it shook the floor. She stopped to let her nerves

settle, waiting for the next flash of lightning to hit in order to look around. Three successive flashes came, and Aggie was disappointed to not find Devin.

The next logical place was the study, and Aggie hurried along the hall. Sliding open the study door, Aggie stepped into darkness. She scanned the masculine room as intervals of lightning came and went, checking past the desk and the large leather chair behind it. All sat neat and tidy.

Biting her lip, Aggie stared into the darkness, sighing. She was going to have to light a lamp and search every room in this place. And then the stables. And then, hell, she would grab a horse and fight her way to the Circle if it meant finding Devin and getting some answers.

Aggie spun on her heel to leave, just as a lightning flash filled the room, and out of the edge of her eye she saw a slight movement in the corner of the room. A leg twitched in front of a chair facing one of the floor-to-ceiling panes of glass that lined the entire north edge of the room.

She moved to where she could see who was in the chair, already knowing the answer.

Facing the thundering storm, Devin sat in a winged leather chair, his forehead buried deep in his propped-up hand. He wasn't sleeping—his leg movement that had caught her eye had already clued her to that. He was just sitting in the dark, facing the rain.

A sudden, deep insecurity gripped Aggie, and she almost backed out of the room. But with a quick breath to steady herself, she planted her feet, concentrating on the instinct that told her to stay.

"Do you leave our bed often?"

There was no response, no movement from Devin's inert frame. Was he drunk? Disgusted with her?

Aggie took a few steps closer and cleared her throat. Maybe her voice was drowned out by the pounding rain.

"Do you leave our bed often?"

Still no response. Worry hit Aggie. Her challenging questions usually elicited some sort of response, even if it was of mockery.

She strode across the long room and stopped next to his chair. No movement or recognition of her presence. She didn't see a glass near him, but the smell of brandy wafted up at her.

Aggie ignored her mounting fear and went in front of him, kneeling as she set her hand on his robe-covered knee. Her voice came out soft. "Devin, do you leave our bed often?"

Her knees pressed hard onto the parquet floor. She watched his hand-covered face, letting seconds slide into minutes as she was determined to wait this out. No amount of ignoring would get him out of answering what, to Aggie, had suddenly become the most important question in the world.

The wind whipped harder, slashing the rain onto the window behind her. Lightning flashed, illuminating Devin's shadowed face and hidden eyes. Aggie waited.

An eternity passed, and Devin moved his hand from his forehead, setting it along the arm of the chair. His eyes opened, only to stare past Aggie at the window.

"It is the rain." His coarse voice set the hairs on the back of her neck on end.

Aggie waited.

"The rain." A touch of anger crept into his voice.

Her hand moved ever so slightly on his leg, urging him on.

"The rain wakes me…memories, guilt, they haunt me, have plagued me for far too long."

"Guilt?" Aggie brought her other hand to his leg.

"Look at the rain, Aggs. Turn around and look." Devin leaned forward and grabbed Aggie's shoulders, gently twisting her around. She sat on the floor, tucking her legs under herself, and wrapped an arm along his calf. As she stared at the pelting rain, lightning would strike the sky, and in those moments, Aggie could see Devin's face reflected in the glass—hard and tortured, as memories consumed him.

Devin leaned back in the chair. It took all of Aggie's willpower to wait through the silence and not turn back to him.

The pit in her stomach grew, and when he finally spoke, it dropped, taking her breath.

"My father killed my mother during rain like this. I watched. I stood paralyzed. My mother cried for me to help her, but I could not move. Not one muscle. Not one step."

Aggie froze at the words.

"I watched as he beat her with a metal stoker, hitting her, over and over. The entire time her arms were out to me, as were her words, for help. She died on the floor, arms still begging. I did nothing. It is why people think I am a monster. It is why I leave you when it storms." His blunt voice held no emotion.

She forced herself to take a breath, but she couldn't move a muscle, couldn't tear her eyes off the spot on the window that held his reflection. "How old were you?"

"Twelve."

Bile filled her throat. The gruesome image flashed in her mind, a twelve-year-old boy, witness to cruelty beyond sanity. He had just laid it out for her.

The pain she caught in his eyes at unguarded moments. Why he wanted her to know nothing of his childhood. The slight surprised glance he gave whenever she spontaneously touched him. She had never imagined the horror he held.

Without warning, her own father's face, dying, came into her mind. She tightened her arm around his leg as tears began to slide down her face, her heart breaking at what that one destructive moment in time must have done to him.

She couldn't—didn't want to hear any more of it. But she knew she had to. She also knew she couldn't dare to turn around and face him. Facing the window, facing the storm—this was the only way she was going to hear the truth he had tried to hide.

"How? Why?" Her choked whisper was loud against the rain hitting the window in front of them. "Tell me all of it."

He stayed silent, and just when Aggie thought she would need to prod him, his voice cut through a crash of thunder.

"You once asked about the small dining table. This is the story of why." Aggie watched his reflection as he took a deep breath. "My parents did not love each other. Rather, my mother never loved my father, loathed him at best. I understand he loved her, or at least was infatuated with her at the beginning.

That was his ruin. That was his mess. And he eventually echoed her sentiments. He married her for her beauty. She married him for his money and title. After I was born, the necessary heir, she collected a number of lovers. She flaunted them. She was deep on laudanum most of the time." Devin's voice remained detached.

"Despite the animosity, if the three of us, mother, father, and myself, were present in the same household—usually it was here at Stonewell—my father demanded we all take dinner together. I was four when I first remembered this hell. Our dining table ran near the length of the hall. Mother would sit on one end, father would sit at the other, and I was exactly in the middle. Conversation was never had at these dinners. Rather, my mother would berate my father, his lacking in bed, through all the courses, her voice echoing down the table. Father ignored her. He reveled in the fact that he could still make this one demand on his wife. I heard everything. I felt everything. Those were the coldest moments of my life."

Devin's legs moved, stretching out aside Aggie. She moved her right hand up, wrapping it under his robe around the warmth of his thigh.

"For the longest time, I wondered why she didn't love us. Why she looked at me with disgust. I gave up on her long before father did."

Fresh tears filled Aggie's eyes. She could only picture Devin as a little boy, face falling time and again as his mother discarded him.

"My father moved into town almost exclusively, and mother stayed here, a line of lovers tromping through the halls. I stayed in town with father. She was mean. He was bitter. I was lucky to stay in the household of bitterness. I finally escaped both of them when I left for school. The night it happened, it was on a rare occasion we were all at Stonewell, and father and I had left for London. A storm came up, just like this one, forcing us to return."

Lightning flashed as Devin paused, giving Aggie an agonizing glimpse of his taut face.

"When we arrived back at the estate, we were soaked, tired, hungry. Father was walking down the hallway before me and passed by the dining hall."

Devin's entire body tensed around her. Aggie's fingers tightened into his leg.

"My mother and one of her lovers were on the dining table, naked. On the table. To my father, the table was a symbol of the last bit of control he had over his wife. He snapped. He picked up a fire stoker. The man ran. But my mother just laughed. Ridiculed him. Cruelty in every word. He attacked her. He killed her. Then he climbed out of an upper window, screaming at God. I don't know if he slipped or jumped to his death. The entire time I heard him ranting above, I stood in the dining room, paralyzed, the dark rain pounding on the glass behind my mother's body. Taunting me with every echoing drop. The first thing I did after their funerals was to destroy the table."

Devin went silent, his body still.

Aggie prayed for lightning, she needed to see his face. Excruciating minutes passed, but when the light flashed, she took in every line of Devin's face reflected in the glass. He stared straight ahead into the rain, a set mask of hardness. He was waiting for judgment.

Judgment she had no right to entertain.

As still as possible, she took a deep breath, struggling to gain control of her emotions, to quell the shards that ran through her stomach, to stop the flow of tears staining her face. Her tears would not be seen as lamenting all a young boy had lost. No, Devin would see the tears as pity. And she would not give him a reason to believe she pitied him.

After long moments of silence, Aggie regained control. She turned around, balancing on her knees between his legs. She placed a hand on each of his thighs.

Aggie watched Devin's averted eyes, waiting patiently. After a few blinks, he dropped his gaze to her, meeting her eyes.

"You cannot forgive yourself, can you?"

Surprise crossed his face and, after a few seconds, he shook his head.

"And you cannot forget either, can you?"

Devin closed his eyes for a long moment. His chest rose and fell in deep breaths. Breaths that harbored the weight of unyielding demons. He shook his head again, giving a tortured exhale.

Aggie near doubled over from the anguish she saw etched on his face.

She lifted her right hand and laid it gently along his jaw. "Then I will watch the rain with you."

Without waiting for him to open his eyes, without asking for answer, Aggie turned back around, tucked her feet under her, and wrapped her arms around Devin's leg.

She set her head on his thigh, and watched the rain hit and roll down the glass before her.

~ ~ ~

She was asleep now. Her head, lighter before, was now heavy on his thigh, but her arms still gripped tightly about his leg. Her breathing was light, even.

Devin mindlessly caressed her hair as he stared down at her. He had looked at nothing else but her since she had turned back around several hours ago.

She hadn't pitied him. She made no demands for him to forget all he had been through. And she hadn't branded him a coward or a monster. Not as so many others had done.

She had simply accepted what he had said, and stayed.

The only other person who had ever accepted him and what he had been through, without judgment, was Killian. And he would not think twice about doing anything for Killian, including death. But Devin also knew Killian would never abuse that loyalty.

Devin's chest tightened. Here was this slip of a girl, who took the truth and then simply accepted him. She was either in love with him, or was the best actress in the world.

It was the latter that had been holding him hard against letting her into that hollow spot in his chest. Even as she scratched, day after day, to get in there.

Damn. What she could do to him. What his mother had done to his father.

Mind firing, he couldn't stop the unknowns. What if she grew tired of him? What if he turned into a decaying, raging shell like his father? Unbearable. What if she took on a lover? The last question hit him hard, and a large lump formed in his throat as anger he could barely suppress gripped him.

Devin looked hard at the top of Aggie's head, willing her to wake up and promise over and over that, no, she would never have another man, and no, she would never leave him. He stilled his hand in her hair, shaking as he fought against grabbing her shoulder to wake her and demand the oaths from her.

Her breath caught with a tiny twitch through her body, and Devin froze. She shifted, arms tightening around his leg as she nuzzled her head in his lap. Back to sleep. Back to peace.

She had given everything to him. Her body. Her heart. Her trust.

All he had to do was give her a chance.

The defining moment in Devin's life, and all the horror of it, slipped from his mind.

He was staring down his new defining moment.

This one he wasn't going to screw up.

Devin leaned down and gently picked Aggie up. He stood, walking out of the study with Aggie still sleeping in his arms. A sudden crash of lightning made him pause and look back at the windows.

It was raining harder than ever. And he didn't care.

He had a wife to wake up and make love to.

CHAPTER 18

He was on top of her, his body hot, his flesh pressing into hers. Mouth on her neck, attacking. Aggie's eyes flew open. This was nothing like what Devin had done to her a few hours ago. Or what she thought he did, she couldn't be sure if that had been dream or reality.

She remembered falling asleep in the study, watching the rain, but then waking up in bed, naked, his lips on the small of her back.

In and out of lucidity she slid, arching against his mouth, his fingers on every part of her body. Gentle, exploring, worshipping each morsel of her skin. Tongue on her belly. Stubbled chin on her inner thigh. Fingertips massaging the muscles in her back. No skin left untouched. Devin deep in her. Slow. Savoring. Even at orgasm, she couldn't tell if she was awake or not, and she didn't dare find out, just in case it was a dream.

It could have been a dream. It could have been reality.

No. This was nothing like that. This was Devin demanding she wake up. Demanding she meet him, touch for touch, scream for scream, no reservations. Demanding she be fully aware to everything he was going to send coursing through her body.

This was carnal, and she was ready for it. After all the emotion she had to squelch last night, she ached for it. She needed it.

Her hands slid down his bare back, cupping his already tense muscles.

She could feel him smile on her neck. "Awake?"

Aggie arched her chest to him, letting the sensations roll. "Can you wake me up like this every morning?"

"Request noted. But you are lucky I let you sleep this long. I have been watching you, hard and waiting, for hours. It has not been easy."

He pulled up from her, hovering for a moment above her face, taking in her eyes. The look sent shivers into her core, traveling down her belly and collecting, building a pounding throb between her legs. She saw it in him. He wanted to possess her, and she needed him to.

Hands leaving his backside, she clasped them around his neck, pulling herself upright as she pushed him flat back onto the bed, straddling. She met his mouth, on fire, tongues instantly in duel, thrusting for control.

Writhing her hips down against him, she tried to connect their bodies. He was more than ready, hard against her folds, but he wasn't going to pass control that easily. His hands held her hips hard, thumbs pressing into her belly, holding her just beyond her need to have him in her. Agonizing.

Aggie pulled from his mouth. "Cruel. You wait for hours, then do that to me?"

He smirked. "My pain is yours, Aggs."

Her instant groan turned into a wicked smile as her eyebrow rose in challenge. "Then your pain, your grace, is about to get extreme."

His smirk widened. "You will accomplish that how?"

She didn't answer, instead, bent down to his chest, her lips ravaging his skin, trailing downward. The hard ridges along his stomach got harder as she teased the area with her tongue. She moved slow, taunting with every touch of her mouth as she moved down, until her chin hit his protruding member.

Devin's rumbling grunt when her lips met the tip of him was worth the trip downward. And the blasphemous yell that exploded from him as her tongue traveled wantonly up and down him, secured her power, but also sent her own throbbing into a frenzy.

But she wasn't done with him. His hips already in motion against her lips, she wrapped her mouth fully around him. His hands tangled in her hair as she took him deep, her tongue flickering on the muscle as she dove repeatedly, reveling in every gasp she elicited.

"Damn, Aggs." The harsh growl matched Devin's hands as he untangled them from her hair and grabbed her by the shoulders, ripping her mouth off of him and smashing her back onto the headboard.

Teeth on her neck, Devin shifted her sideways until she hit the bed post.

Aggie heaved a breath, her back on the hard wood giving no room for her lungs. Taking him in her mouth had done just as much damage to her own need for him, as his for her. Her hands went down to his waist, pulling at him. "I need you in me now, Devin. Now."

He grabbed her wrists, bringing them both above her head, latching her fingers around the post.

"Grab it, because I am going deep into you." His hands went down to her hips, lifting her and impaling her in one fluid motion.

With a screaming shudder, she wrapped her legs around him, and her fingernails dug into the wood as she arched, taking him full and long. Nine searing thrusts, and she twisted uncontrollable, agonizing in her peak. She lost grip on the wood, crumbling against Devin in spasms, but then he slid one hand under her bottom and used his other to push her back up against the headboard.

His hand on her collarbone pinned her to the wood, and his mouth went to her ear. "You're not done, Aggs. You have more. No walls. You are giving me everything."

Spasms ebbing, she nodded, her voice breaking. "God, yes. Everything. Do it. Everything."

His hand went under her thigh, and he pulled out of her, crashing into her again and again. This time, her hands gripped Devin, fingernails deep into his skin, begging, urging every thrust onward. Her legs held him deep in her every time, until he fought his way free, only to dive deeper back into her.

He wasn't wrong, and the build in her core hit fiercely. She could only cry half words at the onslaught, demanding he not stop. Demanding he take her even deeper. Harder. Contort her flesh and make it his.

He came, surging into her, expanding and filling her so completely her body had no choice but to join his in a screeching, blinding light.

She was splayed on him, cheek in the crook of his chest, muscles jelly, when conscious thought came back. And the first thought she had, she said breathless, without thought, without defenses.

"I love you, Devin."

"Aggs…"

She tilted her head to look at his face. He didn't waste a moment before he slid her body upward and kissed her hard and long.

The kiss held everything he didn't say, and it didn't bother Aggie there were no mirrored declarations from him. She said it for herself. Said it to honor what she recognized deep in her heart. This man was her breath. She wasn't going to deny that. Nor would she ever have him doubt it.

As for him uttering the word "love" to her—she wasn't sure she would ever hear that word from his lips. Not with what he had gone through as a child.

She didn't need to hear the words to know what was in his heart. Everything he did for her, to her. What he had shared last night. It wasn't even a question in her mind that he loved her. He did. That, she was sure of. Words would not make it any more or less true.

She pulled from his lips, nuzzling her head under the rough whiskers on his chin. "You woke me up only to exhaust me, you rake."

His chest rumbled under her cheek, and then he kissed the top of her head. "Go back to sleep, Aggs. Your everything needs replenishing for tonight. No, make that this afternoon."

~ ~ ~

Hours later, Aggie woke up to find Devin had already disappeared into the day. She snuggled into her cocoon of warmth under the sheet, reliving every moment of what had happened last

night. Her soul had lifted tenfold, and she couldn't help the grin
that was pasted on her face.

After getting dressed and making her way downstairs, the
lightness in Aggie's step fell flat as she walked by the study, her
ears catching conversation and a voice she didn't recognize.

"I have been following the lead on her brother, and I think I
have something."

Aggie yanked the door open, crashing into the room without
thinking.

"My brother? You found him?" She jostled in front of Devin,
pinning down the man that was just speaking.

Behind her, Devin sighed and grabbed her shoulders.
"Killian, you remember my wife?"

"Oh. Lord Southfork, I apologize." She gave him her most
humbling half smile. "I understand I was rude when we were first
introduced?"

"All is forgiven, duchess. I know you were under a great
amount of stress that day."

"Nonetheless, I was rude. And I am going to be rude again
right now. What have you found of my brother?"

Killian laughed. "You are right. That was an abrupt change of
subject." He looked past her to Devin with a raised eyebrow.

Aggie knew exactly what that meant. He wasn't going to
tell her a thing without Devin's approval. Aggie looked over her
shoulder at her husband. "What about Jason? Tell me."

"I did not want you to know, because I did not want to give
you false hope," Devin said. "He has not been found. But after
you told me how the leader was convinced you had something he
wanted, I asked Killian to explore what work Jason was doing for
the crown in case there was a connection."

She turned back to Killian. "And was there?"

Killian shrugged, still looking at Devin. "The lead is vague
and can go in several directions."

"I understand you are talking in very ambiguous terms, all at
the behest of my husband, I imagine." She took a step away from
Devin so she could face the two of them. "If you still have no real
leads to find this man, I have a way to find him."

"You do?" Dread was already on Devin's face.

"Bait." She looked back and forth between the two men.

"No." Devin grabbed her arm, spinning her fully to him. "Do not even dare to utter the insanity you are thinking right now, Aggie."

"Devin. Please. I have been really thinking about it. It is a way. Maybe the only way. He will come after me. You know he will. You know he is waiting. Watching. Let me go back to London. He will come after me again."

She could see Devin struggling for control against anger, but she didn't care. She needed to get on with her life. To live with Devin in peace. And if her being bait was the only way, then she would do it.

He leaned in on her, his voice harsh. "Aggie. Please do not be stupid. Promise me you will listen to me. You will not go back London."

"Devin—"

"No, Aggie, no. I will gather up your mother and your sister, and your aunt and uncle if need be, and sequester them here, if that is what you need. Just promise me you will not do anything stupid. Promise me. Please."

Aggie clamped her teeth onto her tongue. Devin wasn't ordering like he usually did. He was asking, near begging. His grey eyes pleading with her. It unnerved her. And it made her instantly relent. "Okay. Yes. I promise. It was just an idea."

His eyes closed and he let out an audible breath of relief.

She moved her free hand to his jaw. "I trust you. I do. You will find him."

He opened his eyes to her, but didn't let her arm go. He didn't believe her. She could see that in his face.

She looked over Devin's shoulder at Killian. "Will you please excuse my lack of decency, Lord Southfork?"

"Whatever you need, duchess."

She nodded, then twisted her arm out of Devin's grip. She bent, hiking up the skirt of her dress until she had access to the pistol strapped to her thigh. Removing it and dropping her skirt, she went over to the desk and set the pistol down.

Stepping back in front of Devin, both hands went to his face, each word punctuated harder than before. "Devin, I trust you. You are the one that keeps me safe. You. I do not need the pistol to put my mind at ease. I need you. You will handle this. I trust that you will."

Her hands slipped from his skin.

As much as her mind screamed at her to stay. To demand answers. To concoct a plan. Her heart told her to leave the room.

It was the only way Devin would truly believe she trusted him.

Taking the biggest breath of her life, she turned and walked out of the study.

And let go.

~ ~ ~

Aggie looked down at the apple she had a knife half buried in. After the scene in the library, she needed to get out of the house to clear her head, so she stopped to talk to cook, then grabbed an apple and walked down to the small stream that ran past the great lawn at the back of the main gardens.

The north woods started along the area, manicured greenery giving way to nature, and she found a tree next to the water and sat, leaning against the oak. She started to carve the apple, but stopped. Minutes passed, her mind so overwhelmed it was blank. A red squirrel ran across the bank opposite her, jarring her from her own stillness.

Setting the apple down, she pulled her legs up and leaned forward, stripping off her slippers and stockings. Her feet hit the cool water, swelled from the rain, and she let her toes play along a swirling whirlpool.

She didn't know what to do with herself in that moment.

Last night, Devin had given her something very precious of himself—the truth of what really made him who he was. She knew how hard that had to have been for him. And in return, she had just given him the one thing she had not been able to—complete trust.

But that meant no control. No questions. No wondering. No planning. No worry.

And without all of that, who was she? What was she supposed to think about?

"Duchess, may I interrupt?"

Aggie jumped at the voice next to her. Had she let go so completely—just like that—that she couldn't even hear someone sneak up on her? She bumbled to her feet as she turned to see Killian standing next to her.

"Yes, hello." Smoothing the skirt of her peach muslin dress, she looked past his shoulder for Devin.

Killian looked over his shoulder, then back to her. "Nope, just me. Devin wanted me to talk to you."

"He did?"

"He wanted me to make sure you are okay. He thinks you too often hide what you are feeling. So you know—the whole story of his parents? It is a lot to take in."

Aggie's hands went to her hips. "That is ridiculous. Why would he send you? Why does he not just ask me himself?"

"He does not trust himself. Not on this." Killian rubbed his jaw. "And personally, I want to make sure as well."

"Make sure of what?"

"That you are not hiding anything from him. Disgust. Judgment."

Her eyebrows shot up. "What? He told you to ask me that?"

"No. Of course not. That is for my own reassurance." Killian's easy smile disappeared. "I like you, Aggie. Even if you don't remember meeting me. I know a lot about you, and I like you. But my enjoyment of your antics only goes so far. Devin is like a brother. The only person I consider family. And I will ask things that he will not. Things he does not want to know the answers to."

Aggie folded her arms across her ribcage. "I cannot say that I return the sentiment of 'like' to you right now, Lord Southfork. It is only because of your importance to Devin that I have yet to walk away from your rudeness."

"Forgive me, duchess. I may be rude, but I have Devin's best interests in mind. And you have yet to answer my question."

"Am I disgusted? Am I judging? Yes. Hell yes. Of course I am. His parents disgust me. I never knew them and God forgive me for speaking ill of the dead, but I think they were awful people. I think they were weak. I think they were selfish. I think they were cruel. I think they did something unforgivable to a child, and then crushed whatever shred of innocence Devin still had left that night. And I think he is better off with them dead."

Aggie sucked in a breath, shaking. She had no idea that much anger was in her about it. She hadn't recognized it. But there it was.

"I am sorry. That…that was too far." Aggie closed her eyes, shaking her head and trying to stop the fire that had lit her body. She wiped away the wetness around her eyes. "It was only last night he told me. What they did…I cannot yet bear to think about the horrendousness of it, much less come to any sort of terms with it."

When she opened her eyes, Killian's hard features softened into a smile.

"Good. Then we are of like mind. I must apologize for pushing you into that. I was unsettled by what I saw inside."

Aggie shook her head, confused and heart still pounding. "What?"

"When he asked you to drop your idea about becoming bait. Devin does not ask. He tells. He forces. He makes happen whatever he wants by demands. But inside just now, he was pleading with you. Pleading. It was something I have never seen before. So you can imagine my worry."

Aggie couldn't help the smile that touched her lips. "All that demanding, yet he inspires a great amount of loyalty, does he not?"

Killian nodded. "He does."

"But again, if he is worried about how I reacted, why not just ask me?"

"My perspective?"

"Please."

"He does not always think straight when it comes to that night. And because of it, he has thought of himself in a certain way for a very long time. That can be hard to overcome."

"How does he think of himself?"

"The night his father killed his mother. In that one moment of time, he convinced himself he was either a coward or a monster. And he has been living it ever since. He spent an entire war trying to prove to himself he was not a coward."

"And?"

"Having fought by his side time and again, I can say Devin is the furthest thing from a coward. So much so, I had to save him from himself a couple times."

"He does give you credit for that."

Killian smiled. "He should, the ass. He makes bad decisions in the name of his demons."

Aggie took a deep breath, afraid to broach the second half of Killian's assessment. "And the monster?"

Killian looked away from Aggie, watching the bubbling water for a long moment. Eventually, his eyes swung back to her, heavy with sincerity. "The monster part…I think that part rests with you."

~ ~ ~

Killian disappeared from view, and Aggie sank back down to the bankside, the weight of his words on her shoulders.

Her blank mind a distant memory, she pulled her feet up, wrapping her arms around her legs as she watched the water. That Devin could think himself a monster. It broke her heart, but it also lit a fire in her belly. She would spend the rest of her life, if that was what it took, to show him he was the exact opposite of a monster. She knew exactly what a monster was. And it wasn't Devin.

A memory from London flashed in her mind, and she bit her own tongue. It was long ago, but that she had even spoken the words "Stone Devil" to him. Atrocious. Her gut churned.

Consumed by examining every moment they had spent together, every moment that she must have made him question himself, Aggie didn't hear the sound at first.

The odd noise repeated, again and again until it finally made its way into Aggie's conscious mind. Almost like the call of a falcon, except it was just a bit off.

It echoed from the woods, repeatedly, until Aggie finally pulled up, truly concentrating on the noise. Cocking her head, she waited for it again. It came, and it sounded fake, almost like the secret calls she and Jason used to have for each other in the woods.

No—it couldn't be.

The call sounded again.

Aggie stood, ears straining. No. It couldn't be. No. She pulled the knife from the apple, shoved her muddy feet into her slippers, and started a desperate walk into the woods.

Jason was dead. She never wanted to admit it, but she knew it in her gut. Only death could keep him away from his family for so long.

The call reached her ears once more. Aggie walked deeper into the thick woods on her left.

A cruel joke. Someone was playing a cruel joke on her. She bent over as she walked, hand gripping the knife tightly. She knew she was safe at Stonewell, but she was not stupid, and the memory of being attacked so close to the estate hung in her mind.

Aggie picked through the trees, following the strange calls that continued sporadically. Fifteen minutes into the woods, a thick canopy of trees above her filtered out much of the sunlight. Aggie paused, hand on a tree, willing the sound to come once more. She knew she was close.

A twig cracked behind her, but before she could turn around, a hand came tight across her mouth and an arm engulfed her, locking her arms to her sides. The knife dropped. Aggie kicked as hard as she could, hitting shins, but making no impact.

"Aggie! Hush!"

She stopped. No. It couldn't be. She stood motionless, dazed. The arms around her relaxed, and she slowly turned, terrified at what she would find.

Eyes of a man she knew better than her own met hers. Aggie searched his face—so different—scars. But the eyes were unmistakable. Save for the flecks of brown, her exact eyes.

"Jason." The word choked out as she threw her arms around her brother's neck, burying her head deep into his shoulder. Tears were both immediate and uncontrollable.

"Aggie, I don't have much time."

She ripped her head back to look at him. "How—what—where have you been?"

"Not here," Jason whispered, peeling her arms off his neck.

"But why—"

He shook his head with finger poised over his mouth. "Come."

Aggie nodded and grabbed Jason's hand. He led her deeper into the forest, and ten minutes later, Jason ushered her up, of all things, a tree. Aggie wasn't sure whether to be complimented that Jason still believed she could easily scamper up a tree, or annoyed that he thought she would do so without complaint.

He swung up onto the first branch he had hiked Aggie up to, and followed her up several more thick branches until they were both out of sight from the ground.

Dumfounded, Aggie looked at her brother as he climbed and got comfortable on a fat branch across from her. This was a hulking man, bearing little resemblance to the skinny boy they had said goodbye to years ago. His face was deeply tanned, except for the white scar that ran from his temple to below his jaw. She swallowed hard at the sight. She wasn't sure she wanted to know where he had been all this time.

Catching her appraisal, his familiar mischievous smile appeared. At least that hadn't changed.

"Sorry about the tree. And the scare. Your duke has this place locked down tighter than the place I just got out of. There are five rings of guards around the estate. Ridiculous."

"What? Really?" Maybe she should have been quicker to believe Devin when he said she was safe here.

"Yes. I have been lurking for a week, trying to get to you."

"Why not come to the house?"

"I am effectively dead, and it needs to stay that way for the moment. And I only dare keep you here for a moment. They watch you, and if they find you missing from the creek—"

"Then tell me everything as quick as you can."

Jason arched an eyebrow at her demand, then shrugged. "About a year before father died—right before you and the family were told I had disappeared and was most likely dead—I was working on a special force under the crown that investigates treason. We were mostly concerned with transgressions that happened during the Napoleonic Wars. Best to know who your enemies are, and all."

He shifted his foot on the trunk of the tree, gaining better balance. "I discovered damning evidence against a group of three in acts of treason during the last years of the war. It turned out they were business associates of father's."

The blood dropped from Aggie's face.

"No, father wasn't involved. He did not even know these men until a few years ago," Jason said. "I was missing some critical pieces in the evidence. So I was stupid. I involved father. I asked him to do some light investigations."

Jason paused and rubbed his eyes, shaking his head.

"It is my fault, Aggie. He is dead because of me. I convinced myself he would be fine. I was very wrong. I did not even know until I got back—two days after I contacted father to tell him about the three, I was beaten unconscious and thrown into a ship hold."

Jason stopped, his face tight against obvious guilt. Aggie reached across the expanse to grab his hand and squeezed.

He took a deep breath. "I have only been back two weeks. No one knows I am alive. I found out you were here, so I have been attempting to get to you." Jason shifted on the trunk uneasily. "They killed father. I need to finish this, Aggie."

Aggie's throat had closed up almost immediately into Jason's story. She opened her mouth, and it took a long instant for words to escape. "Yes. Yes, you do."

Jason's head cocked at her, curious, but she ignored it. She couldn't go into all that had happened. Not now. Not yet.

"Two of the three men in the group are dead. I believe the third, Baron Von Traff, killed off his partners, tried to dispose of me, and murdered father."

Movement sounded below them. Aggie looked desperately at Jason, but he just motioned for her silence and shook his head. The footsteps soon retreated.

After long minutes, Jason breathed a sigh of relief. He pointed downward. "That is why it took me so long to contact you. It took me a week to find this one timing lapse in the guards in order to get onto the grounds and close enough to get your attention. Your husband knows what he is doing. Which leads me to a question, why are you being locked away from the world?"

Aggie avoided his eyes. "There have been some incidents. You will hear all about them, I am sure. But not now. You obviously need me for something, or you would not have risked sneaking onto the estate to get to me. Is it because I saw them?"

"Saw who?"

"The men who killed father. It will help with the case? There were five. They were all unmasked. Four are dead now. The fifth—I assume it is Von Traff—I can identify him as father's murderer."

"What?" Jason's voice went lethal. "Aggie, you saw father die? My God. And how do you know the other men are dead?"

The calm steel that had carried Aggie through the last year resurfaced. "No...no. Not now. Just tell me what I need to do to help end this."

He looked at her hard, and Aggie matched his gaze, refusing to fold to the scrutiny. He would see no torture in her eyes. He didn't need to know all that had happened to her. All she had done.

Plus, she was always very good at out-waiting him.

"Aggie, from what I have seen, you are safe here. But are you?
I mean really well protected? No strangers? No visitors? I need to
know your safety is intact. You already know you are a target for
Von Traff, don't you?"

"You have seen yourself. I am extremely safe here—there has
not been one sign of anything out of the ordinary since we arrived
at Stonewell. No visitors. Nothing amiss." Aggie hid her fidget.
Those words would fall under her truth-omitting that Devin was
so fond of, but she wasn't going to add another worry onto Jason
right now.

He breathed an audible sigh of relief, patting her hand.
"Good. Then I can leave for London and try to finish this entire
mess. But first I need the panther. I have looked everywhere, but
have not been able to find it. Do you know where it is?"

Puzzlement crossed her face. "Do you mean the one you sent
us right before you disappeared?"

"Yes. Do you know where it is?"

"I have it. Do I even want to know why you need it?"

"No, but I will tell you as soon as it is safe."

Aggie nodded. She honestly didn't want to know she had
been carrying around the reason for her torture. "I have it in my
rooms, let me run and get it and bring it back here."

She started to slip down her branch. Jason grabbed her arm.

"No, Aggie—is the duke home?"

"Yes, he was in his stu—"

"He cannot know I am alive—I cannot chance he mentions
me to the wrong person."

"I will tell him to tell no one, Jason, and he will not. He can
be completely trusted." She looked at him hard. "Completely."

"Aggie, this is my life, and yours too that could be in danger."
He began climbing down the tree. "Do not tell him yet. A
fortnight and this will all be finished. Then you can tell him all.
Bring the panther here to this tree the morning after next, an
hour before sunrise." He jumped to the ground.

"What? Jason. No. Wait—"

In a blink, he was gone into the forest. He had always done
that. Left in the middle of conversations if he didn't like where

they were headed. It was effective as children, and apparently, just as effective as adults. Especially when she was sitting in a tree.

Aggie climbed down the oak and trekked back to the stream, picking up the dropped knife and her stockings along the way. She chucked the apple into the stream and walked slowly to the house, deep in thought. Jason's abrupt disappearance had effectively forced a promise from her.

A promise she had no intention of keeping.

Aggie entered the garden on the north wing of the house, trailing her hand along the waist-high hedge. Damn Jason for putting her in this position. She was not about to keep this secret from Devin. She trusted him with her life, and she was not about to sneak from their home in the middle of the night.

She would tell Devin everything, and she would bring him to meet Jason, whether Jason liked it or not.

~ ~ ~

"Thompson!" Devin crossed the study and stuck his head into the hallway. "Thompson!"

His steward appeared by the front door. "Yes, your grace?"

"Have my horse readied. I am going to London for a few days with Killian and I would like to leave immediately."

"Yes, your grace. Will the duchess be joining you?"

"No, Thompson, she will not be."

"Is something amiss?"

Devin walked over to him, voice low. "We finally have a real lead on her problem. I will be going back to London with Killian to check out the validity of it. And to loosen some tongues that are staying stubbornly closed. But I would rather she believe I am going to London on business."

Thompson nodded. "As you wish."

Devin started walking to the stairs, then turned abruptly at the bottom of the steps.

"I also want the men on the grounds doubled. And Thompson, I want you to know where she is at all times. I do not want her off the main grounds of Stonewell."

"It will be done."

"I know. Thank you."

Devin disappeared up to his room. Within minutes, he had changed for a hard ride back to London and was on his way outside to his horse. Killian was already waiting on his impatient mount. At that moment, Aggie turned the corner at the front of the house.

"There you are." Devin smiled and strode toward her. "I was just about to start searching for you."

Aggie's eyes narrowed at him. "Really? Why?"

"I just got an urgent message about one of my holdings—I need to go into London to head off disaster." He grabbed her hand and started walking to his waiting horse.

"But—wait—I could come with you?" She looked up at him, eyes almost frantic.

Best to leave quickly, or she was going to hound him with questions. "No, I will only be gone a couple of nights, and I need to leave immediately."

"But, Devin, I needed—"

"I want you here, Aggie. You will be safer here than on the roads with me—I have Thompson doubling the guards on the grounds. Trust that you will be well protected. I would not leave if that were not true."

He leaned down and kissed her hard, lifting her slightly off the ground. He pulled back, letting her go as he stepped up and swung his leg over his stallion.

"But, Devin, you do not understand, I needed—"

"If you are wondering about the investigation—this will give me a chance to break some heads over the stagnancy of it." Devin looked down at her. "And I will check in on your mother and sister."

Devin watched her squint up at him, her hand hovering to block the sun behind his head.

"Thank you. But, Devin, it is just that…"

"Yes?"

She looked over her shoulder, then back up to him. Her hand went on his calf, squeezing it. "Nothing. It can wait until you get back."

Devin smiled and leaned down to cup her cheek. His fingers fought to leave her smooth skin. "I will be home before you know it."

He set his horse into a breaking pace down the graveled stones of the estate.

CHAPTER 19

Aggie swung off the covers and rolled out of the big bed she and Devin shared—not that she had managed a wink of sleep over the past day-and-a-half.

She had been berating herself since Devin disappeared down the drive for not making him stop and listen to her. But he had been in a rush, and it could wait. It had to wait. No harm would come of it. She had to believe that since there wasn't another option.

Maybe Jason would even have Von Traff arrested and put away before Devin got home from London.

Throwing a dark blue walking dress over her head, she looked out at the night. The thick draperies framed a crystal clear sky, with a full, shining moon. She had been studying the patterns of the guards, and she would need to be extra sneaky to get into the woods unseen. The bright moon was a stickler—she had not counted on it being so light out.

Aggie picked up the panther, studying it as her hand trailed the sleek black lines, the strong molded legs, and the small onyx-set eyes. Had she had the answers to her problems this whole time? She put the figure in a pouch tied about her waist, and shrugged into a demi-length navy pelisse. Foot on the edge of the bed to tie her boots, she eyed the pistol lying next to her toes.

She had wanted the security of a pistol enough to rummage through Devin's study yesterday in search of the one she had given him back. But now, looking at it, she realized how very much she had hoped to never have to touch a pistol again. Not after all she had done in London. Not after she had finally let go.

With a sigh, she picked it up and strapped it to her thigh. Wants had nothing to do with needs. And creeping around in the middle of the night warranted some modicum of protection.

Moving quietly through the back of the house, Aggie was in the woods within moments, the guards not the least bit aware of her presence slipping past them. She moved through the woods slowly, avoiding the next ring of guards, and tried to recall the path she and Jason had taken the other day. At least the moon helped in that regard.

She found the tree she had sat in, but Jason was not to be seen. She looked up. A slight move gave him away.

"You are not going to make me crawl up there again, are you?" Aggie whispered, not enthralled with the idea.

"You are late." Jason jumped out of the tree and landed lightly beside her.

"I had to deal with double the guards around the house. Spooking about in the night may be your forte, but I am poor at it. I do not think I will be asked to spy for the crown anytime soon."

Jason chuckled, then spied the pouch about Aggie's waist. His mood turned instantly dark. "The panther?"

Aggie untied the pouch and pulled it out. He exhaled a sigh of relief.

"This will all be over within days, Aggie. Then you can tell the duke everything, and I presume," he looked around, "you can dismiss these guards and stop looking over your shoulder."

Startled, Aggie looked up at him, her mouth open.

"Do not claim that you have not been. Aggie, I do not know exactly what you have been through since father died, but I know by looking in your eyes that it has not been good. God forgive me, I do not think I want to know what has happened to you, for the guilt at my not being here to protect you, and mom, and Lizzie…it would kill me." Jason paused, and stared up at the dark sky.

He looked back down at Aggie. "Life, and how we knew it when we were kids, is lost to us. But I grieve more for you. The innocence that once shone in your eyes…" He touched her cheek, wiping at the single tear that had escaped. "It is gone."

Aggie nodded, tears clouding her vision. Her brother was right.

"I did that. I let that happen. I failed, and it tortures me. I can never ask for forgiveness for it. I just hope that ending this mess will, at least, let the pain be put to rest."

Aggie searched his face through her tears. She wasn't sure if he was talking about her pain or his. Obvious anguish weighed on his entire body.

"I know you would not have chosen any of this, Jason. You do not need my forgiveness, because you already have it." Gently, she reached out and took his hand, turned it over, and placed the panther in it. She looked in his eyes. "Finish it."

Jason nodded and wrapped his arms tight about Aggie in a death grip. She hugged him just as hard back.

Out of nowhere, a clamp viciously latched around her wrist and ripped her from her brother's embrace.

Slipping, it took a moment for Aggie to gain footing enough to look up.

Devin.

His eyes pierced into hers.

"Oh God, no—Devin—" His grip on her wrist brutally tightened. "Devin, no—it's not—" A scream of pain cut off her own words as the bones in her wrist twisted against the pressure, near snapping.

Her body contorted, trying to escape the pain, but she froze when she saw Devin's face. His eyes were cold ice, and Aggie saw death flash in them.

Her heart came up to her throat, stopping all sound.

In the next instant, he whipped her wrist down. Just as quickly as he appeared, he disappeared.

"Devin—no." She stumbled after him. She could just make out his horse's form as he mounted and tore off into the woods.

Aggie started running, screaming. "Stop—no—my brother—"

Jason grabbed Aggie around the waist before she had taken three steps, stopping her.

"Your husband?"

"Oh, hell—yes—he thinks—no, no, no—I froze. I couldn't get it out." She shoved at Jason's arms around her waist. "Hell—

he doesn't understand, he thinks—Jason, let me go—Devin needs to know—let me go, dammit—oh, hell—"

"Aggie," Jason yelled against her ranting, "you will go back to the house, and I will find the duke. I will talk to him."

At that moment, another figure stepped out of the shadows. Jason shoved Aggie behind him, drawing a knife.

"Duchess?" The figured moved.

"Thompson?" Aggie went to her tiptoes to look past Jason's wide shoulders. "It is okay, Jason—this is Thompson, our steward—Thompson, this is my brother."

"Your brother?" Thompson's voice went weak, his reserved demeanor completely broken. "His grace, he thinks—"

"Yes, we know what he thinks, man—take my sister back to the house. I will find him." Jason grabbed Aggie's arm and flung her at Thompson, who gently caught and steadied her.

Jason ran off in the direction Devin disappeared just as the first rays of the day appeared.

Aggie looked up at Thompson, eyes wide with terror, pleading. "Thompson, they will kill each other. Devin will strike at Jason any way he can after what he saw. I have to go after them—they will kill each other—"

Back in control of himself, Thompson grabbed Aggie's arms and gave her a slight shake. Aggie almost crumbled.

"Duchess, they will not kill each other." His voice was sharp, even though Aggie knew he didn't believe the words he was saying. "We are going back to the house to wait."

Aggie looked up at him, numb, and shook her head. He didn't understand.

Thompson put his arm around her and began to guide her limp body back toward the house.

A few minutes passed before the numbness lifted and Aggie got control of her muscles. When she was sure her legs were back under her, she stopped, took a slight step away from Thompson, and looked up at him.

"Yes, duchess?"

"I am sorry, Thompson," Aggie said quietly, then reached back and punched Thompson as hard as her slight frame allowed.

She turned and ran back into the woods after Devin.

She didn't look back.

Didn't see Thompson reel onto his backside from her blow.

Didn't see him get up, shocked and rubbing his face.

Didn't see the club that bashed into the back of his head, knocking him out.

~ ~ ~

Devin left to avoid doing it, but if the bastard was determined to follow him to defend Aggie, he was going to get ripped limb from limb. The woods were too thick to gain much distance on the bastard, and Devin was getting sick of holding himself back. Every step his horse took away from Aggie only aggravated his anger.

He stopped his heaving horse in a small clearing, only to hear underbrush rustling behind him. Pulling on the reins, he turned, and the second the man appeared, he charged. A side kick, and Devin's Hessian dug into the man's side, sending him to the forest floor.

Devin jumped from the saddle, ready to tear his throat out. The man came swift to his feet, shifting into battle stance.

"I am her brother, you ass."

But it was too late. Devin's fist landed solidly into Jason's jaw before the words penetrated his brain. Just as quick, Jason shot one back at Devin's cheekbone.

They landed several feet apart, Devin bent over, hands on his knees, heaving in anger; Jason with a hand on a tree, heaving from having run for an hour.

Devin's hand moved stiffly to his now swelling cheek. His eyes crept to Jason.

"Aggie's brother?"

Jason crossed his arms across his chest and nodded.

"Jason?" Devin asked.

Jason nodded again.

"Not dead then, huh?"

Jason shook his head no.

"Why did she not tell me you were here—alive?" Devin's suspicions began to take root again.

"I asked her not to—I just finally got to her a day-and-a-half ago."

"When on that day?"

Jason shrugged. "Middle of the day. I have been trying to get back for years. Her life, along with mine, and probably yours now too, is in danger. Aggie is the only one who knows I am back, and she knows only because I needed the panther." Jason picked up the panther from where it had fallen from his coat when Devin kicked him over.

"The panther?" Devin's eyebrow cocked.

"Yes." Jason walked to a nearby rock and slammed down the wooden figure. It split, and from the scattered remains, he plucked out several tightly folded documents. He held them up to Devin. "This is what I needed from her. She never knew she had them. And since you now know about me, I may as well tell you the full of what is going on."

"That is what they were after?"

Jason looked at Devin, assessing. "My sister is quite adept at seeing people for who they are. I hope that has not changed, as she is staunch in her trust of you, and I will have to take her word on it."

"Yes, you will just have to trust me." Devin didn't bother to curb his sarcasm. "Who is it? Who are you taking down with those?"

Jason hedged, then sighed. "Baron Von Traff."

"Von Traff?" Devin blanched. He had talked to Von Traff the night of the Appleton party. It was only for a passing moment—hell, that was the night Aggie had thought she saw her attacker. And he had talked to the damn bastard.

"You know him?"

"Only in passing. And he would be dead right now, had I known." He turned from Jason and whistled. His horse trotted to his side. "We need to find Aggie."

"I had your man—Thompson—take her back to the house."

"Good. We need to let her know right away that her husband
has not just killed her brother."

Jason coughed at the insult, but said nothing. Devin gave
him credit for that.

"You can tell me along the way why those papers are so
damn important," Devin said. "And they sure-as-hell better be
important for Aggie to almost get killed over them."

"Killed? Aggie?" Jason froze, shades of white running up his
cheeks. He ran a few steps to catch up to Devin's quick strides.
"She did not mention anyone trying to kill her."

Devin raised an eyebrow at Jason, not breaking his pace.
"No, I do not suppose she would have. I have a few things to
share with you, brother-in-law. Whether you knew it or not, you
put your sister through hell. And you are lucky I am not tearing
you apart for it right now."

~ ~ ~

The two men stepped into the open area of the great lawn
behind Stonewell, and Devin could see that Jason was close to
being physically sick after hearing about Aggie's escapades. Posing
as a hack driver, her voyages into the scum of London, her cache
of pistols, getting shot—and he had even left out the worst
details.

Jason had not said one word during Devin's report. He just
got paler and paler, and Devin took comfort in that—at least he
didn't have the only stomach that curdled at the danger Aggie
purposefully set herself in.

He let the images he described sink into Jason's brain as he
looked up. In full sight of the sky on the open lawn, Devin noted
the early sun-rays were already waning from a storm brewing off
to the west.

As they neared the house, Thompson appeared, stumbling
out of the tree line on the opposite end of the clearing. He
clutched a hand to the back of his head. Both men sprinted to
Thompson.

"Thompson." Devin pulled Thompson's hand away from his head, only to see a mess of blood. "Your head—your eye—who did this to you?"

"Well, your grace, the black eye is from the duchess. She wanted to follow you. I would not let her, so she punched me to set me down. I was getting up from her blow—

"She laid you out flat?"

"Yes, your grace, she did. I, ah," he coughed, "I did not see it coming, your grace."

Both Devin and Jason stifled laughter.

"But as I was getting up, something crashed against my head from behind. It must have been a rock. I only just woke a few short moments ago, and was on my way to the house. Where is the duchess? I have quite the bone to pick with her."

"Thompson, she is not with us," Devin said, panic invading him.

Devin and Jason looked at each other, grey eyes reflecting the same deep fear in green ones. They tore toward the house, frenzied, and searched the entire building, the stables, and grounds, screaming for Aggie.

She was not to be found.

~ ~ ~

Aggie jerked awake and was greeted with two things, darkness tight in front of her eyes, and pain so brutal in her head she was sure a thousand knives were embedded in her skull.

She struggled for calm, trying to orientate herself. A dark cloth rubbed on her eyelashes as she blinked against the blackness, the tight tie of it only exacerbating the excruciating throbbing in her head. Flat on her side, her hands were tied behind her back, a rough rope cutting into her skin. She was jostling in a closed carriage—thick cushions under her, but no wind on her face. Her legs were unbound—a small favor; and aside from her head, she was relatively unharmed.

How long had she been unconscious? An hour, maybe two? She moved her right leg, rubbing her left thigh. Her pistol wasn't there.

"It is gone." A voice, black syrup that echoed of evil, broke through the muddled remains of her unconsciousness. It was him. The voice was unmistakable. She had lived in fear of it too long to be wrong.

Panic seized her. Her father's murderer. She had wanted this. Needed this. Then she had let it all go. Let it go. And now she was blindfolded and tied up. Aggie almost began to laugh at the cruelty of it.

Her senses more awake, the hair on her arms stood on end, every pore ready. This was good—she needed everything on fire if she was to get out of this situation. She concentrated on listening to the hooves on the ground. Four horses sped, rocks kicking up and hitting the carriage below. Her mind was getting clearer, and the painful throbbing began to ebb.

His sneering voice broke through the stale air.

"Did you honestly think I would leave a pistol on you, especially after you and that idiot duke of yours managed to take out four of my men? And now I will have to not only deal with you, but your duke, as well."

No—not Devin. Aggie's mind went frantic, instant tears soaking the cloth on her eyes. Not Devin. He needed to be safe.

Maybe Jason couldn't catch up to him. That was her only hope. If Devin believed she betrayed him, he wouldn't care if she disappeared. He would be done with her. She had seen that in his eyes. The rage. The instant she thought he was going to break her wrist. She should have known better. He would never hurt her. He was not his father. And then he was gone.

She had destroyed him in the worst possible way.

As much as she wanted him safe, it shattered her soul to imagine he would end up thinking of her in the same breath as his mother. But if it kept him safe from Von Traff, so be it. It was the only way he wouldn't come after her, and that was worth it. All she could do was pray he believed what he saw.

Aggie squirmed, twisting her wrists against the ropes.

"Do not bother. The more you try to escape, the tighter the knots will get."

Aggie ceased. There was nothing she could do blindfolded, with arms bound.

Her mind was working again, and what Jason had said to her earlier was beginning to filter through her brain. "Baron Von Traff?"

"Excellent. You have discovered who I am, which makes this all the more timely. I wondered how long it would be before you learned who I was," Von Traff said.

Aggie could feel the heat of his body in front of her, then his hand went to the back of her head. She tried, but failed to jerk away.

"Which means that you will be able to give me exactly what I want."

Damn. She had just unwittingly given Von Traff all the power—not that she was going to tell him anything. She cringed from his touch as he untied the cloth binding her eyes, then grabbed her shoulders and set her upright. He sat back down across from her.

Aggie blinked several times, trying to adjust her eyes to the dimness in the carriage from the drawn windows. She focused on the man across from her, and bile she couldn't suppress burned up her throat. It was him.

She hadn't known she would be so unprepared to see his face again. To see the greasy hair holding onto a bald head, the pockmarked cheeks, the stringy mustache that sat limp over his vile mouth, and the eyes. The evil white-blue eyes.

Her eyes moved down.

The hand that gripped the scalpel.

He was as repulsive as the day he had murdered her father. As the day he had scarred her. Aggie's first reaction was to freeze, but then she yanked up a reserve of the courage she didn't think she possessed, and willed her body into composure.

She stared into his eyes. "And what is it that you want?"

"All in due time, dear, all in due time. This time, I will not be rushed. This time, I am going to enjoy getting what I want."

CHAPTER 20

"Bloody fucking hell," Devin spat out for the twentieth time in five minutes. He paced back and forth in his study, fists white with anger.

Jason sat on the edge of a burgundy leather settee, leaning forward with his hands clasped tight in front of his mouth.

A second exhaustive search had turned up nothing.

"Are you sure there is nowhere else she could be?" Jason asked.

"Yes, positive." The words barely eked past Devin's fury. "There is only one other place she could possibly go, but we would have passed her in the woods, or heard her on the way back. She would not have had enough time to get there. And damn." Devin stopped mid-pace to glare at Jason. "If you would have cared about her just the tiniest bit—you would have insisted she tell me about you, and that whole god-damned scene could have been avoided, and Aggie would be right where she belongs. She would be sitting here right now safe and sound—"

"I do care about her and you sure as hell know it. What I didn't know was that she married a man who would assume the worst of her." Jason stood up, giving Devin a just-as deadly glare. "I didn't want you to know about me, precisely because I was trying to protect her."

"You should know her well enough to know that the man she married could be trusted."

Each took a threatening step toward the other.

"I don't know if I trust you even now."

The study door opened, and Thompson entered carrying a silver tray with dark brandy and two glasses. "Your grace, if I may interrupt."

"No, you may not, Thompson." Devin crossed his arms across his chest as he shifted his glare to his steward.

Thompson ignored Devin and continued on, calm as ever, and set the tray on a side table. "It has occurred to me that the bickering you two are partaking in is not getting the duchess back any quicker. As you two throw your fits, Aggie could, at this moment, be taken farther and farther away."

"Thomp—"

He held up his hand, stopping Devin. "Now, the two of you working together might get you closer to finding her. But unless you both put your pettiness about the other aside, she may be lost to all of us forever." He looked at Jason, then back to Devin. "I am quite fond of the duchess, your grace, and would rather not lose her. It is time for you to find her and get her back. I will have horses readied."

Devin's scowl broke as Thompson left the room. His eyes swung to Jason. "Fine. For the moment. We go under the assumption that Von Traff took her?"

Jason nodded, losing no urgency in his posture.

"You know Von Traff the best. Obviously, he wants those papers." Devin pointed toward the safe that now held the incriminating evidence against Von Traff. "And he does not know you are alive. Are you certain of that?"

"Yes. No one knows."

"But could he possibly know where the papers have been?"

"No, he knew they were sent to my father, but there is no way he would have known the evidence was in the panther—he would have easily stolen it long ago had he known."

"So where would he believe the papers to be, then?"

"Our London house was ransacked, that I saw first-hand and it looked recent. It looked desperate. That leaves our main estate and our country home we use for hunting." Jason rubbed his forehead, searching. "According to our solicitor's records I found, father had been at all three homes—routine visits, I am sure—just days before his death. My best guess is that Von Traff thinks father hid the evidence at one of them."

"Or that Aggie hid the evidence at one of them. Or that she would be privy to any secret hiding spots your father had in the homes."

Jason nodded. "If he took her to one of the houses," Jason looked at the clock on the mantel, "and he travelled fast, he may even be done with one and moving onto the other by now."

"We split up, you take Clapinshire, I will take Mitlan Place."

Devin went to his desk and opened a rich mahogany case to matching pistols. He looked up at Jason. "I assume you are armed?"

"You assume correctly."

Both men, dark and furious, strode out of the house.

"Do you know where you are going? Aggie told you where Mitlan is?" Jason asked as they went to the waiting horses.

"No, she didn't. But I know. I make it my business to know as much about my wife as possible. I will find it." Devin mounted his horse, and with a curt nod to Jason, took off down Stonewell's drive.

Jason thundered on his heels.

~ ~ ~

Aggie stepped down from the enclosed carriage, defiantly graceful, considering her arms were still tied behind her back. The day had grown muggy and still, just as it does before a wicked storm.

Her worry for Devin intensified.

As much as she prayed Jason hadn't found Devin and told him the truth, she was just as afraid that the incoming storm might throw him over the edge.

Twisting her arms again, the rope bit further into her skin. Von Traff hadn't lied about the knots getting tighter. She could feel her left wrist beginning to bleed from the chaffing of the cheap rope.

Von Traff grabbed her arm and pulled her around the carriage, and she realized they had arrived at Mitlan. It was almost unrecognizable—crotchety vines had taking reign of the walls, covering the once proud brick masonry. Why would Von Traff bring her here?

She glanced at the surrounding landscape. It had fared no better. Overgrown weeds were everywhere, and toward the back of the house, Aggie could see the sharp angle of the roof-line beginning to crack, slowly caving in.

Pangs of guilt shot through her. She let this place fall to ruin as it had. She had not visited, had not had staff at Mitlan since her father's death, much less ordered any upkeep or repairs. Jason was going to be so disappointed in her. She would fix it, if she got out of this.

When she got out of this, she corrected herself.

Von Traff dragged her across the walk as quickly as his stumpy strides allowed and pushed her through the front door of Mitlan.

Looking around the dim entry, Aggie was not surprised by the slight smell of mildew that hung in the air, and dusty, cobwebbed corners and walls. Von Traff pulled her further down the hall.

What did surprise her, as she passed by room after room, was the complete upheaval of the place. Furniture, books, linens—the place was in complete shambles. Thieves had obviously ransacked the home, going after any valuables that may have been left here.

Von Traff pushed her into the library. Several small tables were completely overturned, the large ornately carved desk sat at an odd angle, chairs were splintered in half, and not one book remained on the shelves that ran waist-high to the ceiling.

Not one book on the shelves. Why would they remove all the books?

"My apologies for leaving the place in such disarray, but we were not having any luck finding my pardon." Kicking some books aside, Von Traff flipped a wooden chair upright and shoved Aggie into it. She landed awkwardly, twisting one of her hands, and the rope dug tighter into her skin.

Fighting a wince, she looked up at Von Traff. "You did all of this?"

He nodded with a sneer.

"Bastard."

He shrugged his shoulders, then turned and walked out of the room. Aggie could hear his footsteps receding down the hall, then the front door opened and closed.

Frantic, Aggie searched the room. She knew she wouldn't be able to escape with her hands tied around her back, she would be incredibly slow and wouldn't be able to protect herself.

Her eyes scanned the mess. Books strewn in every possible place, splintered chairs, haphazard papers—there wasn't one spot in which the dark wood floors showed. Aggie caught sight of the waist-high sideboard that ran a quarter of the width of the room. The middle of the sideboard had been hacked apart by a hatchet, but most important, a port glass was stuck between torn wood. That glass was intact, but what had happened to the rest of the set? Aggie struggled up out of the chair and across the room, slipping and tripping on all the books and papers crowding her feet.

Reaching the sideboard, she kicked at the paper on the floor until she heard a clink of glass. Shifting a book away with her boot, Aggie spotted a broken triangular shard. She squatted, struggling for a few moments to pick up the glass with her bound hands behind her.

Glass chunk solid in her hands, she stumbled back to the chair, sitting down. She turned the glass in her right hand, holding it between her palm and fingers, and began sawing at the rope. The shard cut into her palm, the warm blood on her hand making the glass slippery.

Back and forth. Back and forth. Aggie struggled for calm. Then a few cords on the rope broke. She sawed harder.

The rope loosened, and Aggie could feel only a few more cords between her and escape. She pressed hard on the glass. It slipped out of her hand, hit the chair, and fell to the floor through the space under the arm-rest.

"Damn." Aggie struggle out of the chair again. Flicking papers next to the chair with her foot, she searched for the glass. Lucky. It landed on top of a book and hadn't disappeared into the mess.

The click of the front door echoed down the hall. Aggie kicked at the books to hide the bloody glass, then spun around, landing in the chair just as Von Traff entered the room.

"Duchess, you really should quit squirming." Von Traff strolled into the room, carrying a stiff black satchel. "You will be doing plenty of that soon enough."

Aggie watched him, producing a facade of calm defiance while she tried to bury her blood-soaked hands into the back of her skirts. Von Traff set the black bag on the large desk, askew from three broken legs. He opened the bag with a snap.

"It has been a long while since I have had a chance to partake in such…entertainment. Your flesh was the last I cut, and it reminded me that I do miss it. We were in much, too much, of a rush last time."

Aggie's eyes grew wide as Von Traff methodically rolled out a piece of red velvet cloth, then pulled from the bag a gleaming silver rod with a dark mahogany handle. The rod ended in a wicked-sharp point, and he laid it gently on the velvet.

"You are a beautiful girl, duchess. I always did like the beautiful ones the best. Male or female, their faces contort in the most fascinating way." He glanced over his shoulder at her, then back to the bag. "You are a treat. I am grateful…it will make this so much more pleasurable."

Five more polished silver hand tools were lovingly procured—a curved double blade, a gutting hook, a sickle-shaped bone-saw blade, a flat straight blade, and lastly, the scalpel. It was the smallest of the blades, and it was the one that sent a glut of terror-filled bile into Aggie's throat.

She panicked, breath out of control, all composure lost. Her feet started to push backward on the paper in front of her.

Her only saving grace was that his back was to her as he fidgeted with all the tools, fondling each dark mahogany handle, perfecting them into a straight line on the red velvet. "Yes, beautiful faces distorting. They are glorious. Ugly ones are already ugly. There is no joy, no accomplishment. But beautiful into grotesque." He hummed to himself. "That is a feat…so much more fulfilling."

Aggie managed to stop her feet and slow her breathing by the time he turned to her.

His cold white-blue eyes pierced her. "Where are they?"

"Where are what?" Aggie knew her voice came out as a tiny squeak.

"The papers incriminating me." He stopped. Looking at her. Assessing her. "The papers that your brother sent home before his demise."

Aggie let out an imperceptible sigh of relief. She knew nothing of papers. Jason had only asked for the panther. That was all she knew. She couldn't have a weak tongue if she was ignorant of what Von Traff wanted. And looking at the row of sharp blades, she didn't trust herself to keep quiet about anything.

"I do not know anything about the papers you speak of." Her voice was much stronger now.

Von Traff smiled, pleased. "I was hoping you would say that."

He turned back to the display of instruments and paused in deep consideration. His humming started again as his hands danced above the instruments. He picked up the very sharp, straight, pointy tool. He plucked the tip with his forefinger.

Von Traff looked at her, and Aggie could see the fear that flashed on her face thrill him beyond anticipation. He walked over to her and bent, his sputtering mouth next to her ear.

"You have given me a great gift, and I promise I will always savor out time together." His sticky breath invaded the pores on her face, and she gagged at the sick smell. "I do want to enjoy this, so the longer you hold out, the better, duchess. Please try."

He moved to stand in front of her, his eyes eating her body.

Aggie stared straight ahead, unblinking, trying not to be intimidated by Von Traff. As long as Devin and her brother were safely away from this madman, she didn't care what he did to her. Now that Jason had the panther, he would have Von Traff in the gallows before he could harm Devin. That was what mattered. Here, this moment, she would just have to endure.

"I have decided to start with something simple. This tip." Von Traff rubbed the point of the tool. "I will drive this tip first under each one of your fingernails, until all have been separated from your delicate fingers."

He smiled as he looked her body up and down once more. "Then, before we put it away, it will be pressed into your left ear, until it pops membrane after membrane. I will leave your right ear untouched, for you will need to hear my demands."

He moved the poker to his mouth, holding it sideways in his teeth as he gripped her arm and spun her half out of the chair, and she landed on one knee. He pulled a short, thick knife with a wide blade and a common, leather-wrapped handle from his pocket. The knife didn't match the rest of the set. Slicing through the rope at her wrists, he seemed to neither note, nor care that the ropes were almost cut through.

He yanked her arm up, and his knee punched up into her gut. Aggie fell back into the chair, wind knocked out. Before she could suck in air, he tied her left arm to the chair's armrest.

His arms caging her, he hovered. "I will ask you one more time before I begin. Where are the papers?"

Aggie couldn't say a word. All she could do was shake her head.

Striking snake, he grabbed her right wrist, and clamped all her fingers inward. All except her pinky, which was wedged straight out in an iron grip. He pushed the finger onto the wooden arm-rest.

The humming started as he jammed the point of the tool slowly under her nail, ripping skin.

The pain was instant. Brutal. She couldn't scream. Couldn't writhe.

All she could do was shut down. Shut down everything in her mind.

Nothing could get in. Nothing could get out.

The pain existed. It was all that did. But that was exactly what needed to happen. Nothing in. Nothing out.

Waves of excruciating torture hit, refusing to yield. Neither did his words. More about the papers. Something about ear drums. Something about eyeballs. Something about nipples.

Vague words, spotty, filtered into her brain, none of them taking root. She was blank.

The void continued until she realized she was standing, and his common blade was flat on her chest, tearing down through the fabric of her dress and chemise.

It clicked her mind back to firing, and she sucked in air, thrusting backward, only to hit the chair and fall back, her hands tied behind her again. When had that happened? The fabric fell away from her chest, exposing her in the most vulnerable way.

Von Traff snatched her upper arm, jerking her back to her feet. His face went in front of hers, appraising her eyes.

"You are back with me. Good." He was sweaty. Sneering. His eyes went down to her breasts. "This is much better when you are aware."

His blade came to her neck, sliding down along her skin until it stopped on her nipple. Cold. Aggie recoiled just enough to gain space from the sharp silver.

"Perfect. I should have started with this." He laughed, vile. "All of these tools are going to travel up and down your body, slicing, carving your most intimate places. You will beg to tell me where the papers are."

Repulsed, Aggie tried to dig her heels into the papers at her feet as he dragged her to the desk. She only managed to slip and fall, but Von Traff's vice grip kept her upright.

He pushed her face-down onto the desk, hand on the back of her neck as she tried to kick from her awkward position.

The sound of the front door crashing open startled them both, but before Aggie could move, Von Traff gripped the back of her hair, jerked her upright, and clasped her in front of him. He instantly had the blade pressing dangerously into her neck.

It was the first thing Devin saw when he tore into the library, and it stopped him dead.

Aggie froze. She was half naked.

Terror filled her as she pleaded with her eyes for him to not believe the wrong thing about the scene before him.

He answered her fear without hesitation. "Let her go Von Traff—it is over. We have the papers." Devin leveled his pistol at Von Traff's head.

Aggie's eyes flew wide. Devin had the papers? How had that happened?

"Do not bother with the empty threats, Dunway. I will kill her without the slightest bit of provocation, then use her body as a shield against your bullet." To prove his point, he pulled the knife harder against Aggie's throat.

Aggie shoved her head backward to avoid the blade.

"Very simple, Dunway, put the gun down and your wife doesn't get hurt."

Aggie watched Devin struggle for a moment, and then the blade on her neck start to separate her skin, warm blood seeping out. His eyes on her neck, Devin blanched and instantly set the pistol down on an upright table.

"Good, Dunway. Wise choice. I was not ready to kill her quite yet. I do like to enjoy their writhing bodies as their blood spills." He smirked at Devin, and let go of Aggie's hair, reaching around to crush her right breast, twisting the nipple.

Contorting at first to escape his grope, Aggie realized his loosened grip was her opportunity. She kicked off from the ground hard, throwing her weight back away from the blade, and then dropped straight to the floor. The knife only nicked her chin as she fell. She rolled away from Von Traff as fast as her bound arms allowed.

It took Von Traff a critical second to react to the surprise move. But it was too late. Devin had already lunged at him.

Lying on the floor, Aggie gave thanks she hadn't been killed by her stupid move. She craned her neck back to see Devin wrestling with Von Traff, trying to get the knife away. Papers and books flew in every direction as the two men struggled. Rolling to her knees, Aggie slid, slipped, then finally gained her footing.

Why in the world had Devin attacked him when his pistol was still lying on the end table? She ran to the desk and assessed Von Traff's torture tools. The curved sickle tool seemed best. She spun, looking over her shoulder to see what she was grabbing.

Sickle blade in her blood-slippery hands, she fumbled with getting the blade on the rope, but once in place, the sharp edge made quick work of the binding.

Devin and Von Traff slammed into the back of an upturned couch next to her. Why hadn't Devin disposed of Von Traff as easily as he could have? He was a master at slicing necks. She had seen that more than once. Was he hurt? What the hell was going on?

The struggling pair rolled, and Aggie caught a glimpse of Devin's face.

It terrified her to her toes.

She had never seen Devin—or any man—so enraged. Was that what his father had looked like so long ago? Was this what Killian had said—Devin made stupid decisions in the name of his demons? Von Traff had grabbed her naked body and now Devin couldn't even see straight.

Von Traff's blades would do her little good, she realized, so Aggie tore across the room, ducking under the wild swinging of the two men. She reached the table with the pistol, checked for a bullet, and had it cocked by the time she turned to Devin and Von Traff.

She set her aim, the gun slippery in her bloody fingers, but Devin and Von Traff continued their savagery.

Von Traff still had the knife in his grip, swinging it wildly. Devin deflected all but one of Von Traff's thrusts, and it cut across his forearm.

Catching eye of what Aggie had in her hands, Devin hit the floor, giving a clean shot of Von Traff. The gun slipped in Aggie's hands.

The baron lunged on top of Devin with a thrust, but Devin deflected the blade from meeting his chest by sheer strength, holding Von Traff's wrist suspended in mid-air.

Aggie froze at the sight of the blade above Devin's heart.

"Aggie—now," Devin yelled.

It was all Aggie needed. She fired.

Von Traff fell back, the bullet hitting his shoulder. But he still gripped the knife and was attacking again before Devin could gain his footing on the loose papers. Devin slipped onto his back, but then kicked out Von Traff's feet the moment before blade hit flesh.

Von Traff slipped, falling heavy, face-down. He went still.

Devin got to his feet. Slowly, he stepped to Von Traff and kicked him over. Von Traff's own blade had pierced his heart, the leather handle sticking out of his chest.

Both heaving, Devin and Aggie stared at the blood pooling around Von Traff.

Devin was the first to move.

~ ~ ~

"Hell, Aggs—" Devin rushed to her, gathering her in his grip. "What has he done to you?"

He pulled back, cupping her head in his hands, searching her face. "I am so sorry I—I never should have left you—it was stupid—I never should have believed—and then I didn't protect you—I—hell—damn the bastard—damn me—are you okay?"

Aggie nodded numbly. Her eyes stayed on Von Traff's body.

Devin tore off his shirt and wrapped it around Aggie, covering her naked chest. He lifted her wrist to remove the gun from her hand, and nearly threw-up when he saw her fingers. Through the blood, it looked like two fingernails were missing.

Fighting the need to suddenly dismember the body behind him, he instead picked Aggie up and walked out of the house.

Devin carried Aggie to his horse, purposefully turning her so she didn't see the two bodies lying near the carriage that had brought her here.

He set her to her feet on the gravel driveway as he checked the saddle. It had begun to drizzle, and Devin swore under his breath. He wanted this to all be over for Aggie, and now they had to ride back to Stonewell in the rain.

Aggie stood, waiting, silent. He turned back to her, only to see wet splotches on her face. He couldn't tell whether her cheeks were moist from the rain or from tears.

His knuckles brushed her cheek lightly, wiping some of the wet away.

"Aggs, I do not know what I would have done if…" He stopped, drawing a deep breath. "I love you, Aggs."

She looked up at him, silent.

Brow knitted in confusion, Devin touched her shoulder and gave Aggie a little nudge. She blinked, looked to his horse, and asked flatly, "Ready?"

Devin paused, staring at Aggie. It was as brutal as a slap to his face. He willed her to acknowledge him. To return his sentiments. But she didn't.

Silently, he lifted her up onto his horse's back, and then joined her.

The rain came harder, and lightning flashed off in the distance as Devin set back to Stonewell. He tucked her into his bare chest as best he could, and tried to shield her from the pounding rain. She stayed silent.

Had he been wrong? Did she not love him? Was he a fool to have believed this whole time she was happy to be his wife, happy to spend time with him, talking, arguing, and laughing? Or had he ruined her love for him when he had so quickly believed she had betrayed him?

He stared down at the top of her head. Her blond hair was thoroughly wet, tendrils clinging to her neck and down her chest.

No matter what she had just been through. He had to know. He had to know if he was wrong about their whole time together. He had to know if he had ruined it all.

He pulled up on the reins, stopping. "Aggs."

There was no response. Devin rubbed her arm, covered by his thin, soaking shirt.

"Aggie."

Still no response. Devin squeezed her shoulder.

"Aggs."

No response.

His bare neck prickling in fear, Devin reached to turn her face up to him.

Her eyes were vacant.

CHAPTER 21

A ceramic vase hit the wall, shattering.

Devin winced at the sound, his eyes not moving from the full glass of brandy he gripped tight in his hand.

Sudden thumping started, then stopped. Devin took a deep, calming breath. The noises of destruction had been getting louder and louder.

"For God's sake, Dunway—I am going in there." Jason started toward the study door again. "She will be hurt."

Devin took one step to his left, directly in front of Jason's exit, and put his hand firmly on Jason's chest, effectively stopping him.

"She already has been. That is the point." Devin glared at Jason. "So no, we will stay in here."

Jason didn't immediately back off, so Devin stared him down, wills clashing.

Taking a step back, Jason relented, went to the decanter of brandy, poured a glass, downed it, poured himself another, and then stomped back to the couch he had been waiting on.

A large thump, followed by what sounded to be the splintering of wood, broke through the momentary silence.

"You had better be right about this," Jason muttered, still glaring at Devin.

Devin went back to leaning on the wall by the door of the study, staring into the amber liquid in his hand.

Yes, he had better be right about this decision. His immediate anger at Aggie for ignoring his declaration of love had shattered the moment he lifted her face to his in the rain.

The complete lack of emotion reflected in her face petrified him. There was nothing there. Nothing.

It had only taken him a moment to understand. She was not ignoring him, she was in shock. Shock in all that had happened to her. Shock in all that was finished.

Then she opened her mouth, rain hitting her forehead. "I do not know…" Her voice had trailed off, unable to finish the thought she couldn't formulate in her state.

But Devin understood. Or, at least he hoped he did. She had been too brave, too scared, too strong, too smart, too hard, too calm—too damn everything, for too damn long.

The last year had made her into steel. But if not tempered right, steel can be brittle. And Aggie had never had time to temper. She had never had time to grieve for all that she had lost. Grieve for her father, her mother, her brother, her lost innocence.

She had accepted all that was given to her and moved on, because that was the only way to survive. And she had survived. Survived with grace. But she had missed a crucial piece. She missed the grieving.

Devin knew what he had to do. He had to give it back to her.

So he had wrapped her tighter into his bare arms, trying to warm her against the rain, and hurried. They rode the remaining hours in silence.

Arriving at Stonewell, an anxious Jason tore Aggie off the horse, he was so relieved to see her safe. He swung her around, not even noticing her lack of emotion until he caught Devin's face, which cued him to look at Aggie's.

Jason's concern was immediate. His sister was blank, and he looked accusingly at Devin. Devin shook his head, forcing Jason to back off as he pushed his hand between them, wrapping his arm around her shoulders and guiding her into the house.

Jason followed down the hallway, but Devin turned and told him to wait in the study. His voice gave no room for argument, and Jason did as requested.

Devin led Aggie further down the hall to the rarely used rose parlor, adjacent to the study. The room was only in use when Stonewell was full of guests, and was one of the most ornate in the house. A red-hued room, it had light burgundy rugs on the floors, floral curtains, red rose-colored couches and chairs, and a harp next to a pianoforte for entertaining in the corner. It also held countless artifacts passed down through the generations of the house—vases, tapestries, ivory inlaid tables, and a barrage of lace scattered about.

Devin guided Aggie to the large sofa in the middle of the room and sat her down. He left to gather a robe, washcloths and a pitcher of water, and wasn't surprised when he returned and Aggie hadn't moved a muscle. She stared straight ahead, eyes empty.

Kneeling before her, Devin gently dabbed away the blood on her neck, on her chin, and then on her hands, wrists, and fingers. When every drop of blood had been erased, her skin clean, he wrapped her in the robe and stopped, eyes level with hers.

"Aggie…Aggs, look at me."

Her green eyes shifted to Devin's.

"Aggs, I need you to do something. Not for me, not for your brother, but for yourself. You need to do this if you are to move on with your life. Our life." He squeezed her leg gently.

"Aggie, you need to grieve. Grieve for your father. Grieve for your mother's loss of sanity. Grieve for the fact you were forced to kill. Grieve for the brother you thought you lost. Grieve for all the time and all the innocence those bastards stole away from you. Grieve for the times you could not sleep because you were too scared to close your eyes. Grieve for everything…and let it go."

His hands moved to cup her face. "This will not be easy, but you have to face all that has happened to you, and deal with it. God knows I wish I could do this for you, but I cannot. You have to do this on your own."

Devin's grip along her jaw hardened. "I need your best, Aggs. Right now. After all you went through, this, this is the moment you need to find your best. Find your fight. I know you have it in you. You need to pull out that last shard of courage that has kept you so strong this far, and make it through this last piece. Make it through and come out the other side. I know you can do this, Aggs. Do you understand?"

Silence. Not the slightest twitch.

Devin's head went down, searching for words. Searching for some way to break through.

Long moments passed before he lifted his head, eyes brimming with moisture. "Aggs, I need you to come back to me. You don't have to be whole. It does not matter to me. I will take the smallest part of you. That is all I ask. Just a little bit of you to come back."

He swallowed, the lump in his throat threatening to cut his words.

"I don't need you to come back to me completely. But you need to do whatever it takes to come back, even a little. Anything. The smallest bit is all I ask, Aggs. I will be here, no matter what. But please. Please try. Please just come back to me. Just a tiny part of you. I swear we will figure out the rest from there."

Devin moved his hands down to her shoulders, then back up along her neck.

"Aggs, please, do you understand what I am saying?"

Finally, a tear trailed solo down her cheek, and she nodded.

Devin searched her face for comprehension, and, finding it, gently brushed the tear with his thumb.

He stood up, took a nearby blanket and wrapped it around Aggie, then left the room, closing the door behind him.

~ ~ ~

Eight hours had passed.

Devin winced as something heavy banged into the floor. It had been quiet for the first two hours. Devin and Jason could hear nothing at all coming from the room. Eventually, soft sobbing floated into the study. Both were shocked when the first glass smashed against a wall. Devin had to pin Jason to the floor to stop him from going in.

Since then, screams, glass shattering, wood splintering, cloth ripping, and an odd pounding-thumping came at a frantic pace from the room. Devin had initially thought this was a good idea, but he was beginning to wonder about the wisdom of his plan.

He took a small sip of the brandy he had been staring at for the last hour and a half. He could not stop her now. Aggie needed to finish whatever she had started in that room.

"I cannot believe you are making her do this. She obviously was not ready to think about all of this so soon after Von Traff's death." Jason stood up, starting a repeat of the argument they had been having since the first glass shattered.

"She needs to do this."

"Why? What good is it going to do her? Give her a few days. Be gentle and she will be back to normal."

"Gentle is not what she needs. She needs to fight. Fight before it overtakes her. You saw her. She was on the edge. An edge she could fall either direction from. I would rather she not turn out like her mother."

Jason jumped. "Our mother? What is wrong with my mother?"

"I thought you saw her in London."

"I did. I checked on her and Lizzie, but it was through a window."

"What was she doing?"

"Sitting. I don't know. Reading, maybe."

Devin sighed. Jason didn't know. "Your mother is catatonic. She has not spoken since your father died. Aggie said she sits, eats, sleeps. No reaction to anything or anyone around her."

"What? No."

"Yes. And I am damn well not going to let that happen to Aggie if I can help it. She would not want that for herself."

A piece of wood hit what sounded like the ceiling.

Jason shook his head, leveling his glare at Devin. "My mother aside. This is not the way. You don't know how she is going to come out of there. This could push her down the very edge you are afraid of. You are gambling with my sister's sanity and I am beginning to wonder if you really do care at all for her, if you did—"

"Shut the hell up," Devin said, voice lethal.

Jason stared at him, waiting, willing Devin to attack.

Devin rubbed his eyes with his free hand. He stared at the floor for an uncomfortable amount of time.

At Jason's cough, Devin looked up at him, allowing Jason to see plain on his face, the torment this was putting him through.

"If I could take," Devin started slowly, voice reverberating with raw emotion, "all the pain Aggie is feeling right now away from her, and add it one-thousand-fold to my own, I would do it in a heartbeat. There is nothing…I repeat, nothing I would not give to or for Aggie."

Silent, Jason sat down, a man unable to help his sister.

Devin was right. There was nothing he could do.

~ ~ ~

It had been quiet in the room for an hour. Devin ordered Thompson to have a bath drawn for Aggie. Jason had fallen asleep on the leather couch, and Devin quietly left him in the study.

He opened the door to the rose parlor slowly, having to lean into it with his shoulder to move what turned out to be a broken table wedged behind it. Once in, he looked about the room under the dim light of the wall lamp, and was not exactly shocked at the complete mayhem that greeted him.

Not one piece of furniture in the room was intact, not one glass, not one vase, not one tapestry, not one figurine, not one piece of lace. Everything had been destroyed.

Devin had expected no less of his wife.

He found her, curled in a ball, sound asleep in the middle of the mess, stuffing from the sofa strewn around her body. Walking gingerly into the room, crunching glass as he went, Devin gently picked Aggie up.

He brought her up to his room where a bath was waiting. Thompson had also delivered tea. Good man. Devin laid Aggie on the bed, stripped her, and then removed his own clothing. Not breaking from her exhausted sleep, she only twitched at his hands on her body.

He carried her to the copper tub and slipped them both into the warm water, Aggie nestled against his chest.

He washed her body as she slept, softly rubbing soap into the scabs of earlier on her fingers, wrist, and the small line at her neck where Von Traff had pressed his knife into her flesh. His stomach turned on itself once again as he examined the contorted scabs where fingernails had once been on her right pinky and ring finger.

"Hmmmm, Devin?"

Devin let out a breath he didn't know he was holding. Those were her first words since the ride back from Mitlan.

"Yes, I am right here, Aggs," he said softly in her ear, caressing her arm.

"I love you."

Devin stilled, his whisper in her ear, "Aggie, are you awake?" As much as he prayed she was, prayed she didn't hate him, he didn't want to wake her if she was actually sleeping.

Aggie slid her head on his chest so she could see his face. "Yes." She looked at him as though he had turned daft.

"Then say it again." Devin demanded, his face hard, for he wanted this more than anything.

"I love you." Aggie smiled, the love unmistakable in her green eyes.

It was all Devin could do to keep from crushing Aggie in the arms he clamped around her wet body. Finally, he let her loose, and spun her in the water so he could fully see her eyes. He cupped her face in his hands.

"I am so sorry I left you, Aggs. So sorry I thought you and your brother...I did not know and I was stupid. And then I did not protect you. It was the one thing I promised to do, and I failed. I have no right to even ask, but can you forgive me?"

Aggie slid forward on her knees, straddling Devin's waist. Her hands went behind his neck, resting on the lip of the tub as she evened her eyes to his. "You did not fail me. You were just a little late. As for the reason you were late," her eyes twitched mischievous, "that, you are in trouble for. For some bizarre reason, I think you do not understand how there could never be another for me. How you have me, heart and soul."

His hand shaking, it went into her wet hair, clasping her tight to him, his head buried in her neck.

"In case you missed it the first time." Devin leaned back, pulling his eyes up to hers. "I will say it again. I love you, Aggs."

With a gasp, Aggie choked him with wet arms. Her head turned to his ear. "Truly?"

"Truly. The worst moment of my life was seeing that knife on your neck. Seeing the blood. Your blood. My life was taken away from me in that one moment, and that will not do. I never want to have to be the man I was without you."

She moved her face so her green eyes could meet his grey ones. "I am finally here. All of me. All of me for you."

With a deep breath, Aggie spun around in the tub, utterly content as she snuggled onto Devin's chest. "When did you say it before?"

Devin shrugged, his smirk hidden from Aggie's view. "That does not matter."

Her fingers traced the wet skin on his chest. "Okay, so when did you know you loved me?"

He smiled, letting his mind wander. "Truthfully, even though I did not give it credit for a long time, it was the night after you were shot. I was in the library, and you came for me. You swayed, could barely stand straight—injured, exhausted. But you still made it to me. You wanted me. You needed me. And then you left."

Under the water, Devin wrapped his arm tight around her waist. "I sat in the library, arguing with my drunk self. It was only a few minutes, but it was an eternity. I wanted the safest thing for you. The best thing for you, even if it was not me. But I did not want to give you up. I could not make myself give you up. And I knew that if I got up and followed you, I could never go back. That would be it."

She turned her head into his chest, kissing his skin. "Then you carried me up to bed."

His lips went to her forehead. "I did. And that was it. I have never looked back—except to thank God I was not a complete idiot in that moment."

She tilted her head up to him. "Thank you for not being an idiot. And I guess that idiot-free choice makes up for your idiot move in the woods with my brother." She pulled up. "Speaking of which, you did not kill him."

Devin laughed. "No, I did not."

"Thank you. I am sure that was hard. I have had to resist once or twice myself through the years. But I am so happy he is alive and back." She set her head back down on his chest, then held her hand up, her last two fingers catching her gaze.

"Do they hurt?"

"Throbbing. But they will heal." She grabbed his chin with her thumb and forefinger. "I will heal. You reminded me that I was capable of that. Thank you."

"From day one, your capabilities have never ceased to amaze me, my love."

She smiled. "Oh, and I broke some things."

"I saw."

"I am sorry."

"Do you not know," he pulled her body up onto his so her face was next to his, "that you are more important to me than trinkets and furniture and priceless artifacts?"

Her eyes went big. "Priceless artifacts?"

Devin shrugged. "A few. But you, right here, talking to me with clear eyes. More than worth it. You are the priceless one. You are my everything, Aggs."

He kissed her, long, gentle, taking his time, with the promise of the life they were meant to lead together no longer waiting, no longer a dream, but here. Here and precious.

Aggie dropped her head onto his shoulder, holding tight with both arms. "Did you know it is still raining out?"

Devin looked through the window into the night, surprised by the torrential downpour.

He hadn't noticed.

~ About the Author ~

K.J. Jackson is the author of *The Hold Your Breath Series* and *The Flame Moon Series*. She specializes in historical and paranormal romance, will work for travel, and is a sucker for a good story in any genre. She lives in Minnesota with her husband, two children, and a dog who has taken the sport of bed-hogging to new heights.

Visit her at www.kjjackson.com.

~ Author's Note ~

Thank you so much for taking a trip back in time with me. The next book in the *Hold Your Breath* series will debut in Fall 2014, and yes, Killian is the star of this one! Be sure to sign up for news of my next releases at www.KJJackson.com (email addresses are precious, so out of respect, you'll only hear from me when I actually have real news).

In the meantime, if you would like to switch genres and check out my *Flame Moon* paranormal romance series, *Flame Moon #1*, the first book in the series, is currently free (ebook) at most online book stores. *Flame Moon* is a stand-alone story, so no worries on getting sucked into a cliffhanger. But number two in the series, *Triple Infinity*, ends with a fun cliff, so be forewarned. Number three in the series, *Flux Flame*, ties up that portion of the series.

As always, I love to connect with my readers, you can reach me at:

www.KJJackson.com

https://www.facebook.com/kjjacksonauthor

Twitter: @K_J_Jackson

Thank you for allowing my stories into your life and time!

~ K.J. Jackson

Printed in Great Britain
by Amazon

25923801R00145